Secret Crimes

ALSO BY MICHAEL HAMBLING

Michael Hambling

SECRET CRIMES

Detective Sophie Allen Book 3

JOFFE
BOOKS

Revised edition 2024
Joffe Books, London
www.joffebooks.com

First published by Joffe Books in 2016
Previously published in Great Britain in 2014 as *Killer Blues*

Cover art by Nick Castle

ISBN: 978-1-83526-855-1

To the memory of my late parents, Nora and Bob.
Always supportive; always encouraging.
I miss them more than words can say.

CHAPTER 1: MUSIC

Friday evening

The note quivered and hung in the air. The guitar was accompanied only by a gentle cascade from the cymbals as the slow blues number drew to a close. The music drew Ed Wilton back to a time long ago when he'd been younger and contented with life. Had he really been happy then? He thought so. Life had been so much richer when Lizzie was alive, when he'd felt wanted and needed and she had been the focus of his life. He remembered that time as being full of laughter and joy. He even recalled coming here, to this very pub, arm-in-arm with her, to attend gigs at some of the earlier blues festivals.

The audience's ripple of applause broke into his reverie. He looked up from his seat, crushed into a corner against the wall. The place was packed. At least he had found a place to sit. He saw the main door open and another group of people try to squeeze in to the crowded lower area where the band was playing. Surely there wasn't room? But they weren't all newcomers. He'd had a conversation with the two women earlier at the bar — Rosemary and Sarah. They'd left to visit one of the other venues but had now returned with two men in tow. He waved but they were busy fighting their way through to the bar. Should he get up and make an attempt to join them? But if he did so, he would surely lose his seat, and would they really welcome his presence now that they had found a couple of other men? So he sat on, sipping his beer, hoping that one of the women would look his way.

The taller man, dark-haired and stylishly dressed, was standing close to Sarah with his arm around her. She was laughing, her hand resting on his shoulder. Fast worker, thought Ed, but she'd made it quite clear that she was out for a good time over the weekend. Ed could see that Rosemary, her quieter companion, was far less confident. He had thought then that they were a slightly mismatched pair. Rosemary had a cooler, more distant demeanour. She was slim, fair-haired and blue-eyed whereas Sarah was a curvaceous, olive-skinned brunette. Now, whereas Sarah was obviously enjoying the close attention of her new partner, Rosemary was showing no such enthusiasm about the shorter man at her side.

Ed watched as the man tried to slide an arm around Rosemary's neck and rest it on her shoulder. She stepped back and shrugged the arm away, obviously irritated. The man looked offended, but Sarah had managed to gain the attention of one of the harassed bar staff. As they took their drinks, the people at the table beside Ed decided to leave. They got up, and several standing revellers eyed the table, including the group of four. Ed slid sideways into one of the bench seats and threw his jacket onto the chair opposite. He waved to the two women and at last they saw him. They walked across, with the men following. Rosemary looked relieved to see him.

'I didn't realise you were still here, Ed. You went missing just before we left.'

'I was in the loo,' he replied. 'I came out to find you both gone, and then I spotted this stool tucked away in the corner. I tried to get your attention when you came in just now, but I guess you were all concentrating on getting to the bar.'

Rosemary smiled and slid into the seat beside Ed. Her companion looked annoyed as he sat down at her other side.

'Brian, meet Ed. Ed's a professional musician. We met him in here earlier.'

Ed reached across in front of Rosemary to shake hands. Brian merely touched fingers then pulled back, almost wincing. He did not smile.

'This is Derek,' she went on, indicating the taller man. He was sitting as close to Sarah as it was possible to get without actually being on her lap. His arm was already around behind her and Ed could see his fingers gently kneading her shoulder.

'Glad to meet you,' Derek replied, squeezing the offered hand. 'Great festival, isn't it? We met up with these two lovely ladies up the road, but Rosemary said the band wasn't as good as this one. They talked us into coming down here instead.'

'This band was recommended to me,' Ed explained. 'Particularly the vocalist. She looks a slip of a thing, but she's got a very expressive, jazz-oriented vocal style. And she sings, not shouts. I've been impressed so far.'

Neither of the two men appeared to be listening. Derek had already switched his attention back to Sarah, and Brian was staring moodily into his drink. He was evidently irritated by Rosemary's brush-off as well as Ed's presence. Ed felt increasingly awkward, but realised that Rosemary was thankful he was there. She was leaning closer to him than to Brian, and smiled as she spoke to him. Ed was under no illusion that she had any romantic intentions towards him.

'I've only recently begun to get over a very messy divorce,' she'd told him earlier. 'I've no intention of starting a relationship just yet. But Sarah is really up for it, although I'm not sure how far she wants to go and how quickly she wants to get there.'

Ed glanced across the table at Sarah. She was nibbling Derek's ear, and his hand was inside her jacket, over her breast.

'Cool it, you two. You'll get us thrown out,' Rosemary said.

3

The couple laughed. They continued to caress and kiss each other for the remaining twenty minutes of the gig. They clearly weren't going to wait too long before taking things further. Brian made further attempts to woo Rosemary and she continued to resist. When the last encore number finished, the small group rose, hesitant. The two men said that their guest house room was small, and the proprietors would probably object if they returned with two women, so they decided to go to the large hotel in which Sarah and Rosemary were staying. A hotel would probably have less stringent codes of conduct. Ed finished his beer.

'I'll just toddle off home now,' he said. 'I'll be in your way.'

'Please come, Ed', Rosemary said, turning to face him. She mouthed the word 'please' a second time.

Ed understood. 'Well, maybe just a short nightcap.'

They walked the few hundred yards up the High Street and crossed a narrow road to the plush hotel where the two women were sharing a room. Once inside they made for the lounge bar. The place exuded peace and quiet after the mayhem of the crowded pub. They settled into plump sofas, each nursing a glass of liqueur. Ed could sense Brian's animosity. He wasn't sure what to do. Ten minutes of small talk went by and the two women visited the powder room — to discuss tactics, Ed guessed.

Brian lost no time in telling Ed to get lost.

'Just piss off, will you? There are two of us and two of them; and you, my friend, are getting in the way big time.'

'I'm not here because I want to be. I'm here because Rosemary wants me to be. And it's not because she fancies me. You must have picked up on her signals. She doesn't want to get involved with you either. She told me earlier that she's still getting over a very recent, messy divorce.'

'All I know is that I was in with a chance until you appeared. So do me a favour and shove off.'

Ed sighed. 'Why do you think they've gone to the ladies loo? They'll be arguing like fury in there over what to do. And

4

I'm not leaving unless I get the go-ahead from Rosemary. If she wants me to go I'll be out of here like a shot, don't you worry. So let's just wait and see.'

The two women came back. Ed could see at once that they'd argued. Sarah snuggled up to Derek, whispering in his ear. Rosemary looked pink-faced and miserable.

'Do you want me to go?' he asked.

'Please don't,' she whispered, and nodded towards the couple opposite. 'You can guess what they want. I don't know what to do now.'

'I have a sofa bed in my lounge if you want it. I'd offer you the bed in my guest room, but my daughter's staying with me at the moment.'

'Do you really mean that?'

'Of course. You'd be most welcome. And Ella won't mind as long as you keep your distance from me. We're supporting each other at the moment.'

'That would be just great. Thank you so much.'

Brian had been listening to the conversation.

'Fuck this,' he said. 'I'm heading off.'

He stalked out of the room. Rosemary went to the shared room to collect a few things and was back within five minutes. She had a few words with Sarah, and then followed Ed into the hotel lobby. They walked the short distance across town to Ed's flat.

* * *

'Hello, Dad!'

A young woman's voice called out as Ed opened the door. His flat was in a small block on a private mews. It was a haven of peace, somewhere he could escape to when the whirl of his London life became too much for him. He'd bought it less than two years previously, some months after his wife's death from cancer. Here he could take stock and remember the good times.

'Hi. I've got someone with me, Ella.'

He beckoned Rosemary to follow him into the lounge.

'Don't jump to any wrong conclusions. Rosemary here is stuck for somewhere to stay, so I've offered her the couch.'

Ella rose from her chair to greet them, giving her father a hug, and then Rosemary. She was a tall, shapely redhead, where her father was slim and dark, almost swarthy.

'Ella takes after her mother,' Ed explained. 'She had the most beautiful auburn hair.'

He turned to Ella. 'I know this is unexpected, but Rosemary is a damsel in distress with nowhere to stay.'

'She can have my room, Dad. I've no problem with the sofa bed.'

'I won't hear of it,' Rosemary responded. 'It's either me on the sofa bed or I walk out. I'm not putting either of you out. You're doing me a big enough favour as it is, Ed.'

'Well, I can at least put the kettle on. That is if either of you would like something hot. I'm having my usual bedtime hot chocolate, and I'll make one for you, Dad. How about you, Rosemary? I can do you one, or make a coffee or tea if you'd rather.'

'Chocolate sounds great. I got out of the habit years ago but I don't know why. It always seemed to help me sleep.'

Ella left the room and they heard the sounds of a kettle being filled and the clink of crockery.

'She's lovely, Ed. You must be proud of her.'

'I am. We had our difficulties when she was younger, but she's taken on her new role as my personal carer really well. She fusses over me like an old woman when she's here, and we're on the phone at least twice a week when she's back at university. I don't know how I'd have coped without her. I'd have muddled through, I expect, but . . .' He shrugged. 'Do you have any children?'

Rosemary's mouth became a thin line. 'No. Paul always said that he didn't want any and I went along with it, even though I secretly yearned for a baby. Then he left me for a

6

younger woman, and I hear she's pregnant. I just can't get over the treachery of it. And it's far too late for me now. Bitter doesn't come near how I feel about it.'

'I think I can imagine.'

'Can you?'

He thought for a moment and then said, sheepishly, 'Probably not. Sorry.'

'I feel so empty now. It's as if something has been sucked out of me and I just can't be bothered with anything anymore. I sometimes look at myself, amazed I'm still keeping going, still together somehow. I could so easily have ended up like Sarah, hopping into bed with any half-handsome man who came along.'

'Is she any happier though?'

'Probably not. Paul always said that I had too much pride. I keep myself too much under control. I always think I couldn't live with myself if I started letting my guard down, but I might be mistaken. Maybe I'd enjoy it. You know, fling caution to the wind and see what happens. It's not as though I have anyone depending on me, not now.'

'But you do have your pride, and maybe that's a good thing.'

'What else is there? That's what I keep asking myself.'

Ella came back into the room carrying a tray with cups of chocolate and a plate of biscuits.

'What do you do, Ella?'

'I'm at university in Bristol, studying dentistry.'

'Wow. I don't quite know what to say. I don't think I've ever spoken to a dental student before. It's very different to what your Dad does, isn't it?'

'I'm very proud of her,' Ed said. 'I know what people think about the music business, and all those celebrities, but it's doctors, dentists, teachers, engineers and the like who really contribute to society. Once we become ill or get a raging toothache or have a child who's disabled, we know who's really keeping our world ticking over.'

'So do you come down to Swanage often, Ella?'

'I like to check up on Dad to make sure he's looking after himself properly, so I get down here some weekends. But he's away a lot in London, and we don't meet as often as I'd like.'

'And is he? Looking after himself properly, I mean.'

'I think so. If he isn't then he hides it from me very well.' Her look at Rosemary was careful. 'I think he's coped brilliantly. I know what he's been through. He's my hero.'

'That's a lovely thing to say, Ella. I think he's probably safe with you keeping an eye on him. I didn't feel that way about my father.'

'I don't think I would have done if things had turned out different. But we support each other. It isn't just one way. And my brother, Murray, does his bit — when he remembers.'

Ed felt that a change of subject was needed. 'How did you meet Sarah?'

'At a divorcee support group in Portsmouth, where we both live. I wasn't coping at all well and decided to go along to see what they had to offer. Sarah was also there for the first time, so we naturally got chatting. And she's been good for me. She's so lively, and she throws herself into everything she does, which is the opposite of me. Like tonight. Brian's probably a perfectly decent man, but I'd need to get to know him better before starting anything. But Sarah, she's right in there, although maybe not quite as direct as she was this evening with Derek. I guess there was a real spark between them.'

She looked at Ed. 'Please don't think I'm condemning her. This is the third music festival we've been to together. At the others I'd just go back to our hotel room alone, and she'd turn up later or the next morning in time for breakfast. And a part of me thinks it's great that she can do that. We've only got one life, and we're not getting any younger so I can absolutely understand what she's doing. I hate it when people get sanctimonious. But I'm a product of my upbringing, so I have a few barriers to break down first.'

Ella yawned. 'I need to get to bed,' she said. 'I've had a long day.'

'Me as well,' Ed replied. 'I'll just get the bed ready. Can you give me a hand, Ella?'

* * *

The next morning Ed knocked on the door of the lounge shortly after seven thirty. He'd heard Rosemary use the bathroom and since he'd just made a pot of tea, he decided to take a cup to her.

'Come in,' came the response. 'I think I'm decent.'

She was dressed and had already collapsed the sofa bed back to its normal shape, stacking the used bedding into a neat pile. The curtains were partly open and weak morning sunlight glinted through.

'Tea for you.'

He placed it on the low table in the centre of the room.

'I'll accept that with thanks, Ed. But nothing more. I have breakfast waiting for me at the hotel. I'm sure Sarah will be bursting to tell me what a wonderful man Derek is.'

Ed noted the dark shadows beneath her eyes. 'Did you manage to get some sleep?' he asked.

She shrugged her shoulders. 'Yes, though I tossed and turned for a while. Too much going on in my head.' She glanced at her watch, then picked up the mug of steaming liquid. 'I'll be off as soon as I've drunk this.'

'Can I walk back with you? It looks such a lovely morning. I'll wait for Ella to show some signs of life before I get breakfast ready. I might stroll along the front for a few minutes to build up an appetite.'

'Okay. I'll call Sarah to let her know I'll be back soon,' Rosemary replied, taking her mobile phone out of her bag. She frowned. 'That's odd, there's no answer. It must be switched off. It's gone straight to voicemail.'

'Maybe she's still asleep?'

'But she never switches her phone off. She uses the alarm to wake herself up if she needs to, and even if she doesn't she still leaves her phone on. I should know, I've often shared a room with her.'

'There's bound to be a reason, Rosemary. I wouldn't worry about it.'

She smiled at him. 'No, I'm sure you're right. I'll walk back to the hotel and see if she wants to join me for breakfast, though I'm a bit worried that Derek might still be around.'

CHAPTER 2: KILLER BLUES

Saturday morning

A brisk, early morning walk is just the thing for clearing a muzzy head. Ed Wilton wasn't the only person using the crisp, sea air to stimulate an appetite. A few runners pounded the pavements but they were outnumbered by the bleary-eyed blues enthusiasts out trying to shake off their hangovers. Out on Peveril Point a couple walked the final few yards of grass towards the rocky shelf of the Peveril Ledges, the treacherous rocks submerged as the tide reached its peak. The old Coastguard lookout station, now staffed by volunteers from the Coastwatch organisation, loomed above them, empty this early in the morning. The man stopped walking and used his binoculars to look at the view north across the bay to the chalk stacks of the Pinnacles and Old Harry. The woman lifted her expensive camera, viewed the same scene through the telephoto lens, and took several shots of the sunlit panorama, then swung her camera westwards to take some images of yachts at anchor in the bay, as golden rays of sunlight struck their glistening paintwork.

'There's something odd in the water,' the man said. He refocused his binoculars on the shoreline much closer to where they were standing. 'Just on the waterline. I thought it was a rock, but it's moving slightly with the waves.'

His partner glanced across at where he was pointing, then swung her camera up and took a shot.

She looked at the image on the camera's screen and zoomed in on it, but it lost clarity.

'It's just some old clothing caught in the rocks,' she answered.

By now her partner had moved to slightly higher ground to give himself a better view.

'Christ,' he said, taking out his mobile phone from a pocket. 'It's more than just clothes. It looks as though there's a body inside them.'

The police were on the scene within minutes. The local force were always reinforced with extra squads during festival weekends, although there were rarely any problems, just a slight increase in cases of drunk and disorderly behaviour, often by locals taking advantage of the extended opening hours in the town's pubs. The extra manpower did mean that a unit was available for an early morning shift. PC Jen Allbright picked her way carefully among the slippery rocks and reached the sodden form lying in one of the pools of water. The head pointed towards the sea and the legs back to the land. The body lay on its front with wavelets breaking across it. Long strands of dark hair wafted to and fro like seaweed. She bent over the head and felt under the neck for a pulse. She glanced back to the grassy area above the low cliff where a small crowd had already gathered. Some held cameras at the ready. She spoke into her radio.

'Jack, get the crowd back away from the edge. Radio in. We have to report this as a suspicious death, so we'll need the full crew out. Good job the tide is on its way out. It gives us a bit more time.'

She gently raised the woman's head slightly, looking to see if it was anyone she knew. Possibly it was a local, known to the police as a boozer, but she didn't recognise the face. She could see signs of bruising on the nose and cheeks.

'Get Barry Marsh here, and someone medical. I don't like what I see.'

* * *

Just over an hour later, Detective Chief Inspector Sophie Allen drove slowly along the narrow approach lane towards Peveril Point. She had to navigate her way through the small groups of people who had been drawn to the vicinity by the sight of flashing blue lights. Several onlookers stared at her in irritation as she sounded her horn to clear the route ahead. When she reached the turning area at the end of the lane she leant out of the window and spoke to the uniformed officer at the gate.

'Get the barrier moved right back to the pier entrance, Jack, and get all these people behind it. We can't have the access road clogged up by crowds of sightseers.'

He nodded and spoke into his radio. 'Okay, ma'am. You can drive on through to the lookout tower. Sergeant Marsh is waiting for you there. I'll get a new barrier set up as soon as someone comes to give me a hand.'

She drove onto the grass and parked her car tight up against the tower's fence. Marsh was waiting, hunched inside a thick jacket. She got out of the car, slipped out of her shoes and pulled on the familiar pair of pink wellington boots. A brief smile flickered across his face.

'I saw that, Barry. Lucky for you it's not grounds for dismissal. Give me the details, please.'

Detective Sergeant Barry Marsh nodded. 'It's good to see you again, ma'am. Someone spotted a middle-aged woman's body among the rocks, just below the high-tide line.'

Allen did not turn. Her short, fair hair blew slightly in the breeze. 'Who found her?'

'A couple out for an early morning walk, almost two hours ago. They called in on a mobile and Jen Allbright came down. She wasn't happy with what she found, so she asked for the police doctor to take a look and for me to come. There's bruising around her face and head, but it doesn't look right

13

for battering against the rocks. She's wearing clothes, but she's got ankle boots on, with fairly high heels. The doctor's down there at the moment.'

'Okay, let's take a look.'

The two detectives made their way through the rocks to a group of figures hunched over a tide pool some yards short of the waterline. Sophie recognised Mark Benson, the local police doctor. He was crouched low over the body, carefully examining the facial injuries. He turned as he heard the approaching footsteps.

'Your people were right to call me in, Sophie. I think some of these head wounds occurred before she died. They had time to clot. The bruising is deep and shows signs of good blood flow to the area, so are also prior to death. There's a deep wound to the back of the head.'

'Could she have fallen and got the head injuries that way? Concussion from the first stumble, if she fell heavily? If she was unconscious she'd have drowned once the tide came in.'

'It's a possibility but I really can't speculate. One thing I did notice is that the head wounds look as if something blunt was involved, and all the rocks at this spot are well-rounded.'

The young constable, Jen Allbright, spoke up. 'Ma'am, she wouldn't have tried to walk down here in those heels, surely? It's so rocky. She would have tripped up as soon as she came off the grass, and even there she'd have been sinking in. She'd have fallen long before she got to the water.'

Sophie looked at the heels. They were practically stilettos. 'What was the weather like here yesterday?'

'It rained all morning and only dried up mid-afternoon,' Marsh replied.

'So the turf up there must be pretty soft. There's no mud on her boots, though I suppose it might have been washed off somehow. How far did the tide come in?'

'It looks as though it got up to her waist. Her head and face might have been under. That's what the couple who spotted her saw — her arms and hair moving as the waves broke over her. But her legs are still mostly dry,' he replied.

14

Sophie felt inside the pockets of the woman's jacket but found nothing. A shoulder bag with thin straps was lying partly under her chest, and Sophie eased it away and peered inside. She spotted a purse, a set of keys, a hairbrush and a small perfume sprayer but no mobile phone. She felt inside the jacket and realised that there was nothing between it and bare skin. She turned to Marsh and spoke quietly.

'She doesn't have any clothes on under this jacket, and her jeans are not fully zipped up. You were right to be suspicious. The forensic unit is on its way, so we'll leave the body to them. Let's have a quick look around to see if there's anything lying about.'

'There were people up on the grass as we arrived. I got them back quickly, but they'll have trampled over any tracks,' said Allbright.

'I'm sure you did your best. But we'll have a look anyway. The area just below the bank won't have been stamped on, so we'll look at that first.'

By the time the forensic squad arrived, the tide had retreated well away from the body. It looked like a sodden mass of clothing, stretched out between the rocks. The detectives left the unit to its work, and returned to the cars.

'The town looks busy, Barry. What's going on?'

'It's our autumn blues festival, ma'am. Pubs and bars are all full of ageing rockers.'

'She's wearing a leather jacket and jeans. Just the kind of outfit for an event like that. Get a message around the local hotels and guest houses to let us know if anyone's missing from breakfast this morning.'

'Might have been camping.'

'So we'll try that next, but we've got to start somewhere. We've got to do it quickly, while people are still in their hotels. Insist that the managers, or whoever, do a full check, even if it means getting people up from their sleep.' She glanced at her watch. 'Eight forty-five. Maybe we'll be in luck. A blues festival, you say?' She grimaced. 'Apt, if it does turn out to be murder.'

'Why's that, ma'am?' Marsh looked puzzled.

'Killer blues, Barry.' She waited in vain for his face to clear. 'It's an expression from years ago. It refers to severe depression, but it was also used to describe a particularly brilliant blues solo, usually by a top guitarist. Eric Clapton? Peter Green? Jimi Hendrix? Don't keep looking at me blankly like that. You must have heard of them.'

'Sorry, ma'am. It's just a bit early in the morning. Yes, I've heard the names . . .' He paused. 'Weren't your parents keen?'

She nodded. 'Peter Green. That was the song at my Dad's funeral: "Need Your Love So Bad." You know, I can't believe it was all of nine months ago.' She shook her head, frowning. 'It doesn't seem possible. Where did the summer go?'

'How is your mother, ma'am?'

'She's thinking about getting married — so she told me last weekend. I think the discovery of his body, and then the funeral, brought everything to a close in her mind. It freed her, in a strange kind of way. She took a while to digest everything that happened, but she seemed more settled once she did come to terms with it.' She sighed. 'I wish it had been as easy for me.'

'Maybe you were punishing yourself, ma'am.'

She looked into his eyes but said nothing. Finally she returned her gaze to the body below them. 'Maybe we'd better get on with it.'

* * *

Less than an hour later they entered the ornate lobby of the Ballard View Hotel. Sophie spoke to an ashen-faced Jenny Burrows.

'I can't believe it, Chief Inspector. It's only been a year since you were here last,' the hotel manager said. 'Is there anything useful I can do?'

'Coffee, Mrs Burrows. Maybe some biscuits? It's going to be a long morning.'

16

DC Jimmy Melsom, Marsh's subordinate in Swanage, was talking to a middle-aged couple who were sitting on a bench seat against the panelled wall of the hallway. He rose, straightening his tie, as he saw her approaching. He looks as if he's put on some weight since the winter, she thought, but at least he's making an effort to dress more smartly.

'Rosemary Corrigan and Ed Wilton, ma'am. She was sharing a room with a woman friend, Sarah Sheldon, but didn't spend the night here. She arrived back this morning. Mrs Sheldon did spend the night here, with a man she met yesterday evening. Or that's what Mrs Corrigan assumed. She didn't answer her mobile when Mrs Corrigan called this morning and isn't anywhere else in the hotel. The description matches.'

'Okay, Jimmy. Stay with them. I'll be back in a few minutes.'

She nodded to the couple, but walked on past them. She needed to see the room, take in the atmosphere and make some guesses about the events of the preceding night. Marsh had a few words with Melsom before hurrying along the corridor to catch up with her. The two detectives passed the bar and lounge, then turned into a passageway that led to a recently-built annexe building. The doorway to the room, the last on the ground floor, was guarded by two uniformed officers. Sophie looked around her. A fire door led out to the garden and the rear car park.

'Fingerprints. Any contamination?' she asked.

'Rosemary Corrigan will have left hers on the outside door handle, but she says she didn't touch anything in the room when she came back this morning. She felt uneasy as soon as she entered, so she just went back out again. But her prints will be all over the place from when she unpacked yesterday evening.'

They slipped into nylon overalls and went in. Heavy curtains made the room dark. Sophie stood, letting her eyes adjust to the gloom, looking at the rumpled duvet on the double bed. The only item of clothing to be seen was an ivory-coloured nightdress that appeared to be made of silk, strewn across the top cover. A single bed was tucked up against another wall, its cover slightly crinkled.

Sophie moved slowly around the larger bed, looking at it from different angles. She glanced around the room, taking in every detail. Her nose wrinkled as she sniffed the tired air.

'There's something in the air. Something sweet and cloying, maybe air freshener spray of some type. But there's something else below it, something almost animal. Maybe it's my imagination.'

Marsh shook his head. 'Can't help you, ma'am. Blocked nose.'

She lifted the duvet at one corner. 'The bed looks as though it's been remade to look as if she didn't sleep here, but it's not been done by a professional. The top pillowcase is a bit crumpled. We know from the other woman that our victim, if it is her, spent at least some of the night here. Tell forensics I want everything taken for examination and I want the bedding analysed, including the mattress.'

She took a last look around before leaving. There were two empty weekend bags tucked up at the side of the wardrobe. Several of the drawers contained clothes and a few items were hanging from the rail inside the cupboard. The two detectives stepped out of their overalls and returned to the reception area. Sophie went across to the couple sitting with Jimmy Melsom and asked the woman to come into a nearby office with her.

'Coffee, Jimmy, please,' she called. 'You're with me, Barry.'

The three of them sat around a table.

'Is it Sarah?' the woman immediately asked, fear in her eyes. 'Dark hair, green eyes?'

'We can't be absolutely sure, but the description fits. I'm so sorry. It must be a shock to you. I also need to tell you that we're treating the death as suspicious at the moment.'

Rosemary started to cry. 'I just can't believe it. Surely there's a mistake? Why would anyone want to kill her? She

18

wouldn't harm anyone. Everyone liked her, she was so full of fun.'

'Let me get some details from you. You're Rosemary Corrigan, is that right? Apparently you felt uneasy when you arrived back at the room earlier this morning.'

'Yes. I don't know what it was. I expected to find Sarah in the room, possibly still asleep. But it was so silent in there. The bed looked a bit rumpled but had been made up, which seemed weird. You'd normally leave that to the hotel staff, wouldn't you?'

'Were you expecting a family room when you arrived?'

'No, of course not. Sarah booked it. According to her it was the last room available in the hotel. I thought it was a bit odd, but I was just happy to have somewhere warm and comfortable to sleep. We agreed that I'd have the single bed and she'd take the larger one. And the room was fine. It's very comfortable and airy, or at least it seemed so yesterday when we checked in.'

'Was there anything else that didn't seem right this morning?'

'It's hard to put my finger on it. There was no answer when I tapped at the door, so I unlocked it and went in. At first I thought she was in the bathroom, but it was empty. It was when I came back into the bedroom. There was something about the atmosphere. It was very different to when we unpacked yesterday. The room was fresh and welcoming then, but this morning the air seemed sort of tired. It's hard to explain.'

'What did you do?'

'I locked the door and went down to the restaurant to see if she was having breakfast. But there was no sign of her. And then the manager came in and started looking around and ticking names off a list. I spoke to her and asked her if she'd seen Sarah. That's when I started to really worry.'

'What happened last night?'

Sophie listened attentively to Rosemary's account of the evening, while Marsh took notes.

'Tell me more about the two men, Rosemary. Describe them to me.'

'Well, Derek was the one who was with Sarah last night. He was tall, probably about six feet. He had dark hair and brown eyes, a kind of Mediterranean look. Really handsome. He was wearing black trousers, a red cord shirt and a tan bomber jacket. There was a spark between them as soon as they met, I could tell. I didn't catch his surname.'

'And the other man?'

'Brian. He wanted to get off with me, but I didn't really like him. He seemed a bit of a moody type.'

'What did he look like?'

'A lot shorter. He had mid-brown hair, and blue eyes that bulged slightly. His nose was a bit turned up. He was in jeans and a black leather jacket. He left about the same time as Ed and me.'

'So you stayed the night in Ed's flat? Did you hear anything during the night?'

'Nothing unusual, and I'm a light sleeper. But I was in the lounge with the door shut. I didn't sleep with Ed, you know. He offered me a place to sleep as a way out of my dilemma. Sarah wanted our room, and I didn't want to go with Brian. Staying at Ed's was the only alternative.'

'Okay. What clothes did you bring, Rosemary?'

'Just enough for a couple of days. It's all in the room, either in the drawers or hanging up.'

'Can you tell me about Sarah? Where she lived, what she did as a job? That kind of thing.'

'I know her address,' Rosemary replied. 'But I can't be sure about much else. She might have worked in a bank, but she also talked about insurance. She was a bit vague about it.'

Marsh took Rosemary back to the reception area. Sophie spoke to Ed Wilton for a few minutes.

'What do you think of their story, ma'am?' Marsh asked, once they were alone.

'Same as you, I would have thought. I'm apt to believe the two of them for now, but I want everything they've said double-checked. Get the locals out looking for our two men. They were at a B and B somewhere in the town. It shouldn't be difficult to find. I'm a bit surprised Mrs Corrigan didn't know where they were staying. But if they were up to no good, maybe they avoided talking about it.'

'Right away, ma'am. It's interesting that Mrs Corrigan also spoke of a strange atmosphere in the room.'

'It was the smell, Barry. I've been thinking about what it was. A faint trace of shit and piss nearly masked by the air freshener and some perfume. But it was in the bedroom, not the bathroom.' She paused. 'It's the smell of someone who's almost paralysed with fright. She lost control of her bodily functions.'

* * *

The forensic team arrived and started their meticulous examination of the room. After interviewing the staff, Sophie and Marsh found time for a coffee. Marsh nibbled on his biscuit.

'Is Lydia still with you?'

'No. She put in for a transfer soon after that last business down here. A bit odd really. She's in Bath now, apparently. She sent me a card thanking me for the help I'd given her, but I haven't heard from her since she went.'

'Really?'

'It took me by surprise. I thought she was happy working for me. I guess I was away a lot around the time she left. It took longer than I expected to get those poor girls identified — the ones you found buried at the farm. Duff and company were clever, you know, certainly in the early stages. They only chose poor, country girls or orphans to smuggle out from Romania. I suppose like so many thugs they got overconfident as time went on, and that's when it started to go wrong for them. Nadia and Sorina were too much of a handful, too bright, and the gang had become sloppy.' She sipped her coffee. 'They were both back here a couple of weeks ago, visiting Jade, and they looked as if they've recovered well.' She paused. 'I was seconded to the Home Office for a while and was getting therapy for the state my head was in. I suppose I wasn't around enough for Lydia to be able to talk to me. I certainly didn't see it coming, her wanting to leave, and it was too late to do anything about it when I did find out.'

Marsh inhaled. 'She thought it was you, ma'am. You know, the woman who tortured Charlie Duff. I tried to convince her that it wasn't, but she wouldn't have it.'

'Christ! So that was it.'

'She'd always hero-worshipped you, ma'am.'

'And in her eyes I fell from grace quite spectacularly.' She regarded Marsh. 'And what do you think, Barry?'

'I was with you when we found him. I know it wasn't you, ma'am. I saw how it affected you, finally finding the man who killed your father. That was no act, and if you'd done those things to him the night before, you wouldn't have reacted like that.'

'That's very loyal of you, but I don't know whether I deserve it. I have a proposal for you, Barry. I don't know what the future holds for you here, what with all this talk of job cuts. I've pondered on it for a long time, but there's no one I'd rather have working for me. So if you could bear to put up with me on a full-time basis, how would you feel about being my permanent second, based at HQ?'

After several seconds Marsh realised his mouth was hanging open and closed it. He opened it again.

'I'd love to, ma'am. There's nothing to hold me here now. I've finally split up with Sammie, and with the uncertainty about the future of the station here, I'd much rather go somewhere settled. You know that Tom Rose plans to take redundancy? We're guessing that it'll just be a sergeant in charge.' He finally took a sip of coffee. 'You've no idea what this means to me. But isn't there anyone else you'd prefer? Someone a bit more qualified? You know, more like Lydia?'

'There are cutbacks going on left, right and centre. I wouldn't get to pick and choose, Barry, and I'd find it hard to accept that. And you're a good counter to me. In some ways Lydia was perfect, but in other ways she was too much like me. I need someone to pull me back down to earth occasionally. And you do that brilliantly. But we will have a DC with us. Someone starts next week as Lydia's replacement, and I don't know anything about him or her. I should have had a DS with me all along, but the powers that be never got around to it because they knew there were cuts on the way. So in a way, if you join me, I'll have the core of the permanent team that I should have had from the start.'

'When do I start? Officially, I mean?'

'Now. I've already cleared it with Matt Silver and the Chief Constable will ratify it. I had a long chat with him last month when I returned to full-time work.'

'I knew you were on leave for a long time. I heard that from the Super on one of his flying visits down here.'

'I needed it, Barry. You saw what a mess I was in. That whole business really wrecked my brain. I thought I'd be okay once we bagged Duff and got all the loose ends tidied up, but I just got worse and worse. I was in and out of therapy for months. It was all due to the hatred I'd felt towards my father. I always thought that he'd run out on my mother when he found out that she was pregnant, despite what she'd told me. A childhood filled with that kind of simmering anger was barely controllable. Then to discover that he'd been murdered and hadn't abandoned her at all was too much for me to cope with. It was all down to the intense guilt I was feeling, at having hated him for forty years.'

'I had no idea. I'm just amazed that you want to continue.'

'It's what I do, Barry. It's what I do best. I'm not ready to chuck in the towel just yet.' She smiled at him. 'Lucky for you, wouldn't you say?'

He nodded. Then his phone sounded.

'We may have a lead on where they were staying.'

'Let's get moving. Time waits for no woman, nor does a murderer.'

* * *

The Hawthorns Guest House was situated just off Victoria Avenue, about half a mile from the seafront. It was a detached building, constructed from the local grey Purbeck stone. Virginia creeper, still in its glorious autumn colours, clung to the walls above the front porch and late-blossoming flowers cascaded from hanging baskets and tubs. Marsh introduced Sophie to the guesthouse proprietor, an anxious-looking woman in her fifties.

'Mrs Julia Fantini, ma'am. She owns the place, and checked in a Mr Brian Shapiro and his friend when they arrived late yesterday afternoon.'

The two detectives were taken to the room booked by the two men. Sophie asked the owner to wait downstairs.

'We'll just have a quick look around,' she said. 'I want to get a feel for the place.'

The twin-bedded room was family-sized, and one of the beds was a double. It was a similar arrangement to the room they'd just visited at the hotel, although this one was smaller. It was neat and clean.

'Well, nothing looks out of place, but we'll get forensics to check once they've finished in the hotel.'

Marsh nodded, and looked out of the window.

Sophie stepped around the beds, scanning the surfaces of shelves and tables, but all the items looked as though they belonged to the premises. The wardrobe was empty, as were the four drawers in the dressing table. Two holdalls lay on the floor in front of the window.

'It doesn't look as though they unpacked,' Sophie said. 'Maybe they arrived, dumped their stuff and went out immediately.'

She carefully unzipped each bag, looking for anything with a name on it, but could find nothing. Each small bag merely held a few spare clothes and an electric razor.

'Travelling light,' Marsh commented.

'Right, let's leave the detailed search to the experts. We need to examine the bookings.'

They returned to the ground floor. The owner was waiting at the bottom of the stairs, her arms folded tightly around her chest. She looked paler than when they'd first arrived.

'A friend's just called and said a body's been found out at Peveril. Is this linked?'

'We can't be sure, Mrs Fantini. Not until our forensic people have been here to check on the evidence. But we'll need to seal off that room, and maybe talk to your other guests. Can you give me the details of the reservation? Which of the two made it, and when?'

'The booking was made about three weeks ago by phone.' Mrs Fantini checked the details on her computer. 'Mr Shapiro made it.'

'That's fine,' Sophie replied. 'Did you pick up anything unusual about them when they arrived?'

Mrs Fantini shook her head. 'Not really. They were in a bit of a rush. They took the key, dropped their bags in the room, then they were back downstairs and out.'

'What time was this?'

'Just before seven twenty. Mr Shapiro asked about pubs and somewhere to eat when he signed in. I told him that all the pubs served food, but that they'd be much busier than normal because of the blues festival. He told me that's what they were down here for.'

'And it was definitely him who made the original booking?'

'Yes. It was done on his credit card.'

'Can I see the details, please?'

Marsh stood to one side and the two women squeezed in behind the desk. Sophie looked at the booking sheet and sign-in book. All completed under the name of Shapiro.

'Did the other man say anything at all?'

'Not that I remember. He stayed in the background.'

'Did they come by car?'

'No. And that's rather unusual. He said that they came by bus from Poole.'

Marsh looked puzzled.

'Are you sure of the time they arrived?' he asked.

'I'm certain. I always note the time and I remember this one distinctly, because the show I was watching on TV hadn't quite finished. I missed the final ten minutes.'

'You couldn't have mixed them up with any other guests arriving?'

'No. They were the last. Everyone else was already booked in and had gone out to see the first performances. They're all here for the festival, you see.'

'How long would you say it takes to walk up here from the bus terminus? Ten minutes?'

'That's what we put on the website, but I doubt it would take two fit men anywhere near that long. And the email I send out to confirm bookings has directions.'

'It would be straightforward, wouldn't it?' Marsh continued. 'Out of the bus terminus, left along Rempstone Road for a few hundred yards and you're just about here.'

'That's right. Those are the directions we provide.'

'Could you smell any drink on their breath?'

'Not that I could tell. And he said they were in a hurry to get out for a drink and some food.'

Sophie interrupted. 'Did either of them return at any time last night?'

'No. We usually lock the front door about eight in the evening, but last night I left it until well after eleven because I knew most of our guests would be coming in late. Even so, I was up until just after midnight. I saw everyone else coming in.'

'What about later? They could still have got in with their key, surely?'

'Of course, but they didn't. We have a tracker on the front door that logs each time it's opened once I set the security alarm

26

on the office. It wasn't activated at all, so no one came in after I went to bed.'

* * *

Sophie and Marsh returned to the car.

'The bus times don't work, ma'am. Not unless there was a severe delay on the route down. One arrives at six forty. If they got that they should have got here long before they did. They could have called in somewhere on the walk over here, but it's unlikely. If they followed the simplest route they wouldn't have passed any pubs or cafés. The next bus gets in at seven thirty, and then they wouldn't have got here in time. The only other possible explanation is that the buses were running late. I'll check when we're back at the station.'

'So, another oddity. And where did Shapiro go when he left the hotel at midnight? According to Wilton and Corrigan he left just before them, and they assumed he was coming back here. But he never made it. Why not? From what our couple back at the hotel said, both men were on the lookout for available women. Maybe the double bed was for that.'

'Shows a lot of confidence, doesn't it? And what does the second one do when the lucky man returns with someone? Stay out until a prearranged time?' said Marsh.

'Maybe they were hoping for a foursome.'

'I'd imagine that Mrs Fantini would have had something to say about that, ma'am. I can't imagine a whole lot getting past her.'

'Let's get back to the hotel. I want to check the times and dates of that booking.'

* * *

Jimmy Melsom was taking statements from the staff at the Ballard View Hotel.

'Nearly finished,' he reported. 'Nothing unusual so far.'

27

Sophie and Marsh visited the manageress in her office and asked to see the booking details for the room.

It had been booked three weeks earlier by telephone, with Sarah Sheldon's name on the reservation. Allen stared at the screen, then stood back, puzzled.

'Barry, this booking was made on the same day as the one at the Hawthorns. And there's less than a fifteen minute gap in the times between them. This one's at noon, the other one was made at ten past. How likely is that to be a random coincidence?'

CHAPTER 3: FRICTION

Saturday lunchtime

'So this might be the last time we'll be using this place?' Sophie asked. She stretched out her slim legs under the table and looked up at the high ceiling. She and Melsom were seated in the incident room at Swanage's Victorian police station. 'It's a shame. I've grown used to it during the past year. It's always had a pleasant feel about it. The whole station, I mean, not just this room. What happens now it's about to close?'

'The uniformed lot are being allocated some unused rooms at the back of the town hall, along with a few car-parking slots. We don't know what will happen to us. Probably a move to Wareham. There's quite a bit of bitterness about it all.' Barry Marsh was preparing an incident board. 'Maybe this building will be converted into flats. Who knows?'

'It's not just due to the cuts, Barry. Crime rates are falling and have been doing so for some time now. It's not been covered in the press because that kind of news doesn't sell newspapers, but it's a fact. Petty and opportunistic crime may be a bit steadier, but society is becoming more civilised. What we're finding is that serious crime is being concentrated more and more into certain pockets of society. And it's not just in Britain. It's been happening across the whole of the developed world.'

'So we'll all find ourselves redundant sooner or later?' Melsom sounded downhearted.

'No. Crime rates may be dropping, but the population is rising. So the numbers will probably remain steady. There'll always be a job for you, Jimmy, don't worry. Anyway, let's get on with a quick review before I decide on priorities for this afternoon. You first, Barry.'

Marsh sat down and took a sip of tea before speaking.

'First odd fact. Despite what Mrs Corrigan said, Sarah Sheldon did ask for a family room. One of the receptionists remembers the phone conversation. Second oddity. The bookings were both made within a few minutes of each other. There was an enquiry about the possibility of a neighbouring room only a short while after Sarah had made her booking. Whoever it was claimed to be her brother.'

'Did they ask for those specific rooms?' Melsom asked.

'Not Sarah, but she did ask for that *type* of room. The receptionist remembers suggesting that the second caller try the Hawthorns. She always tries to put business their way if the hotel is fully booked or too expensive for the caller, because the Fantinis are her parents. And Shapiro's booking at the Hawthorns matches the time and date perfectly. Those two reservations were linked.'

'So the killing might not be random after all? They probably knew each other,' Melsom said.

'It looks as though there was some kind of link, but we can't make the assumption that the murder was pre-planned, Jimmy,' said Sophie. She nodded for Marsh to continue.

'Third odd fact. Shapiro lied to Mrs Fantini. They didn't come by bus. The times don't check out. The buses were running to time and I've had people interviewing the bus drivers on both routes into town. No one matching their description came in by bus yesterday afternoon or evening. What we do have, though, is a vague match with two men who were seen walking out of the town's main car park in Victoria Avenue a few minutes earlier. It was sheer good fortune, since it was dark by then. The times match nicely with their arrival at the Hawthorns.'

'Reliable witness?' Sophie asked.

'I think so. She's a local resident and passed them on the pavement.'

'Why would they lie about something like that?' Melsom mused.

Marsh shrugged. 'It is odd. But it suggests they didn't expect all this to happen, don't you think, ma'am?'

'You're right. Whatever they were up to, they expected it to be trouble-free. But Jimmy's question remains. Why did they lie about their means of transport? My guess is that they didn't want their car identified. Like most places, the Fantinis ask for car registrations. I saw the space for it on the check-in card. So Shapiro opted to park across the road and lie about it. And the car's no longer there.'

'Fourth odd fact. It follows on from the close timing of the booking sequence. It looks as though Sheldon might have misled Rosemary Corrigan into thinking that the two men were strangers to her, whereas she may well have known one or both of them somehow. But if they did already know each other, why couldn't she have just said so? Why pretend that the meeting was accidental?'

'Because it might have led to too many questions from Rosemary,' said Sophie. 'Where did you meet? How did you meet? How many times? Where did you go together? Easier to pretend that you've never met before.'

She turned to Melsom. 'Now it's your turn to tell us what you found out when you interviewed the other guests at the hotel.'

'Not much. I found another group that were in the hotel bar late last night and their accounts match what Mrs Corrigan and Mr Wilton told us. One of them noticed that Shapiro seemed in a bit of a mood. They confirmed that Mrs Sheldon and the taller man stayed for a few minutes after the other three left the bar, then walked towards the stairs together. That also checks out with what the porter remembers. He thinks Shapiro left at about twelve-twenty, followed by Wilton and Rosemary a minute or two later.'

'But no one noticed Shapiro, or anyone else, coming back in later? Or anyone else leaving? Sarah got out of the building somehow, or her body was carried out, probably through the fire door. Could you check whether it's alarmed in any way?'

'There's a back entrance from the garden to the car park, ma'am. You can get into the garden via a footpath coming in from the road down at the back. And there's a side door near the restaurant that leads out to the garden. It's meant to be locked at eleven, but the porter admits that it's sometimes a lot later than that. Even then some guests open it to go out for a smoke and don't bother locking it when they come in again.'

'So we have a possible way that Shapiro got back into the building. Good. We'll get that door fingerprinted as well as the fire door next to the room.'

'But why would he have come back, ma'am?' Melsom asked.

'It could have been prearranged. But all the witness accounts tend to indicate that the two men weren't behaving as if they were particularly close. There may be a simpler explanation. Maybe it was Derek who had the key to the Hawthorns. It's possible that Shapiro left in a huff, got to the front door and found he couldn't get in. Maybe he went back to get the key from Derek.'

'Why not ring the bell and get Mrs Fantini to let him in?'

'Maybe he tried and got no response. She told us she went to bed just after midnight. We'll have to ask her whether she'd have heard the doorbell once she was in bed. Can you do that, Barry? And if it was Shapiro, how did he know about the hotel's rear door leading in from the garden? He wasn't staying there, and, according to Rosemary, he didn't leave the bar area until about the same time as they did. Do you think he could have been here before?'

'Ma'am,' said Marsh, 'do you remember that Rosemary Corrigan told us Mrs Sheldon had stayed out all night when they went to other music festivals? What if she was meeting Derek then? What if this isn't the first time the two of them have met up at one of these festivals, but it's the first time things have gone wrong with whatever they've been up to?'

'Oh, that's clever, Barry. Just the way I want you thinking. Yes. We'll need to track back through the hotel bookings at previous festivals . . . So what could have gone wrong last night?' Sophie glanced at her watch. 'It's time we joined the crew out on the pub hunt. Barry, you go on ahead to any venue that's got a gig on. See that every single person is being questioned thoroughly about our foursome. Other people must have seen them, surely? I want corroboration. Jimmy, you stay and look through booking records to see if any of the names have cropped up before. I'll have another word with Rosemary and check a few things with Mrs Fantini. Then we'll both join Barry in the town. We'll also need to check the cars in all the car parks. Is there a car unaccounted for that might belong to one of the two men, or has it disappeared along with its owner?'

'There was one more thing, ma'am,' Melsom added. 'There are still a couple of residents who haven't been traced yet. The staff think that they'll trail back in during the day sometime. They said there are always a few who find somewhere else to spend the night. Parties and things.'

'Keep on it, Jimmy. I want them all accounted for.'

* * *

Each of the pub gigs lasted for about two hours, but the festival organisers had sequenced them so that visitors had a choice of at least two events at any one time throughout the day. Sophie and Melsom joined the throng in one of the town centre bars, looking for Marsh. The atmosphere was subdued. News of the suspicious death had swept through the small resort, and visitors to the festival were understandably worried. Sophie recognised several police officers, each talking to people in the crowd, using the descriptions that Corrigan and Wilton had supplied, and occasionally showing photos of the pair. She pushed some money into Melsom's hand.

'Get me an orange juice, Jimmy. And something for yourself and Barry. But nothing alcoholic, okay?'

She reached a small group of people standing around Marsh.

'Ma'am, these people were sitting at the table next to our five late yesterday evening. They've agreed to give statements. There's also someone else you should meet. He's waiting in the office. If Jimmy can stay here, I'll take you through.'

They went through a narrow door leading to a corridor.

'It's someone who claims he saw our two guys a bit earlier in the evening than Ed Wilton did. He's a roadie with one of the bands and was moving equipment.'

The two detectives entered a tiny office where a heavyset man, dressed in faded denim, was standing beside a uniformed officer.

Sophie held out her hand. 'I'm DCI Sophie Allen. You have some information for us?'

'Yeah. I'm sure it was them. They were standing just outside the doorway to the patio, and I was trying to get our kit in from the van. They were right in my way but wouldn't move until I told them to shift themselves. And they didn't act like normal punters.'

'What do you mean?' Sophie asked.

The man scratched his bulging stomach. 'Well, most people try to be helpful. Some even help me shift the kit. But these two just gave me a look — it was meant to scare me. Fuck's sake. I told them to fucking move or there'd be trouble. They shifted a bit after that. But they weren't happy bunnies, and I don't just mean with me. They were uneasy about something, but I couldn't tell what.'

'Did you hear anything they were saying?'

'No. But they were definitely disagreeing over something. They weren't there all evening. When I was reloading the van after the gig, they'd gone.'

'And you're sure it was them — the two we're asking about?'

'Yes. And one of them . . . I think I've seen him before somewhere.'

'Do you mean here? At Swanage? This weekend or some previous blues festival?'

'We've never played here before, so it must have been somewhere else. But I can't be absolutely sure. He just seemed kind of familiar, know what I mean? I was thinking about it just now, before you came in. It could have been at some other festival.'

'How many do you play?' Marsh asked.

'About six or so each year. The rest of our gigs are in pubs along the south-east coast. We've never been this far west before. But I don't think it was at a normal gig. It could have been daytime so it was probably at another festival. We've done an occasional jazz festival, so it might have been at one of them.'

'Can you put together a list of festivals you've played at over the past couple of years and include it with your statement?' said Marsh.

'Sure.'

Sophie broke in. 'Which one was it? The one you've seen before?'

'The shorter one. I reckon he was the boss. I didn't recognise the other one. Rude bastards.'

They left a local detective to take a statement.

'This makes it even stranger, Barry. If they were disagreeing, what was it about? There's something complicated going on here. Whatever they were up to, something went wrong, and Sarah's death last night was the consequence. We need to find what other festivals there are, and start looking for links.'

Marsh's phone sounded. He listened in silence.

'We have an address for Sarah Sheldon in Portsmouth. The address she used on the hotel's reservation slip matches what Rosemary told us, and the local force in Portsmouth have just confirmed it. They'll have someone to meet us there and a forensic team on standby.' He took a quick look at his watch. 'In about an hour and a half. Can we make it in time?'

'I've bought a new car, Barry. Just watch me go.'

* * *

The interior of the flat was neat and clean. The hallway smelled of polish and the scent from a vase of slightly faded flowers sitting on a shelf beside the front door. Everything seemed relatively new, all the furniture, carpets and accessories. The lounge had a small bookcase containing recent paperback titles, along with a dictionary and some travel guides.

Sophie inspected the shelves and surfaces carefully, while the local Portsmouth man peered behind the furniture. Marsh opened the drawers and cupboards in a sideboard unit.

A second doorway from the hall led to a brightly painted kitchen-diner. All the utensils and crockery were neatly stacked inside cupboards and drawers. A window looked out over a small, shared garden area where several whirligigs, some encased in plastic covers, stood sentry over the little patch of lawn. Sophie glanced at the bills and letters pinned to a corkboard fixed to the wall. She asked the local Portsmouth detective, DC Phil Barber, to examine the cupboards in the hallway. Marsh finished looking through the drawers, but found nothing out of the ordinary.

The two detectives went into the main bedroom. The room, like those downstairs, was well-lit and colourfully decorated. The furniture was simple and contemporary.

'No pastel shades here, ma'am. She liked her colours.'

'It matches her personality, from what we've been told. We'll just have a quick look through the units to see if anything stands out.'

36

Nothing seemed amiss. Clothes, jewels, books and possessions were exactly the kind of items Sophie would have expected from an educated, middle-aged woman. She glanced inside the rattan laundry basket and under the bed. They walked through to the small second bedroom, which doubled as an office. In addition to a single bed tucked against one wall and the small wardrobe and dressing table, a small desk stood in front of the window with an office chair in front of it. A single shelf of folders and books stood to one side. Sophie looked at the laptop lying on the desk. There was a small laser printer beside it.

Marsh looked under the desk, and opened the single drawer. He took out several memory sticks and slid them into a plastic bag, then turned to the forensic officer, who had followed them upstairs, and pointed at the computer.

'Can we switch the laptop on?'

'The decision's yours,' came the reply. 'But it might be better to take it back to your computer forensic team. The chances are it's absolutely fine, but just occasionally we've come across one that's been rigged to bugger itself up if someone tries to log on. You know, it's been booby-trapped with a clean-up program and all the important stuff gets wiped. It depends who you're up against.'

'Leave it, Barry,' Sophie said. 'We'll take it with us. We don't really know who we're investigating, so we'll get an expert to do it. If we phone ahead maybe someone can be there waiting for us. I don't want to be waiting for days to find out what it contains.'

They took one last look around the room and returned to the lounge. A second forensic man held out a plastic bag containing two booklets.

'An address book and a diary for last year. Only one person's prints on them, and I've made a record. There's no diary for this year, by the way.'

'She probably had it with her, although it hasn't turned up yet. But these will be very useful. We'll examine them back at our place. You have my number. If you find anything unusual, please let me know right away.'

She turned back to Marsh, who was inspecting Sarah's music collection. 'It's a bit odd, ma'am. They were at a blues festival, but none of the CDs here are remotely linked to blues or jazz. It's all fairly middle-of-the-road stuff. Seems a bit peculiar, doesn't it?'

'Maybe. Although some people use the festivals as a way of finding new partners. They may not be interested in the music at all.'

'In that case, why not use an internet dating service? It'd be a helluva lot easier.'

'I take your point. Is there nothing at all?'

'No. She might have mp3 files on her laptop, but there's no player anywhere here. She might have stuff stored on a smartphone and, from what you say, that probably vanished from her bag, but it's a bit curious.' He paused. 'I'm beginning to agree with your idea, ma'am. The blues festival just provided a convenient pretext. If they were up to something, you know, from what that roadie told us, then it's possible none of them, at least the three we're interested in, were attracted there by the music. Remember what Rosemary told us? And Ed Wilton? He said the band playing last night was something really special. Yet Mrs Sheldon and this Derek guy didn't show any interest. They spent the whole hour canoodling. According to them, even Shapiro didn't take much notice of the music. We assumed they were looking for romance. But what if it was something else?'

'Maybe when we start going through her address book and contacting people we'll start seeing the bigger picture. Anyway, let's finish off here for now.'

They knocked at the other five flats in the block. The two who did answer could only say that Sarah had moved in less than two years previously. Sophie asked Barber, the local CID man, to call on the other neighbours early the following week in case any of them could help with background information.

CHAPTER 4: TOUGH QUESTIONS

Saturday evening

'You can stay at my place again tonight, Rosemary. Honestly it won't be a problem.'

Ed Wilton and Rosemary Corrigan were sharing a pot of tea in a small café on the High Street. It was late afternoon and the sky was darkening as rain clouds moved in from the west. Rosemary frowned and took another sip from her cup.

'Ella's still with me until tomorrow afternoon. She's offered to cook something tonight and she's said there'll be plenty for three. And what else can you do? Your room will be off limits for days, surely?' He glanced out of the window. No one had umbrellas up just yet.

'Well, the hotel has offered me a spare room in the staff accommodation, so they have made an effort to look after me. They don't have any other guest rooms because of the festival.'

'That's not surprising. Everywhere's fully booked I expect.' He looked at her tired eyes. 'Well, the offer's there if you want it. And to be honest, I just feel you'd be safer with us. My original plan was to go out again and see another couple of bands this evening, but I really don't feel like it after what's happened . . .' His voice trailed off into silence.

'Oh, Ed, I can't even think straight. I just keep imagining what it must have been like for Sarah and what she went through last night. And I keep thinking, what if I'd been there as well? Would I be dead too?' She finished her coffee and refilled the cup. 'But in answer to your question, yes, please. I'd feel more secure at your place. But only if Ella is happy about it, and only if she stays too. And if the police are okay with it. I watch enough TV drama to know that both of us must be on their list of suspects. Anyway, they want to know where I am at all times. I think they want another interview sometime later, but I'm not sure what about. I don't have many more clothes and I'm not allowed to remove anything from my bag in the hotel room until I get the go-ahead, and that could take days.'

Her mobile phone rang. When the call ended, she looked across the table at Ed.

'It's the police. Can they talk to us again this evening?'

He nodded. She told the caller they would be at Ed's flat.

'Let's walk the long way back,' he said. 'I need some fresh air, and a walk along the front would be just right. We should make it before the rain starts.'

* * *

Rosemary Corrigan perched nervously on the edge of her chair. Sophie was facing her across a low table. Marsh sat to one side, notebook in hand. They'd asked Wilton to leave the room while they talked and Rosemary could hear him and his daughter clearing dishes in the kitchen.

'You've told us that you met Sarah at a divorcees' social evening, Rosemary. Can you expand on that? Think back carefully. How did you get talking?'

Rosemary chewed at her lower lip. She felt mentally and physically wrung out. 'It had been advertised in the local paper. It was held in a room in one of the Portsmouth city centre pubs, midweek, I think, about eighteen months ago. I found it all very strange. Everyone seemed a bit overanxious. It wasn't a very relaxed atmosphere and I wasn't impressed by any of the men there. They were all trying too hard. By then I'd realised I really wasn't ready for it anyway. I was debating whether to have another drink or just cut my losses and go home, when I turned and bumped into Sarah, and she spilled her drink. I apologised of course, being me, but it was just as much her fault as mine and she said so. I remember her saying to me that the evening was a bit crap and did I fancy going somewhere normal? I agreed, so we left and headed down the road to another place that she knew. We got chatting and we decided to meet up the next week for a meal out. And we hit it off. She started talking about these music festivals that she went to. I think I must have expressed an interest because the next time we met, she told me she'd booked the two of us in for a blues weekend at Hayling Island. I was a bit taken aback by the way she'd done it without checking with me, but I decided to go anyway.'

'Did anything unusual happen?'

'Not really. By the time we went, a couple of months had passed and we'd met several more times for evenings out. It became obvious that she was out for light-hearted flings, as she called them. Even so, I was a bit shocked by how easily she paired up with a man. She would flash that lovely smile at some poor bloke, and he'd be hooked. When we went to Hayling Island she didn't appear back in our room until the middle of the night — well, more like two in the morning. It was all a bit of an eye-opener for me.'

'Did the same thing happen the second night?'

She frowned. 'We-ell . . . on the Saturday evening we saw a couple of bands, had a few drinks but stayed together. We'd almost got back to our building when she said she was heading off again. I guessed it was to see Roger, or whatever his name was. I thought it was a bit odd, because she hadn't breathed a word of her plans until then. So I went in by myself. That was when she stayed out all night, and came back just before breakfast.'

'Roger? Are you sure that was his name?'

'No. I can't be sure, but I think so. Although I haven't seen him again. He wasn't at the next one. At least, I didn't spot him.'

'Where was that?'

'Gloucester, in July.' Again the frown and the bitten lip. Sophie waited. 'You know, I've just realised that the same thing happened there. On the Friday evening we went out and she met up with someone, just like before. She stayed out until well past midnight but came back in. On the Saturday night she made no attempt to hit on anyone. Once we were near our hotel, she disappeared again and I didn't see her until the next morning. It was the same pattern.'

'But not the same man?'

'No. There his name was . . . I remember now. The second one's name was Roger. That first weekend, the guy's name was Jonathan. At least I think so. It's so hard to remember.'

Sophie turned to Marsh. 'Is there a way of checking the names of visitors to these festivals? What happens here in Swanage?'

'Not easy, ma'am. Because it's spread across most of the town's pubs, there's no ticket system. People can buy a wristband for the weekend, but it's cash only. There's no list kept, so we can only trace people via the hotels and guest houses. We'd miss out on any day visitors.'

'The Gloucester one was like that,' Rosemary added. 'But the one at Hayling Island was in a holiday park, and we were in a chalet. I remember that we had to check in for that.'

'So we might be able to follow up on that one. And in both cases you never saw who Sarah was meeting on the Saturday night? The assumption was that it was the same man as on the Friday, but you can't be sure?'

'No. And there's something else that's odd. She'd talk about the Friday night man over breakfast on the Saturday morning. She'd be laughing and giggling about it. But on Sunday morning she'd be more tight-lipped. I've never thought of that before.'

'Let's return to this current weekend. Think about the two men, Brian and Derek. Is it possible that you might have seen them before at one of the other festivals?'

'I don't think so. They're certainly not the men Sarah picked up previously, and they didn't look familiar. So, no.'

'Take me back to yesterday evening, Rosemary. I know you gave us a potted account this morning, but I want to know why you left the first pub, the one where you'd been talking to Ed. Was it your idea or Sarah's to go to the one up the road?' Sophie asked.

'Sarah's. And something else has just occurred to me. Her behaviour yesterday was entirely different to the previous Friday evenings. Yesterday she didn't act as if she was on the lookout for a man, despite what she told Ed. She was quieter. That's until we walked into that second bar. Once Derek appeared she was back to being full of life.'

'Did she get any phone calls earlier in the evening?' asked Marsh.

'No. But while I was talking to Ed, she got some text messages. It was just after one of those that she grabbed my arm and said we were going somewhere else.'

'Was there any hint that they already knew each other? Sarah and Derek, I mean,' Marsh continued.

'I didn't think so at the time, but the way she behaved with him was much more forward than I'd ever seen before. They were all over each other. I had to warn them to cool it because I was worried there might be complaints. You know, from some of the other people there, or from the staff. I was actually quite embarrassed.'

'Could you describe exactly what you could see happening between them?' Sophie asked.

'Well, it didn't take long before his hand went inside her jacket. He was squeezing her breasts. And it wasn't so obvious because it was going on below table height, but her hand was inside his trousers. Honestly, she'd never gone that far in public before. Nowhere near.'

'Looking back now, do you think they might already have known each other?'

'Look, I just don't know. They were whispering to each other, but I don't know what they were saying. It was too noisy to hear a thing, what with the band playing and all the people crammed together, shouting at each other.'

'What about when you walked back to the hotel? What was going on then?'

Rosemary thought for a moment. 'I was in front, talking to Ed. Brian was trying hard to keep up with me. Sarah and Derek hung back a bit. It wasn't far. It could only have taken us a couple of minutes. When we arrived at the hotel we made for the bar. It was so quiet compared with the pubs. I settled into a sofa and felt like going to sleep. I remember that the barman brought over a tray of liqueurs and brandies that someone had ordered. I think it was Derek. The next thing I knew was when Sarah nudged me awake and told me that we needed to visit the loo. It was a bit weird really.'

'Why was that, Rosemary?'

'When we got there she got quite bossy. She told me that she was going to spend the night with Derek, and that I ought to loosen up a bit and go back with Brian. Or Ed. It didn't matter which, as long as I found somewhere else to go. It wasn't a discussion. She made it very clear that I was getting my marching orders. Then she walked out. I followed, explained the situation to Ed and he invited me to stay here. That was when Brian left. I collected a few things from our room, said goodbye to Sarah and came out with Ed. I was tired, confused and angry and I let her know how I felt. I was beginning to ask myself whether I wanted to carry on being friends with her, but I didn't say anything. I decided to wait to see how she behaved this morning, and whether she'd apologise. And that was it. I think you know everything else that happened.'

Sophie was silent for a few moments. 'That's fine, Rosemary. I think we now have a much clearer picture of your relationship with Sarah, and what happened yesterday. I just have a couple more questions. How did you get here from Portsmouth yesterday? Can you take us through that, please?'

'We came in my car. I picked her up straight after leaving work at six. I'd normally be working later than that on a Friday, but I'd arranged for my deputy to take over from me for this weekend.'

'Was that at her house?'

'Yes. I texted her when I set off so she knew when to expect me. She was waiting in her front porch with her case. Nothing unusual happened on the drive across, as far as I can recall.'

'You're in retail management, aren't you?'

'Yes. I manage a medium-sized department store. Weekends are our busiest time.'

'So you have a pretty responsible job.'

'In a way, yes. But there's not much room for manoeuvre, not for the individual store manager these days. All the important decisions are made higher up, at head office. We are just responsible for implementing them.'

Sophie nodded.

'It took us about an hour and a half, maybe a bit longer, to get here. By the time we'd checked in and unpacked it was nearly eight. Sarah waited while I changed out of my work suit and touched up my make-up. Then we went out. We managed to get some food in the pub. That's where we chatted to Ed. He was at the bar at the same time.'

'Who chose that pub?' Marsh asked.

'Me. Sarah wanted to go to the Red Lion, but a band had already started playing and it was absolutely mobbed. And I was starving. I pulled her away from the door because I could see that the Swan was a bit quieter. We got some food there quite quickly.'

'Did Sarah seem put out when you got her to leave that pub and go somewhere else?' Marsh asked.

'It's difficult to say. Maybe for a very short while, but I did agree to go back with her later. She was happy with that.'

'You said you changed into informal clothes at the hotel. Does that mean that Sarah didn't need to? Was she already in her evening outfit when you picked her up?' said Sophie.

'Yes. She was in jeans and a sparkly top. And her leather jacket.'

'But I thought she worked in a bank.'

'I'd guess that she finished at five and had time to go home and change. That was what I assumed.'

Sophie changed the subject. 'Did you see anyone you recognised from a previous weekend?'

Rosemary shook her head. 'No. I think we were about the last to check in at the hotel. Most people had arrived earlier and already gone out. And no one at the pubs was at all familiar.'

'What about late at night when you came back to the hotel's lounge bar? Who else was there?'

'I really can't remember. I was so tired by then, all I wanted to do was go to sleep. There might have been a small group around a table in the other corner. I think there was. But I can't remember anything about them.'

'This might be a bit harder for you, but I want to get some idea of the relationship between the two men, Derek and Brian. How close did they seem?'

Rosemary thought for a moment. 'They didn't talk much. But then, it would have been difficult the way Sarah and Derek were behaving. She had her arm hooked into his almost as soon as they met. But they didn't seem to be very alike, not in personality anyway. As far as I remember, they didn't speak to each other much.'

'When they did speak, who took the lead?'

'Probably Brian. Derek was more laid back. Brian seemed kind of edgy. I don't know if it was just last night or whether he was always like that.' She paused. 'There was something about Brian that I just didn't like. I might have imagined it, but once or twice I thought it was something more than just resentment that I wasn't playing ball.'

'Do you know who Sarah's next of kin might be? Are either of her parents still alive?'

'She never talked about her father to me. I always assumed that he must have died some time back. Her mother died just a couple of years ago, I think.'

Sophie glanced at Marsh. He shook his head very slightly. She smiled encouragingly at Rosemary. 'We don't have any more questions for now, Rosemary. You've been really helpful, thank you. We'd like to talk to Ed now but we shouldn't be long.'

Rosemary left the two detectives and joined Ed and Ella in the kitchen. They were sitting at the table, nibbling at some cheese. She sat down heavily, looking washed out.

'They want to speak to you, Ed.'

'Are you alright? You look a bit tired.'

'At least I'm still alive. That's what I keep telling myself.' She gave him a weak smile. 'I'm okay. But they are very thorough. She's quite remorseless. I had visions of a couple of country cops who might be a bit clueless. I really thought I knew Sarah, but after some of the questions they asked, I'm beginning to doubt it. They followed up on every single decision we made yesterday. It's made me think again about the way the evening went. And the sergeant just sits watching, and occasionally throws in another question. I feel like some kind of criminal.'

'Have a glass of wine. There's still a bit left in the bottle.' Ed poured her a glass before he left the kitchen.

* * *

'Tell us about yourself, Mr Wilton,' said the sergeant. 'I understand you're a professional musician and music producer.'

Ed was surprised that the initial question came from the sergeant.

'So you live in London most of the time, and use this flat as an occasional retreat? How often does your daughter visit?' Again it was the sergeant who asked. The DCI watched and listened in silence.

'Two or three times a year. She tries to get to one of the music festivals with me. I arrived yesterday morning, and she got here early evening.'

'But you went out by yourself? Why didn't she go to the gig with you?'

'She had some work to write up for university and wanted to do it while it was fresh in her mind. She was planning to come out with me today.'

'How many festivals have you attended?'

'Over the years? Most of them. I used to come regularly with my wife, Lizzie. She died eighteen months ago.'

At last the DCI spoke. 'I'm sorry to hear that, Mr Wilton. It can't have been an easy time for you. But I hope you understand that we have to ask you these questions, given the circumstances.'

Ed nodded.

'What band did you see last night?' asked the sergeant.

'Blue Moods. They're quite young, but I was given a tip-off to see them. The vocalist is really special.'

'What other bands have impressed you recently? At the last festival for example?' the sergeant continued.

Ed thought back six months and listed a couple of gigs he'd attended.

'Mostly female vocalists, Mr Wilton.' This from the DCI.

'Along with many other people in the music business, I think the female voice is usually clearer and more expressive. Women singers are often willing to work harder at what they do. I recommend acts to a couple of agencies and studio labels, and they want people with real potential. At the moment, as far as vocalists are concerned, that usually means women. Too many guys think they're God's gift to the business and don't live up to any early promise.'

Ed noticed the DCI incline her head towards the sergeant.

'How did you get to meet Rosemary and Sarah last night?' he asked.

Ed described the scene the previous evening. The two women had been waiting at the bar. 'I happened to be beside them, and sat with them while they ate. We were lucky to get a table. We got served just before the place started to get busy, so Rosemary and Sarah got their food fairly quickly. We chatted a little, but they went as soon as they'd finished eating.'

'Who suggested that they should leave?'

'I don't know. I went to the loo, and they'd gone when I got back. I felt a bit let down, because they hadn't mentioned leaving. Though I thought Sarah seemed a bit edgy.'

'In what way?'

'She kept looking at her watch. She also spent a while on her mobile phone. Texting, I think.'

'What did you do then?'

'I'd lost my seat so I got myself another drink and found a stool in a corner. I stayed there for most of the gig. I was surprised to see them come back in later. The band was well into its second set by then.'

'Describe how the four of them behaved.'

Wilton told them of Shapiro's increasing irritation, and Sarah and Derek's heavy petting. He told them about the walk up to the hotel late in the evening.

'Who else was in the hotel lounge, Mr Wilton?'

Ed thought for a few moments. 'A couple of men in the other corner. We were sitting on sofas on one side of the fireplace. They were in chairs at a small table.'

'Can you describe them?'

'Difficult. They were wearing casual clothes. Zipped jackets and jeans, I think. I didn't take much notice, especially since we were only there for ten minutes or so and I was worried about the way Shapiro was acting.'

'Can you explain?'

'He was angry and I could understand why. His chum was getting on with Sarah like a house on fire, and he wanted to do the same with Rosemary. But it clearly wasn't going to happen. I was getting worried for her safety, so I offered her a bed back here. I was glad to help, and relieved when she accepted.'

He went on to describe the scene as the group split up, and the short walk to his flat. Marsh nodded and made some notes. Ed ran his fingers through his hair.

'How did you get that graze on your right hand, Mr Wilton?' The DCI was looking at him.

'I stumbled slightly as we left the hotel last night, and brushed it against the wall. I didn't notice it until later, when I was back here. It's nothing really. I rinsed it and dabbed it with a bit of antiseptic cream.'

She held out her hand and gently took his, turning it to get a better look. Her hand was cool, with slender fingers that brushed against the graze.

'It's slightly bruised underneath the skin,' she said. 'Where exactly did you scrape it?'

'The steps coming down from the entrance. I misjudged one of them at the bottom.'

'Which side were you on?'

Oh, for pity's sake, he thought. 'I was on the left, against the wall of the building.'

'Thank you.' Her green eyes gave nothing away. 'Is there anything else you feel you need to tell us?'

Ed shook his head.

'Mr Wilton, Rosemary asked us for advice about where to stay tonight. I'd have been happier with her at the hotel, but since she was here last night I couldn't raise serious objections to her staying again. Please don't betray her trust. The police station is only two hundred yards away, as I'm sure you know.'

'No. She'll be safe here.' He wasn't sure how to interpret this comment.

'If you think of any other information that might be of help to us, please contact me immediately.' The sergeant looked at his watch, and then at his boss.

Could we have a few words with your daughter, Mr Wilton?' she said.

'Why on earth do you want to speak to her?'

'Corroboration, as I'm sure you can guess. We'll only take up a minute or two of her time.'

Ed walked through to the kitchen.

'This is getting beyond a joke. They want to see you, Ella.'

She nodded and left the room.

'I need a drink,' he announced. 'A big one.'

He opened another bottle of wine, refilled the three glasses and sat down at the table. Neither he nor Rosemary spoke. After a short while he heard the front door open and close and Ella re-entered the kitchen.

'Just confirming times and events,' she said. 'Nothing to get worried about.'

Ed moved to the window and watched the two detectives cross the road. As they walked under a nearby streetlight he could see that the woman had a mobile phone pressed to her ear and was talking into the mouthpiece.

'The trouble is, Ella, I'm a natural worrier. That's what your mother always used to tell me.' He continued watching. 'That's odd. They're walking up the hill, away from the police station.'

His daughter joined him at the window.

'Back to the hotel, do you think?'

CHAPTER 5: THE WEIRD AND WOBBLY WORLD

Sunday morning

Sophie opened one sleepy eye. A chink of light had found its way through a gap in the bedroom curtains and was falling on her face. She felt her husband slide his cold body down under the duvet and raised her head. She spotted a steaming mug of tea on her bedside cabinet.

'Oh, you sweetheart,' she said. 'You perfect specimen of manhood. I love you to distraction when you bring me tea in the morning.' She turned around and put her limbs around his chilly torso. 'Gosh, you're cold. Did we forget to change the timer on the boiler? You poor thing.'

'I'll live. After last night I've got a lot to live for.'

'All your fault, Martin Allen. It was your shoulder massage that started it. Normally all I want to do when I feel as exhausted as that is to sleep. Preferably in bed, but any soft surface will do if it comes to the crunch. My reaction took even me by surprise. I never knew I had an erogenous zone in the small of my back. Mind you, the way my body is ageing it's probably slipped round there from wherever it's really meant to be.'

'Well let's make sure last night wasn't a one-off. Let's make a date for the middle of the week, okay?'

'No promises, but I'll try. And I did sleep well.' She sat up and took a sip of tea. 'I'll just drink up before it gets cold. And it's my turn to give you a massage next. Don't know when I'll manage it, though.'

She snuggled up to him and gave him a kiss.

'Love you. But, I must rise and travel the lonely miles to fair Swanage. Time and tide wait for no beauteous damsel.'

'Sorry to break the mediaeval tone, but the porridge mixture is ready in the microwave. Just press the button. Presumably we should leave Jade to sleep on?'

'Yes. There's no point in us putting our lives at risk unnecessarily. Mothers know these things.'

'In that case I yield before your superior understanding, O great one. You use the en suite, I'll make do with the bathroom.'

* * *

When Barry Marsh arrived in the incident room, Sophie was reading an email.

'Come and have a look at this, Barry. Would you believe what these pen-pushers at HQ think is a priority?'

Her sergeant looked at the screen. 'They want you there at nine tomorrow morning? At this stage of a murder inquiry? But, with respect ma'am, even they're not as stupid as that, are they? There must be something they're not telling us.'

'You might be right. It does say that more information will be provided. Curious. But at least it gives us another permanent member of the team. We need a replacement for Lydia. This is for you and me only for the time being, Barry.' She finished her coffee. 'Now, what are the priorities for today? Did Jimmy get that statement from the roadie we spoke to?'

'Yes, and he's written it up. He made a start on cross-checking all the statements we have so far before he finished last night.'

'Here's what we do. Find out what we can about Derek and Brian. I also want some corroboration of that roadie's story. Even if no one else overheard the conversation, someone must have noticed the two of them out on the patio. We have to make sure he's not a total fantasist. If we could check with the pub staff that he was doing what he said at the times he claimed, that would be partial support. Will Jimmy be able to finish collating all the statements we took from people in the pubs yesterday?'

'Yes. He's due in any time now. But I don't think we should expect too much from them. From what I could gather, the most we got was a few vague recollections.'

'Well at least they help to verify times, Barry. And they help us to check the accuracy of Ed's story. So far it all matches, so there's no reason to doubt his and Rosemary's accounts, but we need to keep an open mind.'

'That makes sense. Festival-goers who were there on Friday night are likely to be somewhere else on other evenings. Our last major opportunity is lunchtime today. People start drifting away on Sunday afternoon. It's only the real hard-core fans and locals who'll stay to the bitter end this evening.'

Sophie thought for a while. 'Do people stick to the same kind of music? Could we find out who was playing at the Red Lion on Friday night and predict where they're most likely to be this lunchtime?'

Marsh shrugged his shoulders. 'Worth a try. Leave it with me.'

'What's really bugging me is the fact that we can't trace either of the two men. Which means their names could be false. In fact, I bet they are. There's something strange about the whole set-up. Has Jimmy made any progress on other music festivals?'

'He got started, ma'am, but only very late yesterday evening. Maybe someone else could take over collating the statements? Then he could get stuck into it right away.'

'Fine. I'll put Jack Holly onto it if you're happy. You and I need to go back to the hotel. I'm still not certain how

Shapiro might have found out about getting into the place from the back entrance. That's assuming he returned and was somehow involved in what happened to Sarah. From what Ed Wilton said, he was only there for fifteen minutes. He spent that time sitting in the bar sulking, not exploring the building. And the barman backed Ed up. So how did our man discover that door? The route through the garden couldn't have been obvious. It was completely dark outside by that time.'

She put photofit images of the victim and the two suspects into her bag, and the two detectives left.

As they arrived at the hotel, the night porter was just going off duty and he had nothing to add to his previous statement. He confirmed that he'd only seen Shapiro coming in after eleven with the three others, and he left a short time afterwards. He did add that he only came on duty at ten, and that it might be worth checking with the receptionist who had finished her shift at ten thirty. This receptionist, Maria, had been off duty the previous day but her colleagues had told her about what had happened. The two detectives remembered her from their visit the previous year during their investigation into the death of her fellow hotel worker, Donna Goodenough.

'I remember the two ladies checking in,' she said. 'They were one of the last. We'd normally get people checking in much later than that, but not for the music festivals. Most people don't want to miss the Friday evening gigs.'

Maria raised a hand to her pale face. She looked miserable. I can't blame her, Sophie thought. Only a year since the nightmare of having a close friend murdered, and this happens. Most people make it right through from birth to death without a murder ever impinging on their lives, and this poor girl has had to cope with two inside twelve months. She was clearly upset but listened carefully to Marsh's questions about Friday afternoon's check-ins.

'There was nothing unusual? Nothing that caught your attention in any way?'

'Not with them, no. Both of the ladies seemed really nice.'

'Is there something else then?'

Maria nodded, her long, dark curls swaying slightly. 'One of our other guests still hasn't appeared. He had a single room for the weekend. I checked him in on Friday and he was seen once or twice during the evening, but not since. His room wasn't used again last night, according to the senior housekeeper.'

'What was the name?'

'John Renton. He gave a Portsmouth address.'

'Maria, please could you ensure that nothing in the room is touched or removed? And let me know tomorrow whether he returns or not?'

The two detectives checked the booking details and obtained a description of Renton. They had a brief word with the senior housekeeper and then left the hotel for a visit to the town centre pubs.

* * *

'Yeah, I remember them. Two guys on the patio up at the Red Lion, with fags. I remember the roadie asking them to shift cos they was getting in his way. He got a right mouthful back.'

Sophie's hunch had paid off. Marsh had identified the band who had been playing at the pub on Friday evening, then had matched their style with bands due to play at midday. They were now in one of the other town centre pubs, talking to a tall, thin young man sipping at a beer.

'I'd been there for a while and the band had arrived and wanted to get their gear inside and set up. That's when your two turned up and decided to stand in the doorway, getting in the band's way. It looked like there were a few cross words, then they calmed down.'

'Did you hear anything that was being said?' Marsh asked.

'No. I was watching but not listening. But it looked like the tall one was a bit put out by the shorter one's attitude towards the roadie.'

'You were very observant, Mr Brodie.'

'Yeah, well.' He coughed. 'I was looking to see if I could make a move on one of them but they were both straight. So I lost interest. When I came back from the loo a while later they'd moved into the bar. What was a bit strange was this other guy standing in the corner. He could have been watching them.'

'What do you mean?' asked Marsh.

'He looked as though he was looking in their direction. But he was only there for a few minutes so I might have been imagining it . . . I probably was. It was pretty busy. He could have been watching anyone.'

'Could you give us a description?'

'Middle-aged, sandy hair. Small tattoo on his left wrist, but it wasn't clear. Jeans, lumberjack shirt. He wore dark glasses. That's what drew my attention. This was inside. Then he turned round and looked directly at me, as if he'd spotted me watching him. His look gave me the shivers. I looked away and when I turned back he'd gone, just vanished.'

'I'm afraid we'll need a statement from you, Mr Brodie. And full descriptions. By the way, did you see two women arrive?'

'Nah. It was like bloody sardines once the band started playing. And to be honest, I don't take much notice of women. Not interested. They're around, they come in and out of view, but they don't stick in my mind.'

'Not even me?' asked Sophie.

'Fraid not. Now . . .' He didn't finish.

'Don't say it,' growled Marsh.

Sophie laughed. 'Barry, don't be so touchy. Take it as a compliment.'

'Yeah, that's what you should do. She's right.' Brodie grinned and raised his glass. 'Here's to the weird and wobbly world.'

* * *

57

Jimmy Melsom had spent the morning on the computer and the phone, searching for information about the two men. He hadn't got very far. Nor had he made much headway on looking for suspicious deaths at other music festivals across the south. He'd made more progress on Sarah Sheldon's background and had traced her ex-husband, Hugh Shakespeare.

'He's the manager of a bank in Southampton,' he reported to Sophie. 'I haven't tried to contact him, but I've got his home address.'

Sophie took a quick look at her watch. 'Fine. I think Barry and I can get over there this afternoon. Maybe at long last we can start to get a clearer picture of our victim. We know that Sarah had a mobile with her, so it looks as though it was taken when she was killed. Can you do your bit, Jimmy, and try to trace that mobile's number? There might be clues in Sarah's address book. Forensics have still got it, so chase them about it. If anything important crops up, contact me immediately. Let's go, Barry.'

* * *

Hugh Shakespeare lived in an imposing, detached house in Bitterne, an upmarket residential area east of Southampton's city centre. The two detectives walked up a short driveway, between tidy flower beds and a neat lawn. They were a little taken aback when a stylishly dressed woman in her early forties opened the door. She spoke with a pronounced French accent.

'Francoise Lassoutte,' she said, after they had identified themselves. 'Please come in. Hugh is in the kitchen clearing away the dishes. He is so *English* with his liking for a roast lunch on Sunday. I let him get on with it.' She smiled. 'My only conditions are that he does all the work and we have French wine.'

'We want to ask him about his ex-wife, Sarah,' Sophie explained.

'Oh, that one. You'd better go into the lounge. I will get him.'

Sophie looked about her as they waited. The photos on display were mostly recent, showing Francoise with a serious-looking man in his late fifties. In some, Francoise was pictured with a teenage girl. There was a single graduation photo of a dark-haired young man. Francoise returned with the man from the photos. He was removing a chef's apron, revealing light brown slacks and a checked shirt. He shook hands and asked them to sit on the couch. He remained standing. Francoise perched on a stool in front of a highly polished, baby grand piano.

'We're here to make some enquiries about your ex-wife, Sarah, Mr Shakespeare,' Sophie said.

'Why doesn't that surprise me?' he responded, with a look of resignation.

'I'm sorry to have to tell you that yesterday morning we found her dead.'

He sat down heavily, and Francoise moved to sit on the arm of his chair, touching his shoulder. He looked stunned.

'That is a shock,' he said quietly. 'You're a chief inspector, so this can't be routine, can it?'

'No, I'm afraid not. She was attending a weekend music festival and was found among the rocks on the shoreline yesterday morning. We're treating the death as suspicious.'

He moved his head to and fro. 'Christ. I thought she would get herself into a mess one day, but not that. Nothing like that.' He looked up. 'How did it happen?'

'That's what we're trying to discover, Mr Shakespeare. It's partly why we're here. You may be able to shed some light on her personality and character so that we can get a better idea of who she was involved with. The motive is unclear at the moment.'

He sighed. 'I wish I could help you, Chief Inspector, but I really don't know. That's why we divorced. She was involved with so many men that I lost count. They were all shallow, disposable relationships. No permanence, nothing of substance. I could have understood it better if she had preferred one man to me, but she didn't prefer any one of them to me. She just seemed to need lots of them. Her life was a constant search for attention and cheap excitement. I couldn't cope with it. We divorced a good ten years ago because I just couldn't put up with all the one-night stands. It nearly destroyed me, and it nearly ruined our son, Peter. He lives in New York now. He moved there partly to get as far away from her as he could. So much for a mother's love.' By the time he stopped speaking his voice had dropped to little more than a whisper. Sophie saw a slight tremor in his shoulders.

'Is that your son in the graduation photo on the sideboard?'

He nodded.

'We may need to get him here, Mr Shakespeare. He'll probably be her next of kin, unless you know of anyone else.'

'I'm not aware of her marrying again, if that's what you mean.'

Sophie nodded. 'We understand that Sarah worked in a bank.'

'Yes.' He sighed. 'That's how we met. We both started at the same time and got on well. We fell in love. Well, put it this way, I fell in love with her. I began to doubt whether she ever felt much for me when the affairs started. It had probably been going on all the time without me realising it.' He looked across at Sophie. 'Do you think it could have been her lifestyle that got her killed? She just picked the wrong man?'

'We don't know, Mr Shakespeare. We're trying to build up a picture of her at the moment. Please tell us more about her if you can. Maybe start with her work?'

'It was strange really. She was so bright, so clever. She had far more potential than me, but she was never willing to put any effort into anything. She was content to coast along in her job while I slogged away, aiming for promotions.'

'You're a manager now?'

'Yes. We were both in Portsmouth, but I wanted a complete change when we separated, so I moved here. I now manage the largest branch in the city. Apart from cards at Christmas and her birthday, we haven't communicated in years.'

'Her birthday? Not yours?'

'No. When I said cards, I meant cards that we sent to her. I never received any back.'

'Is there anything you can tell us about her life in recent years?'

'Not really. I settled down with Francoise three years ago. Her daughter lives with us. She's a student at the university here. Everything is so much calmer and . . . well, as it should be. I haven't really thought much about Sarah for years. She's just a name on a Christmas list. I've gotten over her. So I don't know what she got herself into. I did hear that she'd stopped working for the bank. That was more than a year ago.'

'Do you mean the branch where she'd been based, or the company?'

'The whole network. She was no longer on the bank's payroll, not at any branch, nor any of its other operations. I looked when I heard the news that she'd left. Whether she switched to a different company, well, I can't tell you.'

'What about your son?' said Marsh. 'Do you think he might still have been in contact with her?'

'I don't believe so, but I can't be certain.'

Francoise added, 'what Hugh hasn't told you, Inspector, is that he was close to being a nervous wreck when we met five years ago. I wondered what could have happened to reduce such a decent man to that state. I found out when we bumped into Sarah at a function, soon after I'd started seeing Hugh. She was with a man, but she was still teasing others. She even flirted with Hugh, just as if it was all a big game, as if she couldn't see the hurt that she'd caused and was still causing. Hugh needed therapy when we first met. I could see that and I arranged it. It helped. I don't know if you can understand.'

'Yes, I can. I've been through therapy. It involved hauling some pretty dreadful feelings and emotions from the depths, holding them up to the light and talking about them. It did help.'

Francoise rubbed Hugh's upper back, gently massaging his shoulder muscles. 'She didn't deserve him, Inspector. She was cheap.'

'What's your line of work, Ms Lassoutte?'

'I'm a doctor. A paediatrician at the local hospital.'

Sophie turned back to her partner. 'The other thing we need to confirm is whether Sarah had any siblings, Mr Shakespeare.'

'Not full ones, no. Apparently she had an older sister who was killed in a motorcycle accident when Sarah was still a teenager. And she has a half-brother. She fell out with him many years ago when they were teenagers. They shared the same mother.'

'What was Sarah's maiden name?'

'Sheldon. She was Sarah Sheldon when I first met her and she liked to use the name even when we were married.'

'The name Derek doesn't mean anything to you?'

Hugh Shakespeare shook his head.

'What about Brian Shapiro?'

Again a shake of the head.

CHAPTER 6: COOL BODY

Sunday afternoon and evening

'What would have happened to me if I'd been in that room on Friday night?'

'We don't know, Rosemary. It's impossible to make that kind of conjecture. There are just too many variables. You'd only have been sleeping in the room if the pair of you hadn't met the two men or if Sarah hadn't struck up such a close rapport with Derek. But if that had been the case, the two of you wouldn't have been in any danger. Too many ifs, as I'm sure you can spot. At the moment we have to deal with what actually happened rather than what might have been. But we do take your safety seriously.'

Sophie was talking to Rosemary Corrigan in a small office at the police station.

'So you think I might be in danger?'

'It's impossible to be sure. That's why I want you to remain here in Dorset where we can keep an eye on you.' Sophie stretched out her legs and smoothed out an imagined crease in her skirt. 'I don't want you to return home. You'd be too vulnerable. I have three options for you. You could stay at

Ed's. Whoever carried out the murder must know about you, and if so, probably knows that you stayed at Ed's on Friday night. His flat wouldn't be difficult to find, but it does have the advantage of a locked outer door into the building, then a locked door to his apartment. From what I've seen, the place looks pretty secure. Or you could go back to the hotel. I know that they have a room available for you. At the moment it's crawling with people from my forensic team so it's relatively safe, for a few days at least. The third option, and the one I prefer, is for you to stay in a police safe house. It's more likely to be in the Wareham area than here in Swanage, so you'd be further from Ed. Whatever option you choose, I'd expect you to remain out of view and to take sensible precautions. But I don't want you back at home just yet, or even back at work. It's too risky to have you there alone. I hope it won't be for too long, but you are our best witness for these two men, and they know it. I want to keep you out of harm's way.'

Rosemary thought for a while. 'I'll ask Ed if I can continue to stay there. Ella has gone back to Bristol, and Ed has told me that I'm welcome to stay on, particularly now I can move into a proper bedroom. I think he's a good man. At least I hope he is, so I'll trust him at the moment.'

'We haven't found any evidence to the contrary, Rosemary. I wouldn't have suggested it as an option if I had any doubt of it. But you must stay on your guard. I don't just mean from him, but from any potential source of trouble. I'll have someone check on you regularly and I'll give you an emergency contact button.'

'A what?'

'You hang it round your neck and press it if you feel threatened. It will send a signal directly to us here. I'll walk you back to the flat and have another word with Ed.'

* * *

Late in the afternoon, Rosemary and Ed sat in the lounge of his flat sipping a cup of tea.

'So you've got to stay inside?' he said.

'No. We agreed that I can go out as long as I don't make myself obvious. I couldn't stay cooped up for days, Ed. I'd go round the bend. If I put on a hat, a scarf and dark glasses and make myself as inconspicuous as I can, she's happy with me being out for some of the time.' She gave a wry smile. 'Well, happy is probably the wrong word. She accepted it.'

'Will your work be okay with it?'

'I phoned my boss from the station. DCI Allen had a word with him, and I've been cleared to work remotely. Someone's bringing me a laptop tomorrow morning, and I'll try to keep my eye on things from here. Remote working can be a great thing, you know.'

'I notice you said "can be" rather than "is."'

'I've a huge backlog of admin stuff that needs sorting through. I can settle down in peace and quiet for once. That's if you don't mind?'

She looked so tired and vulnerable.

Ed smiled at her. 'Of course not. But I must warn you that I might play the piano occasionally. Inspiration can strike at any moment you know.'

'Sounds good. I've never had my own, personal pianist playing for me before. It's a deal, then. And since you won't let me pay, once this is over you must come into my store and choose some clothes at staff discount prices. Ella too.'

In the middle of the evening they went out for a walk along the promenade. A stiff breeze was blowing from the west. Swanage nestles in a dip in the land, so the clouds carried by the wind tend to fragment as they approach. The heavy volleys of rain that were falling further west were little more than occasional light flurries here.

They sat on a bench looking across the dark sea to a light twinkling on the Isle of Wight. 'It's the first time I've ever visited this area,' Rosemary said. 'It's really lovely, isn't it?'

'I've been doing the trip for almost ten years, but I'm still amazed every time I take the ferry across from Sandbanks. You come through the built-up areas of Bournemouth and Poole with all the traffic and noise. Then you drive off on this side and it's like a different world. I call it the place that time forgot. Suddenly you're driving through the Studland nature reserve — heath land and wooded areas, with the stunning views of the chalk stacks out at sea. It's so easy to miss the area completely, and selfishly I'm glad so many people do. The place would be ruined if there was much more development.' He glanced at Rosemary. 'Do you fancy a drink in my favourite pub?'

'I do, but I daren't chance it. I promised her I wouldn't. But a drink when we get back in would go down a treat. Is that okay?'

'Of course.' Though he was disappointed.

'Maybe when this is all over, Ed. We'll do it then. Okay?'

She slid her hand across the surface of the seat and found his. She squeezed it gently and moved closer, leaning her shoulder against him.

For the first time in eighteen painful months, Ed Wilton felt some of his emotional barriers begin to crack . . .

* * *

It was after midnight. He was drifting off to sleep after a rest-less spell spent listening to the wind rustling the branches of the trees outside his window. Ed sensed a movement in his bedroom. He tensed and then felt the duvet move and a cool body slid in beside him.

'I need you to hold me, Ed. That's all. Just hold me, please.' She was crying.

* * *

'So where do we go from here?' Rosemary carried two mugs of tea through to the lounge and deposited them on the low table in front of the couch. She glanced through the gap in the curtains, watching the clouds scud across the early morning sky. She pulled her robe closer around her body and sat down next to Ed, leaning her head against his shoulder.

'What do you mean?' he replied.

'You were quite clear that you weren't ready for a new relationship when we talked about it a couple of days ago. Even Ella said that was how you felt. And now this has happened.' She picked up her tea and took a tentative sip. Still too hot.

'That was my rational self talking. You know, the one that plans and organises things. The part that thinks it's in control. What I wasn't aware of was that I'd become a bit like a capped oil well. The pressure was building up inside and I didn't realise it until last night.' He stroked her hair. 'How about you? How do you feel?'

'You've described my feelings exactly. And this morning I feel kind of easy and contented with myself for the first time in months — maybe years.' She paused. 'If I was a youngster I'd say that I was falling in love with you. But I'm not. A youngster, I mean. Not the other thing.' She giggled. 'I think I've lost control of my brain. That came out all wrong.'

'I like your giggle,' he said. 'You giggled a lot last night.'

'I was happy,' she said. 'You have no idea how happy I was. What we did was kind of therapeutic. I was lying in my bed sobbing, unable to get to sleep and I just suddenly realised what I wanted. So I thought, to hell with it. And you cheered me up so much. I always think that sex is kind of funny, you know, the act. I try to imagine how a robotic, automated being would view sex. All that squirming and wriggling. The fluids. All the sounds. It's very kind of biological, isn't it?'

'Well, my understanding is that it's just that. Reproduction? Hormones? Cells? Isn't that right?'

'You're being a clever clogs now. I didn't mean it in that way. I meant in comparison to machines. At least that's what I think I meant. Oh, I don't know. Now you've made me forget what I was saying.' She suddenly stopped. 'Bloody hell. Reproduction. I might be pregnant.'

'What?' Ed sat up with a jerk.

'It's all right. I'll just go and get a morning-after pill from my wash bag. I brought some with me this weekend, just in case. Along with the condoms.'

'Have you been telling us all porky pies?' he laughed. 'You said you weren't like Sarah, and you weren't into one-night stands. And here you are, owning up to having a bag full of condoms and pills.'

She poked him in the side. 'Girl Guides. Be prepared. I suppose a part of me wanted to, but was too scared to do anything about it. And I did tell you that bit.' She sat up. 'Anyway, Mr Wilton, you've successfully managed to change the subject, which was what do we do now.'

'You said that if you were younger you might think you were falling in love. I feel that too. I feel as if, since Lizzie died I've been living in an emotional cold-store, and now you've opened it and let me out. I was lying there in bed last night, hoping. I'd just started to drift off to sleep when you crept in.'

Rosemary made an attempt at Sophie Allen's interview voice. 'Ah, Mr Wilton, I see. That's why you had no clothes on. It all makes sense now. I'll just need to get my sergeant to record this in his little notebook.'

Ed laughed. 'I always sleep in the buff. And if that was meant to be her, I think you're being unfair to our clever police person. Her voice isn't quite as posh as that. Anyway, about this pill of yours. Hadn't you better take it? Before you forget, I mean.'

'And if I didn't? And by some miracle found myself preg-nant at my advanced age? How would you feel, Ed?' Rosemary was suddenly serious.

Ed slipped his hand onto hers. 'Strangely, I wouldn't mind at all. I'd dread the messy nappies, the sleepless nights and the tiredness. But I think I'd be happy if you were happy.'

Rosemary looked at him closely, then flung her arms around him. 'Oh, you gorgeous man,' she gasped. 'Why have you waited so long before appearing in my life? At this moment

I love you more than I would have ever believed possible.' She kissed him on the lips and started to cry, just as her mobile phone rang. She glanced at the caller display and pushed it towards Ed. He answered.

'Oh, hello, Chief Inspector. Yes, she is here but she's a bit emotional at the moment . . . Okay, I'm sure we can pack a few things. Rosemary doesn't have a lot with her anyway. She was talking earlier on about having to get more clothes. You'll send someone across to her house? She's nodding. I think she's ready to speak to you now. By the way, can I bring a keyboard? I'd be lost without my music.' He handed the phone across to his new lover.

'I'm fine, really I am,' she said and listened. 'You want us to move to a safe house? Is that really necessary?' A longer pause. 'Okay, we'll see you later.' She ended the call and placed her phone back on the table. 'Well, I think we'll be in each other's company for longer than we'd anticipated. I wonder what has happened to make her change her mind. I hope this safe house she's found for us is as nice as your flat, Ed. Though I doubt it.' She smiled at him. 'How about some breakfast?'

CHAPTER 7: RAE

Monday

Sophie was woken early the next morning by the sound of a text message. She glanced at her phone and frowned. Barry Marsh had new information about Shapiro.

'I think I may need to move Rosemary somewhere safe,' she said.

Martin emerged from under the duvet. 'What?'

'Barry's just sent me a message that Shapiro might be an ex-policeman with an axe to grind. If he's gone off the rails completely he'll be very dangerous. I can't leave either of them where they are, it's too risky. And I have to make this bloody visit to HQ for some inexplicable reason, just when I can least afford the time.'

An hour after phoning Rosemary, Sophie Allen was at Dorset police headquarters in Winfrith. She was leaning across her boss's desk, almost fizzing with anger. 'What am I doing here, Matt? I'm up to my neck in a murder investigation and I'm told to drive all the way up here to collect my new DC? Why couldn't she come down to me? Has the world gone completely bonkers?'

Her immediate superior, Superintendent Matt Silver, held up his hands in mock surrender, apparently relieved that she was on the other side of a desk.

'It was all arranged in the middle of last week and HR won't budge. I know no more about this than you. Nine on Monday morning, that's all I was told. And it's you only. No one else knows what's going on, not even me.'

'I often notice that, but I don't actually say it.'

'Very witty, Sophie, but I'm not in the mood this morning. I've got a day of meetings on budget cuts, and you can guess my feelings about that.'

'Well, is she here now? I've been in the incident room since seven this morning, and had to break off to drive up here. I suppose HR think we all start at nine, like them.'

'I don't know where she is. Your appointment is with the chief of HR, not me. Like I said, I'm as much in the dark as you. Listen, while you're here, is there anything else you need help with in the investigation? I know we've spoken on the phone every day, but I wanted to say again that you only need to ask. The ACC confirmed it earlier.'

'At the moment I'm okay, Matt. And if this new DC is good, then she will fill the gap left by Lydia. I'm actually feeling quite positive about things in the long term. Barry Marsh has agreed to join the team full-time as my permanent DS, so I've finally got what I wanted. Though it's taken far too bloody long.' She looked at her watch. 'I'd better be going. I've wasted so much time this morning.'

Sophie poured herself a coffee from the jug beside his desk and left the office, muttering to herself. She made her way up the stairs and along a corridor to the HR reception desk.

'DCI Sophie Allen,' she announced to the immaculately clad receptionist. She glanced down at her own faded cord trousers and scuffed ankle boots. At least her tan leather jacket still passed muster, but she really needed a new outfit. She sighed.

'Ms Blake asked for you to wait.' The receptionist fingered his blue and red striped tie, looking a little embarrassed. He pointed to some chairs, one of which was occupied by a tall young woman. She was smartly dressed, with dark hair styled in a short bob, sitting stiffly upright, leafing through a magazine.

'Phone through and tell her that I'm heading up a murder inquiry. If she doesn't see me right now it'll become a double one, with your boss as the second victim. Okay, sweetheart?'

He picked up the phone and made the call, quoting her exact words, including "sweetheart." Sophie muttered and, ignoring his look of alarm, stalked past the desk and opened the door. Sandie Blake, Head of HR, was alone in the office, setting down the phone.

'Sweetheart? What was that about?' she asked.

Sophie shrugged. 'Don't ask me. Maybe he's got the hots for you.' She looked pointedly at her watch. 'Make it fast, please. The murder bit was true.'

'I know. The ACC's PA has already been on to me. Take a seat.'

'Do I have to? Can't you just condense what you have to say into ten words, then let me go?'

'No, I can't. So take a seat. Please.'

Sophie sighed and sat down. She sipped her coffee.

Sandie picked up a sheet of paper. 'Your new DC is the person waiting in reception. But you need some information first. And it must be confidential — to you and any other officer in direct command of her.' She paused. 'Her name is Rachel Gregson. Until two and a half years ago she was Raymond Gregson. Rae, spelt with a letter E, is transgender.'

'Right. And how does that affect things, exactly?'

'It doesn't. That's the point I have to make clear to you. She must be treated like any other detective constable. And as I said, only you and your sergeant are to know. As far as everyone else is concerned, she's just another woman DC.'

'Well that won't be a problem for me or my sergeant, Sandie. But let's be realistic. People are likely to guess sooner or later. My understanding is that female to male TSs are far more successful at going unnoticed. This way round is a lot harder. Isn't that right? So we'd better be prepared. Anything else I need to know about her?'

'She asked for me to put you in the picture. Everything else is in her documentation. She's got that with her. This sheet of paper that I've been trying to pass to you, and you've been studiously ignoring, is a summary of the procedures to be followed in this situation.'

Sophie took the sheet and glanced at it. 'I thought people in her position were quietly shifted into back-room jobs, with little contact with the public in case anyone takes offence? Though to me that's always seemed offensive in itself. What's important is how well someone does their job, surely?'

'You're thinking of uniformed officers. It's been decided that detectives are in less direct contact with the public anyway. And as far as I can tell, every case is to be treated individually. We were very impressed with her at the interview. She asked to be kept in a role as similar as possible to her previous one. She's ideal for what you want, Sophie. She fills almost all of your requests, far more than anyone else in the frame. And she comes across really well.'

'Seems fair enough. Point me in her direction and I'll be on my way.'

Sophie put Matt Silver's spare coffee mug down on the HR chief's desk and left. The receptionist gave her a nervous smile as she passed.

The young DC stood up when Sophie approached.

'Hello, Rae. Glad you've joined the squad. It's bedlam at the moment, and we need you.'

She held out her hand. Rae was wearing a neat, dark blue skirt and a well-fitting tailored jacket in blue corduroy. Sophie could make out the neckline of a pale pink jumper under the jacket. Low-heeled ankle boots completed the outfit. Rae took her hand tentatively.

'Ma'am.'

Sophie ushered her towards the stairs.

'My good friend Sandie in HR has filled me in on your background. You've had a difficult time, I imagine. No regrets?'

'No. It was the right thing for me. For the first time for as long as I can remember, I feel right in myself. I'll work hard for you, ma'am.'

'I expect nothing less from anyone who works for me, Rae. And I like your outfit. I have a teenage daughter at home who acts as my unofficial style adviser, so I'm fairly up to date.'

'I thought quite a bit about what to wear. I suppose my clothes are a sign that I've arrived where I've always wanted to be.'

Sophie looked again at her watch.

'We need to get moving. Time's slipping away like the wind, and even I, Sophie Allen, can't slow it down. I'm only human — despite what you may have heard. I see you have a file for me.'

'Yes, ma'am.'

'Slip this in.' She handed over the policy page as they got into her car. 'While I'm driving, you can read it all out to me. Then you'll know everything that I know, and you can fill in any gaps. I'll need to tell my sergeant, Barry Marsh, since he'll be your immediate superior. He's a careful and thoughtful bloke, and I'm sure you'll get on well with him. But you may need to give him some time before he relaxes.'

'You've taken it very well, ma'am. I'm grateful. I know you weren't told in advance.'

'Well, I've been through it before, a few years ago when I was still in the West Midlands. That time it was a female to male transition, so it was easier for him. People get a much easier ride that way round, as far as I can tell. It's easier to create a more androgynous, slightly masculine look, I suppose.'

'It's also the hormones he'll have had. Testosterone is much more powerful than the oestrogen I take. The effect kicks in quicker and is much more marked. It even causes the voice to get lower. Oestrogen does nothing for that.'

'Your voice isn't bad. Have you been for coaching?'

Rae nodded. 'I paid for the lessons myself. It's possible to get them on the NHS but I decided not to wait. I hope it was worth it.'

'I'd say it was. You sound midway, if that makes sense. It certainly doesn't stand out as masculine. I guess the only problem is when you're on the telephone, because when people can see you, they get the whole you, and you're very convincing visually. Your skin tone is good, Rae. Half the battle is trying to maintain a good complexion and I'm afraid I'm losing that particular one.'

'I don't think you are, ma'am.'

Sophie accelerated out onto the main road, heading east towards Wareham. 'Do you want to tell me about your background? Your reasons? I mean the stuff that isn't in the file? Don't feel that you have to, by the way. It's just that you're earmarked as a permanent member of my team if the trial period works out. It might help us understand each other.'

'It's not a problem, ma'am. I suppose I fit the pattern pretty closely. My childhood wasn't particularly unhappy. My parents were great. But I didn't fit in well with the other boys in my class, even when I was at primary school. I gravitated towards the girls, though I don't think I was overtly feminine in any way, certainly not pre-puberty. I just didn't enjoy the rough and tumble of being a boy and I kept myself to myself for much of the time. Once I was in my teens I occasionally had these strange feelings of wishing I could be a girl, at least some of the time. It wasn't constant, it wasn't particularly strong and it didn't dominate my life, but more and more often I found myself connecting socially with the girls of my age rather than the boys. In my mid-teens that feeling got stronger and I suppose that's when I realised that maybe something wasn't quite right. That's when I took some wrong steps, all in an attempt to get myself back on track, as I saw it. I started to copy the behaviour of other boys, but tried to outdo them. I drank, I swore, I was vile to the girls I went out with. I'm not proud of that time.'

'But you came through it, obviously.'

'My parents knew that something was wrong, but didn't know what to do about it. All the time I was battling with this conflict inside of me and I felt as if I was being torn apart. Then two things happened over the course of a couple of years. I went on a couple of army taster sessions, looking for the ultimate masculine, macho lifestyle that I thought might cure me, if that's the right expression. But I became almost physically sick because it was all so repellent to everything I really felt, and so I joined the police instead. Still fairly macho, you see, but a bit more moderate. And the second thing was that I fell for a young woman who saw through me. She could see how unhappy I was and she started trying to draw out my feelings. I loved her, but I couldn't let her know it. I think she loved me. The trouble was that as she tried more and more to get me to look at myself, the worse my behaviour towards her became. I treated her like shit for a while, I really did, and I'm ashamed of it.'

Rae fell silent. Sophie sensed that the young DC was becoming upset. 'You don't have to tell me all this, Rae. If it's causing you pain, you can stop.'

'No, it's okay, ma'am. It's probably good for me to get it out in the open. I've not really had a good chance to talk things through with anyone since I stopped my counselling sessions after I transitioned.'

'Well, if you're sure you want to continue, that's fine. But look, why don't you read me the stuff in your file first? Then decide if you want to tell me the rest of your personal account once we've got that out of the way.'

Rae read through the contents of the personnel file that Sandie Blake had prepared. Then she returned to her story.

'Hettie and I had been together just over a year when we realised that things just couldn't go on the way they were. I was still feeling depressed, and was feeling physically sick again, just like a few years earlier with the army trials. I was making Hettie miserable. Things came to a head and I told her how I really felt about my life, and my place in the world. The strange thing was, she wasn't really surprised. She told me how much it all fitted together. It was her that got me to contact a counsellor and a transgender group . . . I walked in on a social event and I suddenly knew I had found my spiritual home. Hettie knew. She came with me, to give me support and she could see how things suddenly fell into place for me. I found inner calm and peace, probably for the first time since my early teens. There was never any doubt in my mind once I'd been for some psychiatric assessments. Some of the other girls who were there for consideration at the same time as me, were discussing possible best answers to questions that might be put to us during the assessments. Trying to outwit the system. I didn't bother. I just responded with what I felt in my heart and I sailed through, a perfect example of gender dysphoria. I had surgery two years ago and here I am now, just as you see me.'

'Are you still in contact with Hettie?'

'Oh, yes. We're best friends. She's getting married next spring and I'm going to be one of her bridesmaids. She met a bit of resistance from her fiancé's family about it, but being the person she is, she stuck to her guns. I'm looking forward to it, even though I'll be full of nerves.'

'And have you had any relationships yourself since you transitioned? Have you got close to anyone else?'

'Not really. The problem is that I still don't like men very much, nor the thought of getting intimate with one. Maybe that would change if I met the right bloke, but he'd probably have to be one in a thousand. I still like women much more, but a lot of lesbians distrust male to female transsexuals. You know, they think we're pretend women. Maybe that's true in a way. Anyway, the right man hasn't appeared yet, though I still think it's more likely to be a woman. Or maybe a TS man. I met quite a few during the group counselling sessions.'

'Bernie, who I worked with for a while in the Midlands, had similar thoughts about relationships. He's the female to male TS I mentioned earlier. I think he's found someone now, though I don't know the details. We're not in contact any more. Well I hope things work out for you, Rae, especially with the job. As I said earlier, you're joining us at a hectic time and you're going to be too tired for anything much.' Sophie smiled wryly. 'I'm already running on adrenalin, and it's only two days since we discovered the body.'

* * *

On arriving in the incident room, Sophie introduced Rae to Marsh and Melsom, and then showed her to her desk. She called Barry Marsh into her office and explained Rae's situation.

'No one else is to know at the moment, Barry. Just you and me, as her superiors. Under no circumstances can you talk about this to anyone else. If anyone asks, do not confirm it. Instead, just sidestep the question and speculate. Her deep voice could be due to childhood tonsillitis. Anything else could be put down to possible hormonal problems. What I'm saying is that it's better to have a response ready prepared than to be caught on the hop. If there are issues with other staff, I want to know. Don't keep things from me. For this week, you and I can have a quick chat together each day, no more than a minute or two. From then on, once a week will do. You're down as her official immediate superior, but this kind of thing is probably new to you. Is that right?'

Marsh nodded. 'Doesn't she want to be open about it?'

'We decided that this is the best way, considering we're up to our eyes in this case. I don't want people losing focus and, believe me, this would be a huge distraction. Maybe in the fullness of time we'll decide differently, but not now.'

'I thought we could put her onto background checks at first. There's a lot we don't know about all these people. That means I can free up Jimmy for more direct inquiries,' he said.

'Sounds good to me. I'm off to see Benny Goodall now. He'll have already started the post-mortem and I want to have a chat while it's all fresh in his mind. I'll see you all later. Thanks for that message this morning, by the way. I've set the wheels in motion to move them to a safe house.'

'Does it need to be both of them, ma'am? Surely it's only Mrs Corrigan who's in danger? Ed Wilton only met them by chance.'

'He was a witness, Barry. And meeting by chance might equally well apply to Rosemary.' She turned to Marsh with a slight smile. 'Anyway, I have a feeling that the two of them might now be an item. I'm a soft-centred sentimentalist at heart, you know. I don't want to put a spanner in the works at this early stage.'

* * *

Sophie caught sight of the tall frame of Dorset's senior pathologist ahead of her in the hospital corridor as she approached his office.

'Morning, Benny!' she called. 'How are you on this bright, sunny morning?'

A particularly hard flurry of raindrops hit the window beside him, and he turned.

'All the better for seeing you, O golden-haired one. How's Martin?'

'A bit down. Work problems, so I'm sure he'd appreciate an evening out with you in the pub, if you fancy it. I'll leave it to you. How did the PM go?'

He ushered her into his office. 'Interesting. As you surmised, some of the bruising was caused prior to death, and there's a fairly serious contusion on the left side of her head that would have concussed her, and some severe bruising around her midriff. But she died from drowning.'

'Really? So she was alive when she was dumped on the shoreline?' Sophie sat down on a soft chair.

'No. The water in her lungs was from a tap. The only sea water was in her mouth and nose.'

'So she was concussed by a blow to the head, then drowned, then taken out and dumped in the rock pool? Is that what you're saying?'

'I'm not saying anything, Sophie. I don't do speculation, as you well know. It was also fairly obvious that she was sexually active prior to death. Very sexually active.'

'What do you mean?'

'We found traces of semen in all three major orifices. It's all safely bottled up and off for DNA analysis. But there were no signs of rape. No significant rupture of any tissue, and a lubricant had been used in her anus.'

'So it seems as if it was consensual?'

'No evidence to the contrary is as far as I'd go. But as I said, there were no signs of tissue damage to the throat, anus or vagina. Make of that what you will.'

'Is there any evidence of the order of events? Did the sex happen before the blow to the head?'

'Okay, I will hazard a guess on this one, and I'd say very probably the sex did occur earlier. It's hard to imagine how such sex could happen with an unconscious body. And since the semen traces were still present, she obviously didn't have time to bathe or shower afterwards. But what are your thoughts? You're the detective.'

'From what you've told me? She had sex with three men, maybe at the same time. Something quickly went wrong and she was hit around the head. She was drowned in the bath or basin while still unconscious. Then they dressed her, smuggled her out into a car, and dumped her body on the shoreline, hoping it would look like a simple case of falling and drowning while drunk. Did she have much alcohol in her blood, by the way?'

'Some, but not a hugely excessive amount. She was over the drink-driving limit, but wouldn't have been incapacitated. She didn't have any underwear on, by the way, so that fits in with your theory.'

'Yes, I remember. She had nothing on under her jacket. We also spotted that the zip on her jeans was only half pulled up, and one of her boots was also not fully zipped. It all helps to back up the story.'

'A bit of an adventuress, was she?'

'Apparently, and very attractive from what I've heard. Would you agree, Benny?'

He laughed grimly. 'Seeing a body on a mortuary trolley is not the best place to make judgements like that. I used to try to imagine what they would have looked like full of life and vigour, but I gave that up years ago. This one? Yes I'd guess so . . . You're teasing me, aren't you?'

'Would I ever? Anything else of interest? The shape of the wound to the head for instance?'

'Something heavy with a blunt edge, I'd imagine. The cut is about three inches long and caused significant bleeding, but I can't visualise what could have caused it. No doubt your forensic people will have some theories about that.' He paused. 'Oh, there was something else. She had a number of small tattoos that might help with identification. A butterfly in the small of her back, a flower on her left upper arm and a heart on her right wrist. Now, do you fancy a spot of lunch before you drive back? It'll just be in the canteen, but you look as though you could do with a few minutes to relax. I know I could.'

* * *

'How are you settling in, Rae?'

Barry Marsh had taken a mug of coffee across to the new member of the team. He placed it carefully among the piles of documents on the young DC's desk.

'I haven't really had time to stop and think about it, sir,' she answered. 'It's been non-stop since I arrived. But that isn't a complaint. It's actually been really good.'

'That's a murder investigation for you. A few hours each day to eat and sleep, then back to the grindstone.'

'You've worked with the boss before?'

Marsh nodded. 'This will be the third time. And I'm joining the team permanently from next month. Which really means from now on. If you'd said to me a year ago that I'd be second in command of a speciality murder and violent crime unit, I'd have laughed at you. But here I am, and here you are.'

'Should I be worried?'

'She's fair-minded, if that's what you mean. What you see is what you get. But don't underestimate her. If you do, she'll run rings around you. Don't be taken in by that "I'm just an ordinary cop" act she puts on. She isn't. She's got an Oxford degree in law and a masters in criminal psychology on top of it. She's probably got more brainpower than you and me combined. But she's also got this very ordinary background, born to a teenage mother in a Bristol council flat.' He looked down at his new assistant. 'Not sure I should have told you that, but it'll help you not to make wrong judgements about her. Please keep it to yourself.'

'Sure thing, boss. But I'm glad you did.'

'Rae, if anyone starts to create problems for you because of your background, bring it to me. I don't want the DCI bothered by any distractions in the middle of this investigation. I'll deal with anyone who makes trouble.'

'I hope there won't be any problems.'

'So do I, but we've got to be realistic. Sooner or later someone is going to start stirring, and it's better to be prepared. Where do you live, by the way?'

'I'm renting a little place in Wool. It's very convenient for getting to HQ. I'm not sure about the long term, though. If things go okay, I might consider buying a place.'

'So you'll drive down here each day while this investigation is ongoing?'

'Yes. Not today though. The boss brought me down and is taking me back when she goes home.'

Marsh glanced at his watch. 'We're having a short briefing mid-afternoon after she gets back from seeing the pathologist. We didn't have one this morning. Better get ready.'

* * *

'Brian Shapiro,' Sophie said, 'might be an ex-cop from Portsmouth. From what Barry has discovered there was a uniformed cop matching his description who was sacked some five years ago. And the more I think about it, the more it worries me. That's why I decided to move our two witnesses out of harm's way. I want to double-check the details of his service record. That's a job for you, Barry. Winkle out as much as you can about him. Jimmy, any progress on Derek?'

'Nothing yet, ma'am. I can't find a mention of anyone with his first name and fitting his description on any system that I've searched. That's a bit odd in itself, though I haven't finished yet.'

'It's bound to be difficult without a surname. Keep looking, Jimmy. I also want you to find out what Sarah Sheldon has been up to for the past year. According to her ex-husband she quit her job at the bank. But where did she go? Rosemary said she was working at a bank. Maybe it was a different one. Maybe she was lying and she was doing something else entirely. We need to know. It's possible forensics have finished work on her laptop and it might give us some clues. Can you check up on that, Rae?'

Marsh looked at her quizzically. 'Is there something I don't know, ma'am?'

'I know nothing more than you, leastways not yet. I just feel uneasy about it. It's too complicated, Barry. I'm sure there's a bigger picture here, and we've only stumbled across part of it.' She paused, as if gathering her thoughts. 'There is something else that's bothering me. I checked with the hotel earlier and this man Renton did not reappear at all over the weekend. I asked them to keep the room untouched and locked if he didn't return, so I really need to go and have a look. I'll take Jimmy with me.'

* * *

The two detectives took the short, steep walk up to the High Street and the Ballard View Hotel. They took a key from the duty manager and went up to the room. It was along a narrow corridor on the top floor, off the back stairs. It was a single, small but with an en-suite bathroom. Sophie and the junior detective searched through the drawers and cupboards, all of which proved to be empty. Sophie stood in the middle of the room, frowning.

'The problem is, Jimmy, that forensics are overloaded with my stuff already. If I ask them to sweep this room as well, I'm going to make myself the most unpopular senior officer on the force. And the chances are that they'll find nothing. But If I don't, we might miss something important and never know it. So what should I do?'

'I don't think it's linked, ma'am. This room's on the wrong floor and on the other side of the building from Mrs Sheldon's. There's nothing out of place. There's not even anything in the waste bins, so what would be the point?'

Sophie looked at him and slowly nodded. 'You're right,' she said. 'Those bins are completely empty, aren't they? Yet the room hasn't been cleaned since he left. So whoever was in here took his rubbish with him. Curious, don't you think? We'll get the room checked.'

* * *

For the first time in months, Barry Marsh was feeling happy about his work. The spectre of redundancy had been looming over him like a thick fog and the uncertainty had been playing on his mind. He was relatively young, too young to be let go, but he'd worried about being moved somewhere he didn't want to live. Now he was back to walking with a spring in his step. He greeted people with a cheery word. Goodness, he even whistled while shaving in the mornings. He had broken up with his long-time girlfriend, Sammie, and was alone. But at long last he felt valued again. DCI Allen's words when she'd offered him the chance of becoming a permanent member of her team had meant more to him than she could possibly have imagined. He was determined not to let her down. That was why he was the first person in the incident room each morning and the last to leave at the end of the day, working longer hours than the DCI herself.

He stood in front of the incident board, looking over the images, names, locations and links, musing on the possible explanations for the set of circumstances they were investigating. The phone started ringing. He picked up the receiver and gave a curt greeting. He listened to the message in near-silence, and then went to Sophie's office.

'Ma'am, we have confirmation of that message from this morning. Someone called Shapiro left the Hampshire force a couple of years ago. But there was also a rumour that he quit before he could be fired. He was abusing vulnerable women. Ones that he'd met during investigations.'

'And who is your contact exactly?'

'It's Gwen, ma'am. From Southampton. What she told me was unofficial, since we haven't put in a request yet, but it's probably saved us several days. She knew about it because he worked in her area for a while before transferring, and he was under a bit of a cloud even then.'

'I didn't realise you'd contacted her.' Were her eyes beginning to sparkle? 'Ah, I see. How long have you been seeing her, Barry? Not that I'm being nosey. Well yes, I am being nosey, aren't I?'

He smiled weakly and rubbed his ear, a habit of his whenever he felt embarrassed. 'We're not an item. Not yet, anyway. We've only been out for one meal together, just last week. But we did talk on the phone late last night. That was when Gwen warned me Shapiro might be a former cop. It's why I texted you early this morning. I hope I didn't tell her too much.'

'I doubt it, Barry. It wouldn't be like you. And if it helps, I like her. I know we've only met once or twice, but she's the kind of person I feel we can depend on.' Sophie thought for a while. 'It's interesting, but it still doesn't explain why Sarah was killed. Could she and Derek have been in some kind of relationship? There are a couple of other things we can check right now that might help us think. You phone the hotel and the B and B. Check how long the rooms were booked for. We assumed it was only for the weekend, but I don't think we've confirmed it. I need to find the list from forensics of what Rosemary and Sarah had packed in their bags. Okay? Back here in five minutes.'

Marsh returned to Sophie's office a few minutes later wearing a frown. 'How did you know?' he asked.

'I didn't. Guess would be more accurate. I remembered that something didn't seem right when I saw the clothing lists, but it didn't register at the time. You can see that Rosemary packed clothes for the weekend. The kind of things that I'd pack for a couple of days away. But Sarah's list was more than twice as long, with enough clothes for a week. That could be explained if she were a clothes freak who always packed lots more stuff than she'd need. But I didn't pick up that impression from Rosemary when she talked about their earlier weekend breaks. They both travelled fairly light. So, how long was the hotel room booked for?'

'Until the end of the week.'

'So the weekend would progress as normal, but on Sunday Sarah would have told Rosemary that she wasn't returning to Portsmouth with her. And her room at the hotel was family-sized. I've been wondering about that, but it makes some kind of sense. She and Rosemary had a bed each, but there's a double for her and Derek. But what was she up to? Was she juggling two men at the same time? Did they know? Did Derek tell Shapiro that he was staying on after the weekend?

86

And who was the man called John Renton, who was in the hotel that night? Could he have known Sarah?' She paused. 'You know what might help us a bit, don't you? If we could get more detail on Shapiro somehow, now we think he's an ex-cop.'

'I've already done it. I asked Gwen to get some facts sent through as soon as she could manage it, so it should be with us in the morning.'

'Great stuff, Barry. I knew I'd made the right decision when I offered you the job. Now it's really time to go. If I don't there'll be a good chance my dinner will be lying scorched in the bottom of the oven. Either that or Jade will be standing by the kitchen door ready to hurl it at me when I finally arrive home. Think yourself fortunate that you don't have a teenage daughter who takes her role as Monday's chef rather too seriously.'

'You could always blame me, ma'am.'

Sophie laughed. 'I intend to if it comes to that, don't worry. She'll forgive you things that she won't let me get away with. Tell Rae I'll be ready in five minutes, will you?'

* * *

In the late evening Rae was in her new home, a small flat in Wool, sipping a coffee. She thought her first day had gone well, and that she had fitted into the team of detectives better than she'd feared. Life had never been easy for her but she'd been so successful at keeping her inner anxieties and stresses hidden that no one knew of the shrieking chaos that often whirled around in her brain. Even her closest family members didn't know. Most people could be themselves, happy in their own skin at least some of the time. But what if, like her, there had always been a deeply rooted mismatch between the external appearance and the internal sense of self? Well, it was all over now. Here she was, in the kind of role she'd always dreamed about. Now she was somewhere where she'd already been taken seriously, and had been given responsibilities by other professionals who didn't seem to care about her background. The big boss, the DCI, had acted so naturally that it couldn't possibly have been a facade. Even though Barry Marsh had been quiet, she'd gained the impression he was always so, and that he'd gone out of his way to be welcoming. She wouldn't let them down. She switched on her stereo and inserted a disc. She sat and listened to a Mozart piano concerto. It was her late grandfather's favourite music. In many ways he'd have been proud of her, she knew. He'd been a police officer for most of his working life, having joined up after leaving the army in 1946. But how would he have felt about her new life as a woman? She hoped that, like her parents, he'd have shown at least some understanding.

Rae finished her coffee and sank back into the chair, pondering on the current case. She thought about the weekend music festivals that she knew. One of her cousins played sax in a semi-professional jazz quartet and helped to organise an annual jazz festival in Bath. Would he have any insider knowledge? Would he be willing to speak to her? There was only one way to find out. She picked up the phone.

CHAPTER 8: JAZZ

Tuesday morning

'So who is he exactly?' Sophie Allen turned from her position at the window. She'd been watching a ragged-looking crow as it struggled to land on the branch of a tree growing next to the police station car park. It was eight in the morning and she'd been gathering her thoughts ready for the early morning briefing when a tentative knock at her office door had preceded Rae's head peeping around the frame. The story she related was not entirely welcome.

'My cousin, Matt Rosewell. He's a peripatetic music teacher. Clarinet and saxophone, but really he'd like to play jazz full-time. He's in a small jazz band and helps to organise a local jazz festival in Bath.'

'I'd have preferred it if you'd cleared it with me first, Rae, before contacting him.'

'Sorry, ma'am. I realise that now, but last night I just felt that I wanted to make some headway and he was the obvious person to ask. I really wanted to . . .'

'Impress me?' Sophie suggested.

'Well, I guess that was part of it, yes.' Rae looked crestfallen.

'So what did you learn?'

'The organisers of most festivals are aware of the match-making that goes on. He said it would be hard to miss, even at jazz events. The stewards at the venues are told to look out for single women or small groups and try to ensure their safety. There have been a small number of assaults on women late at night, mainly when they've had too much to drink.'

'But nothing at the level we're investigating?'

'He was aware of one possible assault but didn't know the details. There were rumours two years ago that a woman had gone to a late night party in a hotel room and had been forced into group sex, but he couldn't be sure how reliable the story was. That was when the stewards were told to be on the lookout.'

'How much did you tell him?'

'Nothing, ma'am. I didn't mention the case or where I'm based. We spent most of the time chatting about me. I was very careful not to give anything away.'

Sophie sat down and rested her chin on her hands.

'I'm paranoid about things leaking out to the press, Rae. I admire your initiative and your wish to impress Barry and myself. And I have to admit that you've uncovered something that could be potentially useful so the gamble paid off, but in future please check with one of us first. People aren't stupid, Rae, particularly teachers. I know because I'm married to one. Your cousin will be wondering about your query, I can guarantee it. If he reads the papers or watches the news he'll have heard about the murder. It won't take much for him to twig the real reason for your call. All he has to do is to talk to the wrong person and it gets to the press, and then I'll have to go into damage-limitation mode, and I hate that.' She paused. 'I can see you're puzzled. You're asking yourself why I'm taking it this way when you found out something useful, aren't you?'

Rae nodded.

'Because in most queries like it, nothing useful results. So what, you'd probably say. Nothing lost. But tell me this, if your cousin hadn't given you anything useful, would you have told me that you'd made the call to him?'

'No, I suppose not. I wouldn't have seen the point.'

'So if a press question had come in from Bath about a police interest in Somerset jazz festivals as a result of your call to your cousin, I'd have been at a complete loss as to the reason. And me being me, I'd have tried to find out what had stirred their interest, and if I'd traced it back to you I'd have been so enraged at the time I'd have wasted that you'd have been out on your ear. Do you understand now?'

'Yes, ma'am. I'm truly sorry.'

'But as it happens, you've got a lead so you can run with it, once we've discussed it with the team.' She paused. 'Ignore that. On second thoughts I might take it myself. Normally I'd have left it to you, Rae, but I need to visit Bath in any case. But you can do the background for me. Find out what you can about this supposed assault, but do it through police channels, not your cousin. Well, not unless you fail to make any headway. And keep Barry or myself fully in the picture in future. Understand?'

'Yes, ma'am.'

'We'll discuss it in half an hour with the team. So well done and not so well done, both at the same time. Get yourself a coffee and see what you can discover before then.'

* * *

The incident room was looking lacklustre despite the best efforts of the local officers to smarten it up with some posters. Since the decision had been made to close the police station and move to cheaper accommodation, no money had been forthcoming for sprucing up the doomed Victorian building and it showed.

Sophie opened the briefing. 'Please chip in as appropriate. We're still short of a great deal of useful information at the moment, so perceptive comments and questions will earn lots of brownie points. Can we start with you, Barry?'

'We now know more about Brian Shapiro. He was a uniformed cop in Hampshire, working for a while in Southampton's east end before transferring to Portsmouth. There he was suspended and charged with abusing his position by having sex with vulnerable women he met while working. The women who made the complaints refused to testify so the cases never came to court. He was sacked. This was about four years ago. A photo of him came through earlier this morning and I've copied it for you. I also took it to the Hawthorns and had Mrs Fantini check it. She's pretty sure it was the man who booked in on Friday evening with the same name, Shapiro. I've got the booking details but the address he gave is false. The only way we can trace him is through his credit card and bank, but I haven't got that far yet.'

'Can't we get an address from his time on the force?' asked Jen Allbright. She had been moved from her normal duties to help with the investigation. Her local knowledge from the time she spent on the beat was second to none. She had excellent observational skills.

'Trouble is, since he left the Portsmouth unit he's been seen on the fringes of the criminal community. According to my source he's moved from his previous address. He and the others have been so careful to cover their tracks the chances are that the address the bank's got might not be up to date. But we'll see.' Marsh settled back into his chair.

'Jimmy?' Sophie prompted.

'Still nothing about a Derek that matches our description on any records. It would be so much easier if we had a surname to work with. But I have found a bit more about Sarah Sheldon. It confirms what you found out on Saturday, ma'am. She worked as a false-claims investigator for one of the big insurance companies. Well, not out in the field. She was doing the clerical side of things, computer checks and the like. She's only worked there for the past year or so. The offices are in the city centre.'

'Go and speak to them. Find out from her boss and her colleagues what they thought of her. Have a look through her desk, and if she has a work laptop bring it in. Get a copy of any of her personal files held on the company system, particularly emails. Check if they can get a record of her browsing history, or anything else useful. You may need to see someone from their IT team about that. As soon as we've finished this briefing, okay?'

'On my own?'

'Yes, on your own. You're a big boy now, Jimmy. I'm sure you'll do it right. Just don't rush it. Once you're there, take it slowly, carefully and thoroughly and identify anything that might help us build up a picture of her through her work.' She paused. 'Rae may have found a prior incident at a jazz festival in Bath a couple of years ago. Any more details, Rae?'

'Yes. It's still on record as an open investigation by the local police team. No one's ever been apprehended for the attack, if it can be called an attack. The details seem to be that a forty-five year old woman, who may have had a bit too much to drink, was invited back to a small party in a hotel room. She thought she was with one man who'd been chatting her up, but once there she was given more drink then pressured into group sex with several men. She reported it the next day and claimed it was against her will. The local force never got anywhere because the men had gone by the time they got to the hotel and the address given for the booking was false. They'd paid the bill in cash so there were no bank details to check up on. Her descriptions of the men were a bit hazy, so they didn't have much to go on. And the results of a medical examination carried out late the next morning weren't clear. There was no evidence of violence being used. She admitted she had expected to have sex with the man she'd paired up with, but not with others.'

'How many?' asked Sophie, tucking some stray strands of short, fair hair behind her ear.

'She wasn't sure. Either two or three in total, she thought. But her memory was hazy.'

Sophie thought for a few moments. 'I've decided that we need to follow up on it. It seems uncannily similar to the picture we're building up of Saturday night. The one big difference, of course, is that no one was killed. Rae, I want you to build up a list of all the jazz or blues festivals in the South West or central South. Get dates for them, stretching back, say, four years. Then get onto the local police in each case and see if there were any similar incidents reported during the festivals. Also contact the festival organisers in each case and see if they heard any rumours of incidents of this kind. Could you help where you can, Jen?'

The uniformed officer looked pleased. 'Of course, ma'am.'

Marsh spoke. 'Should one of us visit Bath and speak to the victim there? And the police who interviewed her?'

'Yes, of course. I'll do that, Barry.'

Sophie studied her notes, not looking him in the eye. Marsh nodded slightly.

'The formal results of the post-mortem on Sarah are in and they back up what Benny Goodall told me. She'd been sexually active, probably with two or three men, and had enough booze in her system to have clouded her judgement. The blow to her head would have rendered her unconscious and she died from drowning in tap water. There are sets of faint finger-sized bruise marks on both sides of her neck, consistent with her head being held tightly from behind. I'd guess that was while she was being held under water. By the way, I've asked the forensic crew to check all the waste pipes in the hotel room, just in case some fluids are still trapped in them. It then looks as though her body was smuggled out of the hotel through the door to the garden. They must have had a car there. Our two suspects claimed they didn't have one when they checked in to the Hawthorns. However, we think they parked one in the Victoria Avenue car park instead of taking it to the guest house, though it was gone the next morning. We've a possible sighting of the vehicle on Friday evening in that car park, and the witness reports a couple of men getting out and taking some luggage from the boot. Apparently it might have been a small, red car. I've asked Tom here to put some uniformed officers onto a house-to-house to see if any of the local residents noticed a car coming out of the Ballard View Hotel's parking area in the early hours. Then the same for the lane out to Peveril. We might be in luck and find someone who spotted a suspicious vehicle, but don't be too hopeful. It was fairly misty and drizzly after midnight on Friday night, so visibility was poor. So let me sum up. Jimmy's following up on Sarah Sheldon and her work. Rae can finish off her probe into previous music festivals. Barry, you and Jen are going to concentrate on the men, starting with Shapiro. I'm off to Bath to see if I can track down the woman Rae mentioned. Have I forgotten anything?'

Marsh spoke. 'We ought to make copies of that photofit of John Renton that Jimmy made up with the staff at the hotel, then check it around the pubs. You know, Brodie the gay guy, and the roadie with the band. They seemed observant. And maybe with the bar staff at the Red Lion?'

'I can organise that, Barry,' said Tom Rose, the station's senior officer. 'I expect this will be the last big case I'm ever involved with before I leave. I'll get Jack Holly onto it and, if necessary, I'll help him out myself.'

'I'm sure he'll thank you for that,' Sophie said. Jen Allbright was Holly's usual partner, and knew his idiosyncrasies well. The rather staid constable would not welcome having the town's chief of police accompanying him on his investigations. 'And our Mr Brodie is going to really enjoy being questioned by someone as straight-laced as you, Tom. Or even Jack. Be prepared, that's all I can say. He's a very entertaining guy.' Sophie smiled. She tidied her notes together and stood up. 'Let's try to meet up at six this evening. Happy hunting, everyone.'

* * *

The drive to Bath took longer than Sophie had anticipated. The road runs almost due north from Wareham, twisting and turning through rolling agricultural land. The driver who is unlucky enough to find herself behind a slow-moving vehicle can do little but sit tight and curse. Sophie did plenty of cursing. Tractors were replaced by lorries, followed by late-season caravans. She calmed herself by listening to some Bach on the car's stereo.

She'd phoned before setting out and an officer was waiting for her. It took less than an hour to gather all the information she needed. Then she asked her contact to point her in the direction of the fraud investigation offices. Lydia Pillay looked up from her desk at the sound of approaching footsteps. Sophie saw the worried frown that settled on the young DC's dark face.

'Hello, Lydia,' Sophie said. 'I was hoping you'd be here. How are you?'

'I'm fine, ma'am.' She put down her pen and gave Sophie a guarded smile. 'I half-expected you'd appear one day. I suppose you want an explanation?'

'No, not really. Barry told me his theory about why you left. I do feel partly to blame, being away at the Home Office for so much of the summer. But you must have realised I wasn't well even when I was around, since I was always heading off for therapy sessions.'

'So you're disappointed in me? For taking the chance and jumping ship while you weren't there and fully fit?'

'I suppose I am, yes. It puzzled me. I wouldn't have stood in your way, Lydia. I've always thought too highly of you to stoop to any underhand tricks to keep you. Like so many other things that were happening to me at the time, your leaving left me bemused.'

'Maybe it wasn't entirely what Barry thinks. I've always loved Bath ever since I was a student here. And I'd already met my new boss on a course I went on. When he contacted me with news of the job, I just jumped at the chance.'

'But it was partly due to what Barry had guessed? That you thought it was me who assaulted Duff?'

'It's not as simple as that. I know you didn't actually do it. Barry convinced me of that.' She paused, as if picking her words carefully. 'But I know you were involved somehow. I still think that. Do you deny it?'

Sophie said nothing.

'You see?' Lydia continued. 'It's what I always knew. But Barry's right. There's no proof whatsoever, so no chance of any investigation. And anyway, would I want you convicted? For goodness' sake, I can understand why you would have wanted him to suffer. That evil man killed your father, and murdered all those other people. And even though I wasn't there when you dug up those girls' bodies, I could see the effect it had on everyone. Duff deserved it all. But it altered the way I felt about you. I felt claustrophobic, as if I couldn't breathe. So when the chance came, I jumped. Can you blame me?'

Sophie sighed. 'No, of course not. I don't hold grudges, Lydia. Or at least I try not to. God knows, I was in such a mess anyway that I couldn't have coped with any more, so I just forced myself to accept it. At least I'm a bit more balanced now, or I hope I am. I just wanted to let you know that you can always depend on me if you need my help or advice, or if you need a reference. I'll always do the best I can for you.'

'I'm grateful. I guessed that would be the case. And I know you always had faith in me.' Lydia pulled a tissue from her bag and dabbed at her eyes.

'Can I give you a hug?' Sophie asked.

Lydia nodded and stood up. Sophie put her arms around the young detective and pulled her close. Lydia didn't see the tiny tears shining in the corners of her eyes.

* * *

Sophie rang the doorbell of a smart, terraced house on the north side of the city centre, and stood back. There were flower boxes painted red on the front windowsills with geraniums still in bloom. A smartly dressed woman in her late fifties answered the door. She looked guardedly at her caller.

'Brenda Plant?'

The woman nodded. Sophie held out her warrant card. 'I'm Detective Chief Inspector Sophie Allen from Dorset police. I believe you might have some information that could be of use to me in a current investigation.'

Brenda looked at Sophie carefully.

'You'd better come inside,' she said in a slightly raspy voice. 'You're lucky to catch me in. I usually work on Tuesdays, but I swapped days this week to allow a colleague a day off.' Sophie followed the woman through a rather dim hallway into a large kitchen, well-lit from a south-facing window.

'I hope you don't mind coming into the kitchen. I'm in the middle of some baking.'

'Not at all. I'm impressed. Maybe I'll pick up a few tips. I'm probably one of the world's worst bakers. My teenage daughter is really into it though. Even my husband has given it a go on occasions, with surprising success. Well, maybe not so surprising since he's always been a better cook than me. He takes his time, whereas I get impatient and try to cut corners whatever I'm cooking. It's a question of temperament, I guess.'

Brenda spooned a fruit cake mixture into a large cake tin, smoothed its surface and slid it into the oven. She wiped her hands and sat on a tall stool facing Sophie across the table.

'What can I help you with?'

'It's a tricky one, Mrs Plant. I don't want to cause you any distress, but I'd like to get some details about the assault you suffered during the jazz festival two years ago.'

'Surely the local police can tell you everything you need to know?'

'They can give me factual details, yes. But there's nothing like a face-to-face talk to help get a feel for the events. Can I tell you why I need this information?'

'I saw on the news there was a possible murder at a blues festival in Swanage at the weekend. Is that it?'

Sophie nodded. 'The circumstances sound very similar to your own experience. If there is a link, it will help me, but it might also help your local police make headway with their investigation into your own assault. They told me it has stalled because of a lack of evidence. I have some photofit images with me if you'd like to see them. I saw the ones you helped to create two years ago, and they might be the same men.'

Brenda sighed. 'I guessed when you first spoke at the door. Okay, I'll do it, but it won't be easy. I've been trying to forget about it for the past year.'

'I know that the worst part is often the long-term psychological damage, Brenda. I've been through trauma therapy myself recently, and I know how hard it can be. But unless we do this they might escape again, if it is the same men. And this time it's murder.' Sophie slid the two photofit prints of Derek and Brian across the table but held back on the one for John Renton. Brenda looked at them and nodded her head. 'Yes,' she said quietly. 'I think it's them.'

'Are you sure?'

'Yes.' She shuddered. 'Take them away, please.'

'You don't recognise this one?' Sophie showed her Renton's image.

'No. He might have been there for all I know, but he wasn't one of the men who had sex with me.'

'How many were there, Brenda?'

'Two men and a woman, I think.' Tears welled up in her eyes. 'I shouldn't have drunk so much. I couldn't deal with it. And it wasn't rape like you read in the papers. They weren't violent and I didn't have any physical injuries. But I didn't want it, and I couldn't stop it once it started.'

'It wasn't your fault. You must believe that. Just because you were drunk doesn't give them the right to force themselves on you. They're the criminals, not you.' She paused. 'Can you tell me how it started?'

Brenda walked to the sink and poured herself a glass of water.

'There was the jazz festival proper, with tickets or arm-bands and things. But at the same time some pubs had jazz groups playing for free. I was in a pub, along with a couple of friends. They were married, whereas I was recently divorced, so when they decided to go home I stayed on.' She pointed at Shapiro's image. 'This man was with a small group at the bar, but he left them and came over to sit beside me. He started chatting and we got on really well, or so I thought. Maybe it was just the drink made me think that. Much later on, when the gig finished and the pub was emptying, I saw that his friends had gone, and we were alone. He suggested going back to his hotel room and I agreed. I'd never had a one-night stand before. I thought I'd been missing out somehow. And he was a pleasant enough bloke. Or so I thought. I didn't realise how much drink I'd had until we got outside. I could walk, but I was really unsteady I guess. It's all a bit hazy. His hotel was nearby. I can remember standing in the porch for a bit while he went in. I guess he was checking that the coast was clear, and we wouldn't be spotted by any staff. When we got to his room he poured out some brandies. I can half-remember being on the bed with him and getting my clothes off. There were just the two of us at first, but then the other man and a woman appeared from somewhere, and I think I struggled to get off the bed, but they held me back. The woman made me drink some more brandy, and everything went really hazy. I have dim memories of being with her, and then two men together. I think I passed out. They'd gone when I came to the next morning. You know that the local police have never been able to trace them?'

Sophie nodded. 'Yes. They're pretty sure they left in the middle of the night, from what you told them. The only one who was officially staying in the hotel was the one you returned with, but all his details were false. It's very similar to my current case.'

'But she was killed, the one at the weekend. Do you know why?'

'No. It's a puzzle. Maybe it was never intended, and things got out of hand somehow.'

Sophie showed her a photo of Sarah Sheldon.

'It could be her but I can't be sure. She was heavily made-up and her hair was a bit shorter.' Brenda started to cry. 'I felt sick with myself when I came to the next morning, terribly ashamed. How did I let myself get lured into it like that?'

'It wasn't your fault, Brenda. It was a clever trap, and you just happened to be the person who fell into it. It could have been any woman out in Bath that night. Please don't blame yourself.'

Tuesday afternoon

Barry Marsh still checked up on Jimmy Melsom. Jimmy didn't resent this. He was well aware that there were occasions when he fell into his slapdash ways of the previous year. His involvement with two high-stakes murder inquiries that winter should have brought about a change in the way he approached his work, but sometimes he couldn't seem to help being careless. Thus, before leaving for the Portsmouth offices of Sarah Sheldon's employer, Melsom sat down with his superior and they drew up a rough plan of the kind of questions he should be asking.

Jimmy kept the list firmly in his mind while he was being introduced to Sheldon's boss. The middle-aged woman didn't get out of her seat to greet him. He was forced to reach across the desk in order to shake her hand and then he could see why: she was grossly obese.

'Could you confirm the type of work that Sarah did for you, Mrs O'Neill? I have a rough idea, but I just need to fill in the details.' He sat down on the chair opposite her, assuming this was what her slight arm movement had meant.

'We investigate possible fraudulent claims. There's another team that scans all the claims, looking for the signs. If they find something suspicious we're asked to find out the detail. We do the phoning and track back through the records. There are four of us, or there were when Sarah was here.'

Melsom was writing in his notebook while she spoke. He looked at what he'd written and pursed his lips.

'What kind of claims?'

'Car accidents. Household insurance. Travel. The whole lot, really.'

'Does each person deal with everything, or do you allocate a particular type of claim to each person?' Melsom felt pleased with the question. He thought it was the kind of thing his boss would ask.

'Everything really. Requests come in from higher up and I just share out the jobs.'

'Wouldn't it be more efficient to have your people specialise?'

She gave a kind of minimal shrug. 'Suppose. Hadn't really thought of it.'

'How long had Sarah worked for you?'

'Just over a year.'

'And what was her attitude to work? How did she fit in?'

'She was okay. She got things done quickly. Too quickly, sometimes.'

'What, in a slapdash way?'

Eileen O'Neill hesitated. 'No . . . She was just quick.'

Melsom looked around at the three other workers in the office. The place wasn't quite the hive of activity he'd expected, yet he could see a small stack of documents waiting in Eileen's in-tray. Oh well, he thought, mine is not to reason why.

'And how did she get on with you all?'

'Okay, I suppose. It's not as though we socialise or anything. We just work together.'

'What time did she leave on Friday?'

'Early. She'd worked late a couple of days last week and that meant she could finish mid-afternoon. I think it was about three.'

Melsom found it difficult to get much more out of Sarah's boss, so he asked to see the dead woman's desk and computer. He was surprised to be left alone at the workstation. Eileen wandered off down the corridor. One of the other workers came across to speak to him.

'You won't get much out of her. Really, she has no idea. And we did see Sarah sometimes after work, despite what Eileen told you. It's just that she never came along, so we gave up inviting her. She's a lazy so-and-so. From what I hear she won't be around much longer.' The speaker was a young woman in her mid-twenties. 'I'm Becky Smith, by the way.'

Jimmy smiled at her. 'Thanks. So what did you think of Sarah?'

'I liked her. I think the others did too. She was a lot older than the rest of us, and she seemed to know what she was doing. She latched onto it pretty quick after she joined us. And she didn't get on with old cantilever-buttocks at all.'

The young woman giggled at Melsom's look of surprise.

'That's what we call her. She's so lazy as well as being, well, that size. Rumour has it that she's in for the high jump and that Sarah was going to be offered her job. We were all looking forward to the change, because Sarah was really organised and was so good at what she did. Eileen didn't like her for that, and also because she was so attractive. Sarah could be really wicked too. It was her that thought up that name for Eileen when we were out in the pub one night. Cantilever-buttocks. It's good, isn't it? I could never have come up with a name like that. Wicked.'

'A bit cruel though, isn't it?'

'It's not really to do with her size. The real reason is she's just not a very nice person. I've got a couple of podgy friends and I'd never call them names like that.'

'Did Sarah ever talk about any friends? A boyfriend?'

'Not really. I think she may have had an on-off relationship with someone but she didn't talk about it much. I can't remember his name.'

'Could it have been John?'

Becky shook her head.

'Brian? Derek?'

'Derek. That was it. But she never mentioned a surname.'

'What makes you think it was an on-off relationship?'

Becky thought for a while before replying. 'She never actually said so, but I sort of put two and two together. You know, from little things that she did say, and the moods she was in sometimes.'

'Before the weekend did she say anything about what she was going to do? The music festival?'

'We knew she was going away for the weekend and she finished early on Friday. But she didn't say much about it, just that she was going to Swanage.'

Becky walked away as Eileen came through the door, but the office senior merely returned to her own chair. Jimmy examined the contents of Sarah's desk. Nothing out of the ordinary. He looked through a desk diary, but it only seemed to contain work-related entries. He kept it anyway.

He then logged on to her computer, using details the receptionist had given him when he'd first arrived. He had also arranged for someone from the IT Department to assist him. He began to look through Sarah's stored work. There was nothing that stood out among the files, but he copied them all to a flash drive that he'd brought with him. The emails were more interesting. There were a number of private messages mixed with those related to work. He noticed a few emails that seemed to come from Sarah herself and realised that she must have had a separate web-based account. He attempted to log on to her web account and was pleasantly surprised when the system allowed him in. Sarah had saved her password to the computer. Jimmy scanned down the list of messages, and then he called Melissa, the technician from IT Support. She was there within a few minutes.

'I want all of these messages copied,' he said. 'I know you can do it for her company email account, but these are on the web. Can you do that too?'

'Difficult. There are about fifty messages here. Why don't you select them all and forward them to your own email address? That might be the easiest way. While you're doing that, I'll get her company emails copied for you. It'll probably take me about twenty minutes.'

'Good idea,' he said. 'Is there any way I can get a copy of her browsing history?'

'Yes, I can do that. Anything else I can do for you while I'm here? It's just that I'm on my own this week, so I can't afford to be away from my desk for too long.'

'No, I don't think so. Did you have many dealings with Sarah? I'm just trying to build up a picture of what she was like.'

Melissa shrugged. 'Not really. Some of the people here are really useless at using computers, but she had a good idea of what she was doing. Once she'd settled in she hardly ever needed to call us for help. I liked her from what I saw of her. She picked things up quickly. I always wished there could be more like her here. We knew that if she called us it really was a problem, not something stupid she'd done wrong. And I remember that once, when I did sort out a problem for her, she brought me in a box of chocolates the next day. There's not many that do that, I can tell you.'

'Did she ever talk about her life to you? Friends? Relationships?'

The technician shook her head. 'Sorry.'

Melsom followed her out and went to find the senior personnel manager.

'Eileen O'Neill was Mrs Sheldon's boss,' he said. 'I've already interviewed her and I got the impression that they didn't get on. Was there a plan to reorganise their jobs?'

The woman facing him across the desk pursed her lips and clasped her fingers together. There was a silence.

'I'm not sure I can discuss company plans in this way,' she said eventually.

Jimmy tried to imagine what the DCI would say. He put on his most authoritative voice. 'This is a murder inquiry. I'm afraid I must insist.' He held his breath, but there was no response. 'I picked up on some unhappiness within the team,' he added.

Fleming nodded.

'We did have some plans in place, yes. Ms O'Neill hasn't, er, been drawing the best out of the team, so we've had some initial discussions to find her a suitable alternative position. Sarah Sheldon had been asked to take over for a three-month trial.'

'When was this due to start?'

'Next month.'

'Both of them knew about it?'

She nodded.

'Is there anything else I should know? Any other difficulties?'

She shook her head. 'No. And I don't for a moment think that Eileen had anything to do with Mrs Sheldon's death. The idea is preposterous.'

'We needed to know about it, though. Thanks. By the way, had she booked this week off?'

Fleming consulted her screen. 'Yes. We expected her back this coming Monday. So she took five days off in total.'

'Okay. Could you thank Melissa for me? She told me she was on her own this week but she still found time to be very helpful.'

'Yes I will. She's a great asset. She's very highly qualified. Her boss came up through the ranks. He's a nice guy, though. Also very helpful. He's on holiday this week too.'

Her eyes held Jimmy's for some time. She seemed to be trying to tell him something.

'Umm . . . the *same* week as Sarah, you mean?' Jimmy said eventually.

'Exactly.'

'You mean, you think they'd planned it?'

'Who am I to say?' she added. Her eyes went wide.

'What's his name?' Jimmy asked.

'Paul Derek. He's our network manager. No one else knows this, but there's a pattern of them booking days off at the same time. I suppose that it could all have an innocent explanation, but then I could be a secret princess from a faraway land, couldn't I?'

Jimmy frowned. Derek . . .

'And it was him who suggested she should apply for the job here. Again, that's not on any official document, but I overheard them having a conversation about it shortly after she'd started. Good hearing is a real blessing in a job like mine, believe me.'

'I think I need to see his file,' Jimmy answered. He moved to a quiet corner of the room and phoned Sophie Allen.

* * *

It took Jimmy Melsom two hours to drive to Swanage in the heavy, late-afternoon traffic. When he finally arrived, Rae was alone in the incident room.

'Where is everyone?' he asked.

'Another body's been found washed up, further along the coast. No strong reason to link it to ours at the moment, but the boss is suspicious. They've gone across to take a look.'

'Whereabouts?'

'Burton Bradstock. I don't know it. Do you?' said Rae.

'I think it's somewhere near Bridport, but I can't be sure. Was there any information about the body?'

'Just that it was a male, probably middle-aged. That's all.'

Rae turned back to her work. She looked up to see that Jimmy had sat down on the other side of the desk.

'Things going okay, Rae?' he asked.

'Yes. I feel as if I'm settling in fine. Early days yet, though.'

'You've got a hard act to follow, you know.'

'Really? Who was that?'

'Lydia. She was a fast-tracker. Joined up from university. She got on really well with the boss.'

'Why did she leave?'

'Dunno really,' he shrugged. 'We're out in the sticks here. Maybe that was it. But she was nice as well as clever.'

'Well, I hope I'm nice too, Jimmy . . . Even though I'm also a graduate.'

'Oh. What subject?'

'Marine engineering. But I found out that I don't really like ships very much. This suits me much better.'

'Unusual subject for a woman, wasn't it?'

She smiled warily. 'That's a bit of a sexist comment, isn't it?'

'No, I didn't mean it like that. One of my pals did engineering and he said there were only a few women on the course.'

'Well I'm one of those few women. Even though I didn't become an engineer, I'm still glad I did the degree.'

'Do you fancy going out for a drink sometime? I mean when we've got the time, once this case is over?'

Rae hesitated for a few moments. 'Yes . . . but can we make it a group thing? With the others?'

Melsom looked disappointed.

'I'm not really into men, Jimmy. Sorry.'

'Ah, I thought there was something about you.'

'Could you keep it quiet, though? You're the only person I've told, and I'd rather it wasn't spread around.'

* * *

Burton Cliffs are world famous. The highly-layered sandstone of the cliffs glows gold when sunlight strikes it. It wasn't glowing now. A force four westerly wind was driving dark rain clouds in from the Channel. Sophie and Barry Marsh were facing into the wind as they trudged along the shingle beach towards a forensic tent below the eastern end of the cliffs at Burton Bradstock. Sophie pointed to the top of the cliff.

'It's almost directly under the clifftop viewing area. There's a lane that ends there. You can get a car close to the edge at that point.'

Marsh didn't answer. He was trying to pull up the zip on his jacket, but it had reached its limit. He settled instead for sinking his hands deeper into his pockets. They reached the edge of the crime scene zone and identified themselves to the uniformed officers on duty. They made their way to the tent.

'Hello, Benny,' Sophie said. 'Anything useful for us?'

'As you can see, my dear lady, the body has been really bashed around. So there's not much I can tell you just yet. This one's going to have to wait until I do the post-mortem back at base.'

'Can we have a look?'

'Be my guest. But don't complain to me if you don't like what you see. It really isn't a pretty sight.'

The face was shapeless and unrecognisable. Only the clothes retained any colour.

'Any idea of how long it's been here?' Sophie asked.

'For a few days, I'd guess, tangled up in this rubbish among the rocks. It's spent some time in the water, but I can't tell you how long at the moment.'

'How could it lie here undiscovered for so long?' Marsh mused.

'It's autumn and the weather hasn't been particularly good, so there won't have been a huge number of people along here. And since that tragic death under the rock fall recently, people are probably wary about walking along too close to the cliff edge. It happened just a few hundred yards further along,' Sophie answered. 'And Benny's right. If it's been tangled up in that bit of old fishing net and the sea-weed, people could have walked by and just not noticed it. The smell of the sea-weed would have helped to mask the stink.'

'Were you hoping for someone in particular?' Benny asked.

'Hoping but not expecting,' Sophie replied. 'That way I'm never disappointed.'

'You have too wise a head on those slim shoulders, O golden-haired one. You are in danger of being set apart from the rest of the human race.'

'Stop talking nonsense, Benny. I'm not in the mood.'

He shrugged. 'Okay. I'll send you a message about the post-mortem once I clear a slot for it.'

'Sorry, Benny. I didn't mean to be rude.'

'I know. See you soon, then.'

'But I do think it might be linked to our case.'

The pathologist stopped packing his bag. 'Really?'

'It's the shirt, Benny. Red corduroy's a bit uncommon, isn't it?'

'So I will be seeing you again soon. I'll bear it in mind.' He gave Sophie a hug, then left.

'What is it between you two?' Marsh asked.

'We were at university together and shared a house with a couple of other students. It was Benny who introduced me to Martin. He always claims it was the worst mistake of his life but he's just teasing when he says that. At least I hope he is. He was the best man at our wedding.'

'Ah, I understand. It's puzzled me for a long time. Should we take a look around while we're here? I know the search team has already been over the area, but I'd like to get a feel for the place. We've only got about twenty minutes of daylight left.'

They spoke to the uniformed sergeant, and then walked beyond the scene. Sophie kept looking back at the cliff top, trying to judge the distance and angle.

'He said it was almost directly under the car-turning area and viewpoint on the cliff top,' she said. 'I want to go up there. Let's get back to the car.'

Several squad cars were parked at the end of the cliff top lane, with police tape barring access to the cliff edge. The constable on duty informed them that the area had been searched thoroughly, but nothing suspicious had been found. The two detectives looked down on the temporary tent below. Even though the sea was beginning to calm, the noise of the surf and grinding shingle carried up to them.

'What do you think, Barry?'

'It's an ideal place to dispose of a body. I did wonder if it could have been carried here by the tide from further along the coast, even from Peveril, but I'd guess that's unlikely. The currents are all wrong and it would have to have been pulled round Portland Bill, then come back close into the shoreline here. How likely is that?'

'Not very, but what do I know? Maybe we'd better check with an expert before we ditch the idea completely.' She looked out to sea. 'There's some deep water out there, isn't there?'

'Not sure. I know the area around Swanage has a lot of sudden variations in water depth. There are shallow reefs and ridges next to very deep holes. There's an extremely deep hole right beside the Peveril ledges. But I don't know about here. It's too far west for me. Why do you ask?'

'There's always the chance that it came in from the sea, maybe from a boat. It might be nothing to do with us at all.'

'Do you really think that?' Marsh said.

'No. I think it's Derek. The height matches, so does the hair colour and clothes. And that deep red, cord shirt is a bit of a giveaway, isn't it? And that means there was more going on inside that little group than we realised.'

'If it is our man, when do you think it happened?'

Sophie shrugged. 'He might have been killed at the same time as Sarah, but I think that's unlikely. It would have meant that Shapiro had two bodies to get out of the hotel. So probably it was a while after. Maybe the next day, but not much later than that. He hadn't changed his shirt. If he was a ladies' man, he'd be careful about his grooming. Possibly there was a dispute. But this is all guesswork, and you know that baseless conjecture just isn't my style. Let's get back. You drive and I'll phone in and set the wheels in motion.'

* * *

Jimmy Melsom and Rae Gregson were still in the incident room when the two senior detectives arrived back in the early evening. Rae looked up as they entered.

'A phone call just came in from forensics, ma'am. They've sent you an important email.'

Sophie logged on to her computer, read the message and printed out the attached document.

'How important is it, ma'am?' Marsh asked.

'Very. Traces of Sarah's blood on the duvet taken from the hotel bedroom. And more on the chair back. The report says that the chair was a soft-cushioned one, a dark red colour. Does anyone remember that?'

'Yes,' Marsh replied. 'It seemed a bit out of place compared to the other furnishings.'

Sophie glanced again at the paper in her hand. 'There were also traces of blood in the U-bend of the bathroom basin. Also interesting, don't you think?'

'According to the post-mortem she had quite a deep head wound, ma'am,' Marsh said. 'That must have caused bleeding. And if she then had her head shoved in the sink to drown her, some of that blood would have washed off.'

'We didn't find anything in the room that could have caused that head injury, did we? So they took it away with them. It was something blunt and heavy . . . Unless she was kicked unconscious, then dumped temporarily in the chair. That might explain the midriff bruising as well. If someone was wearing heavy boots, well . . .'

'God, that's awful,' Rae said. 'So something happened to turn the men against her, after they'd had sex? Is that what it's beginning to look like?'

'It may only have been one of them,' Sophie mused. 'Particularly if today's body turns out to be Derek, which is what we suspect. Maybe he didn't like what was happening. That's if he was murdered.'

'What do you mean?' Marsh asked.

'There's always the possibility that he just walked off that cliff, Barry, if he really felt something for Sarah. Maybe things in that hotel room got out of hand too quickly for him to do anything about it. Maybe he couldn't live with himself afterwards.'

Sophie perched on the edge of one of the tables. 'Now, Jimmy, tell us all about this important discovery you made at Sarah's office. You were a bit incoherent on the phone.'

CHAPTER 10: TAINTED MEMORY

Tuesday evening

The safe house Rosemary and Ed were occupying was situated in a quiet cul-de-sac in Wareham. It was a small, unremarkable house among other similar ones. They hadn't been confined to the property, so they spent some time each day wandering around by the river. They had just come back from a circular walk around the ancient Saxon walls surrounding the town centre.

'I'm not sure that was what I expected,' Rosemary said as they hung their coats up in the hallway. 'I thought some of it would be stone.'

'I don't think the Saxons were into stone ramparts,' Ed replied. 'But even though they're earthworks, they're still pretty impressive. It must have taken a lot of people a lot of effort to put them up.'

'I suppose the world must have been a dangerous place to warrant all of that labour. It's not productive, is it? It must have used up time that could have been spent on raising more crops or building better homes. And they wouldn't have been stupid enough to build them for no reason. It must have been a violent time.'

'According to Ella, we have a very violent history. Her boyfriend is doing a doctorate about violence in the middle ages. Just get him started on how people treated each other back then. The statistics are frightening. The newspapers are always saying we live in dangerous times now, but don't you believe it. Modern life's a picnic compared with what those people had to go through. Cruelty was just a fact of life.'

'And murder, I expect,' Rosemary added quietly.

'Sorry. I should have spotted where that clever little speech of mine was likely to lead. It's a weakness of mine, showing off the knowledge I pick up second-hand. I'll learn to control it one day.'

Rosemary squeezed his hand. 'Well don't try to control everything, will you?'

* * *

In the middle of the evening they were snuggled on a couch in the lounge, sipping the last couple of glasses from a bottle of wine. Rosemary's phone rang. When the call was over, she turned to Ed.

'The DCI will be here in fifteen minutes. Apparently there's been a couple of important developments today, although she wouldn't tell me any details. Coffee, I think.'

Ed straightened the cushions and began tidying the room. 'Why am I doing this?' he asked. 'Anyone would think it was my own home.'

'Well, all I can say is, I'm glad your mother brought you up right.' Rosemary laughed.

DCI Allen looked tired when she appeared at the door a little later. Rosemary and Ed watched her sink into an armchair and swallow the coffee in two mouthfuls.

'More?' Rosemary asked.

The DCI nodded. She gave them a short account of the day's events.

'So, is the name Paul Derek in any way familiar to you, Rosemary? Did Sarah ever mention that name?'

Rosemary nodded slowly. 'She did mention the name Paul a couple of times, I'm sure of it. But it wasn't often and I never asked her about him. I don't remember the surname Derek.'

'When was this?'

'Maybe six months ago? A year at the most. It couldn't have been much before that because I only met her eighteen months ago.'

'What was the context?'

'Just when we were out for a drink together, I think. Or maybe on the phone . . . Yes, that was it. We'd agreed to meet for an evening out together but she called to postpone it. She said she had a date. I think it was only a month or two after we met and before we went to the first music weekend together. I remember asking her how it went, but she was a bit cagey and didn't tell me much.'

'And what about the other time?'

'That's a hard one. I really can't remember much about the detail. I think I asked her whether she had seen him again. She laughed and said, "of course." But nothing else was ever mentioned.'

'But no mention of the surname?'

'No.'

'So she didn't talk to you in any depth about what was going on in her life? No girly gossip about relationships?'

'I've always thought girly gossip was just something that happened on TV dramas. Sarah didn't open up about it, and I didn't ask too much,' said Rosemary.

Sophie paused. 'When you first met she wasn't in her latest job. She started at the insurance company about a year ago. Did she talk about her reasons for moving to the new job?'

'I don't think it was a complete change. I mean, she wasn't on the front desk at the bank — she was in admin. And her new job was also in admin. As far as I can remember, she just wanted a change, but I don't know the full story. She wasn't allowed to tell me any details about the new job. At least, that's what she said. She was even a bit cagey about what company she worked for. I don't know why and I never asked. I'm beginning to realise how little I really knew about her, and how little I must have wanted to know. I suppose it shows that we didn't completely hit it off. I can't have been really interested. I never realised that until now.'

Sophie turned to Ed Wilton. 'When we spoke a couple of days ago I asked you for the facts about Friday evening. I didn't ask you about your impression of Sarah. I'd like to get that now. Just give me your gut feelings when you first spoke with her.'

Ed stroked his chin. 'My first impression was that she was lively and outgoing. She smiled and laughed a lot, chatted freely and seemed to have a very cheerful personality. She tended to dominate the conversation, so Rosemary here didn't get much of a look in. But all that faded quite quickly. I got the impression that once she decided I wasn't her type she stopped making an effort. That's when I got to chat to Rosemary. This was all when I met them earlier in the evening. Later on, when they came in the second time, she was all over Derek and didn't have time for anyone else. By the time we got to the end of the evening and were leaving the pub I wasn't impressed with her at all. I've wondered since then if there was a reason for her attitude.'

'What do you mean, Ed?' asked Rosemary.

'Well, sometimes there's a reason why people behave in a very superficial way. Some kind of emotional trauma or a really serious let-down by someone, possibly well in the past. The surface cheerfulness masks an underlying problem. The whole thing is an act. They can only keep it up for a short while and only to one or two people at a time. It possibly indicates a feeling of inferiority. I've wondered if Sarah was secretly envious of your more stable personality.'

'You haven't mentioned this before.'

'No. We've been a bit bound up in ourselves, haven't we? It's one of those things that you kind of feel, but don't talk about unless it comes up. You were a bit envious of what you saw as her adventurous nature. But I think she could well have been even more envious of your calmness.'

Rosemary frowned slightly. 'I don't think so. And I knew her a lot better than you. I always felt that she pitied me slightly for my scruples.'

'What about Derek?' said Sophie. 'What were your initial feelings about him? Again, don't think too hard.'

'I quite liked him,' Ed replied. 'He seemed an amenable sort, and I didn't feel he was putting on any kind of show. But he soon became so busy canoodling with Sarah that he completely lost interest in the rest of us.'

'I agree,' Rosemary added. 'He seemed quite upfront and pleasant. Unlike the other one, Brian. There was something about him that I just didn't like, right from the start.'

'Did Derek ever mention his work?' Sophie continued.

'Now you come to mention it, he did. I think he said he was in IT in some way. But I didn't follow it up,' Rosemary said.

'What about Brian? Did he talk about his work?'

'No. Or if he did, I wasn't listening. I was trying to ignore him, hoping he'd just go away.'

'I got the impression he might have been in the security business,' said Ed.

'Why didn't you mention this before?' Sophie asked sharply.

'I've only just remembered. It wasn't mentioned directly in the conversation. It was when we were coming out of the pub. The doorway was a bit crowded with people leaving, and someone in front had forgotten something and tried to turn back. Brian said something about supplying bouncers to keep order in the pubs, but I was only half listening.'

'Okay. This all helps. Please phone me if you remember anything else. I'd better be going. It's getting late and I need at least some sleep.'

As she stood up Sophie noticed that Rosemary was biting her lip.

'Is there something else, Rosemary?' she asked.

There was a moment's hesitation and then Rosemary nodded. Sophie waited.

'I think she might have been taking money for sex. Sarah, I mean.'

Sophie sat down again.

'It was our last weekend, the one at Gloucester. When she came back late in the night she thought I was asleep, but I woke up when she opened the door. I was still sleepy and didn't say anything. As she dumped her bag on the bedside table an envelope fell out and a lot of banknotes slipped out of it. She counted them and slid them back. It looked like more than a hundred pounds.'

'It could have been there all the time,' Sophie said.

'But it wasn't. I'd watched her put stuff into that bag before we went out, and there was no envelope of cash. I can't think of any other explanation. It worried me for a long time, but I never had the nerve to ask her about it. That was when I started to feel ambivalent towards her, and wondered if I should still be going away on these weekend trips. But she'd already booked this one.'

'What did you decide?'

'I couldn't make my mind up. I thought I'd see how things went this weekend and then come to a decision. And then all this happened.'

Sophie nodded and stood up again. 'You did the right thing to tell me, but I must also add that you shouldn't jump to conclusions. There could be other, perfectly innocent explanations.'

'Yes. It's just that I can't think of one.'

Wilton showed the DCI out, but she paused in the hallway.

'I need to talk to Rosemary alone, Mr Wilton. Can you stay here or do something in the kitchen for a few minutes, please?'

'Of course,' he said and walked through to the back of the house.

Sophie returned to the lounge. She sat down opposite Rosemary and thought for a moment before she spoke.

'I need to ask you something quite sensitive, Rosemary. I need to do it out of Ed's earshot, although it doesn't involve him.'

Rosemary sat forward on the edge of her seat.

'Did Sarah ever make a pass at you? Or did she indicate in any way that she'd had relationships with other women?'

Rosemary's face turned pink. She looked down at her hands.

'Why didn't you tell me, Rosemary? What happened?'

'It was at Gloucester too, but earlier in the day.' Rosemary spoke so softly that Sophie had to lean forward to hear what she was saying. 'We'd had some wine at lunchtime and I was a bit tipsy. We got back to our room and she came on strong to me. We ended up in bed.'

There was a silence. 'And?' Sophie finally asked.

'I was confused. It just felt so different. I really didn't know how to deal with it. It was days before I could even begin to think about what had happened. I was kind of ashamed and excited at the same time. In the end I decided it wasn't for me and I told her so. I only came to Swanage on the understanding that it wouldn't happen again.' She raised her eyes to Sophie's. 'I've come to the conclusion that it doesn't mean I'm a lesbian, maybe just a little bit bi. I also think it was just her. She was so lovely. She had such a beautiful body. The thought of doing it again with a different woman appals me. Does that make sense?'

'Of course. And I think your description of yourself fits Sarah as well. She clearly liked men but was willing to involve women if the context was right for her. I'm not condemning you or her, Rosemary. And this will stay just with me for the time being, so please be reassured. But I did need to know. Well, I'd better be off.'

In the kitchen, Ed was sorting through the contents of the fridge.

'I guess you think I was a bit harsh on Saturday evening when we questioned you both in depth. But it had to be done, Mr Wilton. And everything you said checks out so far.'

'Including the graze on my hand?'

'Yes. We found traces of your tissue on the wall of the hotel, just as you described. So you can rest easy. At the moment, anyway.'

She left and Ed returned to the sitting room.

'I'm feeling miserable now, Ed,' Rosemary said.

'You had to speak up about the money you saw her with. The police had to know, even if there's nothing to it.'

'I know. But I feel I've tainted her memory somehow.'

CHAPTER 11: MUCKY BITCH

Wednesday morning

Sophie and Rae arrived at Sarah Sheldon's workplace early the next morning. They had arranged the visit the previous day. Karen Fleming, the HR Manager, showed the two detectives into her office, and seated them by a low table.

'I wondered if the big guns would arrive at some point,' she said. 'But this is sooner than I expected.'

Sophie laughed. 'I'm not that big, Mrs Fleming. I'm not even a weapon. But here I am, because what you told DC Melsom yesterday could be of vital importance to us.'

Sophie placed her bag on the table in front of her and nodded to Rae. The young DC sat down and took out her notebook and pen. Sophie smoothed her powder-grey skirt down to her knees, and settled back into the chair. During the drive to Portsmouth she'd talked to Rae about the importance of dressing to impress. Personnel managers, she'd said, were often of crucial importance in a large organisation. Jimmy Melsom had been able to provide enough information about Karen Fleming for Sophie to figure out the best way to stroke her ego. If Karen was doing her job right, she'd know a lot more about the workforce than was noted in the official employment records, and they needed to gain access to this information.

Sophie had chosen to wear a grey jacket in soft leather and grey knee boots. 'A black outfit can be too severe,' she'd said. 'But grey or blue outfits look formal without the starkness. Grey's quite sexy really, according to my husband. And it's funny how appearance can charm a woman just as much as a man. I suppose you could call it the psychology of power flirting.'

Sophie smiled again at Karen Fleming, widening her eyes slightly. 'Paul Derek,' she said. 'Tell me about him.'

'He's a good worker with a proper sense of responsibility, and a nice bloke,' she replied. 'He's worked here for a little over five years. He impressed me when he came for interview and I haven't had cause to change my mind since.'

'What about his people skills? IT staff can be a bit prickly and sometimes don't understand the problems ordinary workers have with systems they're unused to.'

So smoothly done, thought Rae. The DCI had given away no hint that the subject of their conversation was currently lying lifeless on a trolley in the pathology department at Dorchester hospital.

'He's fine. He has an approachable manner and is conscientious about his job. Though most of the staff contact work is done by his assistant, Melissa Taylor. He's more back-room.'

'Can we see his file, please? I know my DC had a brief look yesterday, but I'd like to have a closer look.'

The file was ready and Karen Fleming pushed it across the table. The first page gave a summary of his personal details and employment record, along with a photograph. It was the man they knew as Derek, found dead under Burton Cliffs the previous day. Sophie nodded slightly at Rae.

'I'd like a copy of everything in this file please, Mrs Fleming. I'd also like to know about his family circumstances.' Again the smile, lips a little apart.

'He's divorced. It happened about two years ago.'

'Was the divorce amicable do you know?'

'I'd guess not, but you'll have to speak to him about that. To his credit, he's never let it get in the way of his work.'

'Are there any children?'

'Yes, two teenage sons. They live with their mother, Pamela Derek, as far as I know. Paul saw them some weekends.'

'Do you think Mrs Sheldon might have been involved with him at the time of his marriage breakdown?'

'Officially, of course, I wouldn't know. But I'd guess they were an item even then. I told your man yesterday about her applying for the job here on Paul's recommendation. But she turned out to be an asset. She was a bright, intelligent worker who did her job really well. That's why we were considering her for promotion. The news of her death has come as a real shock to us. I'm concerned about how it will affect Paul. Can you tell me how he is?'

Rae kept her head well down.

'No, sorry. Could you show me her file as well, Mrs Fleming?'

Karen Fleming pushed a second, thinner folder across the table. Sophie looked quickly through it. Jimmy Melsom had missed nothing of importance.

'I'd like this copied too, if you'd be so kind.'

Karen Fleming nodded.

'I'd also like to see a complete record of their holiday dates, from when they each started working here. Would that be possible? Also any conferences they went on, training courses, that kind of thing. Could they have attended any courses together?'

'Unlikely. Paul's were all technical in nature, and would have been totally unsuitable for an administrative operative like Sarah. But I will cross-check for you.'

'Thank you. Social functions, work parties and the like? Did they attend any together?'

'Not that I'm aware of. The couple of events they did attend, they stuck with their own colleagues, as far as I remember. You could ask their workmates, but I think they kept their relationship quiet.'

Sophie nodded. 'But why would they need to bother? They were both divorced, weren't they? I'm assuming it wouldn't have been a problem for the company if their relationship came to light. They were working in completely different roles and departments. Didn't you ever wonder?'

'Yes, I did,' said Karen. 'And you're right. There would have been no conflict of interest because of their jobs, so it wouldn't have been a problem for us. I never asked them about it nor told anyone else of my suspicions, because it was irrelevant. But their reasons for keeping it secret . . . that intrigued me. I can't help you, though. I've never settled on a satisfactory explanation. At times I've even thought that maybe it was all just a big coincidence and I misheard that conversation I told your colleague about.'

She looked at Sophie expectantly, but there was no reaction. Rae had finished taking notes. Her boss leaned back in her chair and looked at the personnel manager. She gave a slight twitch of the lips.

'I want all of Paul Derek's personal possessions collected from his office. Rae here will supervise that. I want all of his emails, personal computer files, flash drives, company phones, diaries and notebooks identified and assembled together. I want his phone record for the past three months, showing all his calls. Six months if it's available. I presume he had a work laptop. I want that. His online schedule and record books. Any confidential records the company has on him that are not already in his file. I want the contents of any staff locker that he had. Anything on a coat hook in a cloakroom, if there is such a thing. And anything else that your Melissa identifies as being his. Don't worry, Karen, it won't add to your staff's workload. A team of forensic experts will be arriving shortly.' She looked at her watch. 'In five minutes, to be precise. They'll be gone within a couple of hours, although we'll be leaving a network specialist to work with Melissa going through your servers to look for any other items that Mr Derek may have stored. And there are a couple of other things. Firstly, I don't want the subject matter of this conversation discussed with anyone at the moment, not even your own bosses. I'll explain the situation to the executive manager myself. Secondly, a recommendation. I think you should look to appoint a temporary replacement for Mr Derek from this moment on.'

'But he'll be back next week. We've already organised it so Melissa can cope on her own.'

'Trust my judgement, Karen. That's all I can say at the moment.' Sophie stood up and moved towards the door. Then she stopped and turned. 'Possibly, in the long term, you might be looking for a permanent replacement. And that really is for your ears only.'

The personnel manager stood open-mouthed as they walked out.

The computer forensic team had arrived on schedule and were now in charge. Sophie had spoken briefly to the executive manager and the two detectives were heading for the car.

'That was very impressive, ma'am,' Rae said.

'The benefits of rank and experience, Rae. It's like a chess game really. The trick is to work out in advance which opening gambit to play. It's also important to have a second plan ready to use if you've misjudged your initial approach. But now comes the difficult bit. I have to speak to Paul Derek's ex-wife. We need to find out how old the sons are, and decide who the next of kin is, in order to get the body identified. Maybe he has parents still alive. I'll do that while you supervise things here. I'll come back for you as soon as I can, then we'll pay a quick visit to his home now we have his address.'

* * *

Paul Derek's ex-wife looked harassed and careworn. Her hair was a tangled mess and her face was lined and blotchy. Sophie showed her warrant card and explained to Pamela that she was calling about her ex-husband.

'What the fuck's he been up to now?' snarled the woman.

'I'd like to come in, please, Mrs Derek. We really can't talk about this on the doorstep.'

Sophie followed her through a dingy hallway into an untidy sitting room. She stood while magazines and half-empty chocolate boxes were cleared from the sofa. Pamela turned down the volume on the television but left it on. Sophie waited until the woman was seated and then broke the news of her ex-husband's death. Pamela's reaction was surprisingly emotional, and she sobbed for several minutes.

'This has been hard for you, Pamela. I know that your marriage ended a couple of years ago, and I'd guess that the split was a difficult one. Is there anything you feel you can tell me right now?'

'It was that fucking woman,' Pamela said. 'She got him hooked on all that group-sex rubbish. The mucky bitch. She got him trapped. He wanted me to do it as well, but there's a limit, isn't there?' She took a breath and appeared to calm down. 'Sorry. It just came as such a shock. You'll be thinking I still loved him or something, but I don't. That all finished well before he walked out on me. In the end I gave him a choice and he chose her. In a way I was glad, cos I just couldn't handle it. And there were no feelings left, just memories. That's why I cried when you told me. It was the memories.'

'Did he ever use Derek as a first name, rather than Paul?'

'Yes. He'd been called it when he was a teenager. You know how boys call each other by their surname sometimes. Then, when he started using those websites to look for sex partners, he'd use Derek rather than Paul. I hated it. I'm thinking of changing my surname back to my maiden name. The name Derek makes me feel dirty.'

'How old are your boys?'

'Andy's nineteen and Kenny's seventeen.'

'Now I have to tell you the hard part, Pamela. Paul's body was found on the shoreline in Dorset. It looks as though he fell from the nearby cliffs. At the moment we're treating it as a suspicious death. We'll need Andy to identify his father's body, and I'll have to arrange that for some time in the next day or two.'

'We'll all come. Andy can do the official bit, but Kenny and I should be there to support him.'

'It's your choice, Pamela, and I really respect you for it. It's a very thoughtful gesture.'

'That's all that's left now, isn't it? Gestures. What else is there?' She paused. 'Dorset? Isn't that where that woman's body was found at the weekend? I don't read the papers or listen to the news much.'

Sophie nodded. Pamela's eyes suddenly came alive.

'Was it her? Fucking Sarah Sheldon? It was, wasn't it? Well, all I can say is, he did the right thing after all. Even if he did top himself afterwards. If it was him killed her then well done, my Paul. Good on you. The only decent thing you've done in years.'

* * *

Once more DC Phil Barber from the local unit accompanied the two detectives. Paul Derek had lived in a small flat in north Portsmouth. They found little out of the ordinary in the small, rather bare apartment. They brought a couple of address books and a laptop back with them for further forensic investigation. When they arrived back at Swanage, a message from the pathologist was waiting, giving the time for the post-mortem examination on Paul Derek.

'Just enough time for a coffee and biscuit, Rae. Would you like to come to the PM? Though I only go to the first part, the external examination. When I was a young and over-keen DC in the Met, I steeled myself to stay for the whole of my first post-mortem. I ended up unconscious on the theatre floor. I was badly concussed from the fall and they kept me in overnight for observation. And that wasn't the worst of it. Apparently as I fell my skirt caught on something and ripped, and my bright purple knickers were on show to everyone in the room. You can guess what the rest of the unit had to say when I got back to work two days later.'

Rae was rather taken aback by this. 'Yes, I'd like to go, ma'am. And I won't tell anyone that story.'

Sophie laughed. 'I think they know. I gave up trying to be discreet years ago. It just doesn't work for me.'

* * *

'Severe bruising to the head in three places, rear left, front right and top. Deep gash rear left. Broken nose, torn left ear.' An assistant trained spotlights on each probe of the senior pathologist. A second assistant was noting his observations on a form even though he talked into a recording device as he proceeded.

'Several teeth missing or loose. Dirt and grit in the mouth and nostrils. Cuts and grazes over the facial skin, some fairly deep. You'll notice, Sophie, that there are far fewer skin abrasions on the limbs and torso, where the tissue would have been protected by his clothing. But there are still injuries.'

He probed the chest area and upper limbs. 'Several broken ribs and some severe bruising. A fracture of the left arm just below the elbow. Some minor abrasions of the skin tissue on his hands. One broken finger on his right hand, the middle finger, and a bruise to the neighbouring finger.'

Benny Goodall examined the legs. 'Similar to the upper limbs, with bruising and some abrasions. We've X-rayed already, and there's a fracture to the right fibula and damage to the right hip joint.'

He stopped and looked at Sophie. 'No significant tearing of the nails, and no grit under them. I ordered a blood test when we got him here yesterday. Benzodiazepine in significant residual amounts.'

'Ah, so he was heavily sedated?'

'Probably unconscious.'

'And his injuries are consistent with a tumble down that cliff-face?'

'I would say so.'

'And the condition of his fingers and nails tends to reinforce the idea that he wasn't conscious at the time?'

'Wouldn't you say so? Most people falling down a cliff would try to grab hold of the surface, almost instinctively I would have thought. The head and limb injuries are not consistent with a free-fall, with a crashing stop at the bottom. They look to be in line with a tumble, catching on those ledges and outcrops. Normally we'd expect significant finger and nail damage. There's nothing of that here.'

'Well, it helps me to picture what might have happened, Benny. Very helpful. Anything else I need to know at the moment?'

He shook his head. 'Not with this one. I'll get the details emailed across to you as soon as I can and I'll call you if we spot anything unusual. But something interesting has cropped up with the head wound in the first body. We found microscopic traces of wax in the skin.'

'What kind of wax?'

'Shoe polish.' He raised his eyebrows.

'So it was caused by a kick after all? It cropped up in conversation earlier, but we were only speculating. It seemed such a deep wound. Heavy boots of some kind? Is that what you're thinking?'

Benny Goodall nodded.

Sophie and Rae made their way back to the car.

'He was very helpful,' Rae said. 'I thought that pathologists were generally more guarded than that.'

'He's a close friend, Rae. He knows I won't misquote him, we have an understanding about it. Look, we haven't had anything to eat since breakfast, and I'm famished. How about a late lunch in one of the local cafés? There's a really good one in the town centre. It has an interesting history. Its main room is reputedly the one used by Judge Jeffreys when he held the Bloody Assize in the town.'

'Sorry, ma'am. I've got an engineering background. I know nothing about history.'

'All the better, then. I can tell you about it while we're shovelling our food down. We don't have too much time.'

* * *

Back in Swanage, Barry Marsh and Jimmy Melsom were discussing the man who'd gone missing from the hotel after Saturday night.

'So there's been no sight of John Renton since then?' Marsh asked.

'No. Tom Rose did some double-checking at the hotel, but nothing has come out of the booking details. It was an internet booking made with a credit card. It was fully paid for in advance, so the hotel had no reason to query the reservation. The address given at the time of the booking matches the one for the credit card account. Phil Barber from Portsmouth called in to say that he'd visited the address, but that there was no one in. The neighbours say that he's in the army and at the moment he's in the middle of a six-month tour of duty in Afghanistan. So it couldn't have been him at the hotel, could it, Sarge?'

'No, but if it wasn't him at the hotel, who was it? And how did he get hold of Renton's credit card details?'

'Not that hard, is it? I give mine out all the time when I'm doing a phone booking for a concert or a holiday.'

'You mean we assume the person on the other end of the phone is only recording it on the official system, but they could be making a quick note for their own use?'

'Yeah. We're all so trusting, aren't we? But the person taking the details could reuse them, maybe after waiting a few weeks. As long as it's for nothing outrageous it might not even be noticed when the account holder checks their statement. Does anyone go through their statement item by item? I don't. I just trust that everything's as it should be and the total is about what I expect. But maybe it's not even that. It could be someone else who knows Renton's details legitimately. You know, a close friend or someone in the family.'

'What does the bank say?'

'There's nothing odd in the pattern of spending. Just normal sorts of things. And it's consistent. There's been no recent change in the kind of stuff on the statement, according to the bank.'

Marsh thought for a while. 'Get the past couple of years' statements for the account. Get on to the MoD and find out Renton's unit and where they've been stationed for the last three years. I want the two compared. Okay?'

CHAPTER 12: GLAMOUR SHOTS

Wednesday afternoon

Lydia Pillay was unhappy. The previous day's unexpected encounter with Sophie had set off a cascade of unexpected emotional responses. She'd already realised that she'd made a mistake when she'd walked out on her Dorset job to join the unit in Bath. The feeling had been growing for weeks, but she'd managed to push the thoughts away. The visit from Sophie had brought all her concerns back into her mind and she was finding it difficult to ignore them. The fact was, she really didn't like her new boss. She'd met him on a course and he'd talked about the financial crime unit he was running. She'd been impressed by him and by the job as he'd described it. But the reality was quite different. She found herself as the junior in the team, forced to spend a large proportion of her working days on menial tasks. She was given little responsibility, was not making any use of the experience she'd gained from her training and her years in Dorset and was wondering whether she'd merely been appointed as some kind of token ethnic minority officer. Moreover, she now realised that financial crime just wasn't for her. Why hadn't she seen this before?

She knew why. She just hadn't bothered to think through the full implications of the new job. It had been staring her in the face, but she'd chosen to ignore it. Lydia was a "people person." She enjoyed working out the intricacies of human interaction, and that's why she'd loved her job with Sophie Allen so much. She sighed. And as if all that wasn't enough, there was her new boss. He was shallow, only interested in his own career path and those investigations that would raise his own profile. It was very apparent now, but why hadn't she seen this at the interviews? She realised now that she had, but deliberately chose to ignore what had been staring her in the face. It was all because of her stupid desire to get away from a boss she adored but whose apparent actions had caused her so much anxiety. So here she was, stuck in a job that didn't, and couldn't, make use of the skills she had, in a team that gave her menial jobs to do, and working for a boss who preened and postured his way through his working life.

What could be done? She looked around her. The office was quiet, with most of its usual occupants out on a case. Just one other officer remained behind, sitting on the other side of the open-plan office. He seemed absorbed in his task, so Lydia sat thinking for a while, then slipped out of the room. She took out her mobile phone and made a phone call about jazz festivals in the area. She'd recently met a rather handsome young musician who she knew helped on several committees. She wanted an excuse to see him again so this would kill the proverbial two birds.

* * *

Rae was looking at a list of the items on Sarah Sheldon's laptop. She cross-checked these on the machine itself, which now sat on the desk in front of her. There were numerous photos, mostly of Sarah and friends enjoying themselves at parties and social events. Rae recognised the face of the dead man, Paul Derek, in several of them.

The laptop also contained a folder of letters — a CV and several job applications, including the one for her most recent post. There were recipes — jams, cakes, some simple meals. Then Rae found three digital images. The first showed Sarah sitting on a man's knee. The photo was centred on Sarah, and no details of the man were visible other than his neck, his jacketed left arm encircling her chest and his deeply-tanned neck. There was a small, heart-shaped tattoo on his wrist. The most arresting aspect of the image, however, was what Sarah was wearing: an ornate corset, deep red in colour, with attached, sheer black stockings and matching knickers. Sarah's face was heavily made-up with thick black eyeliner and mascara. The second image showed Sarah posing alone for the camera, wearing the same outfit. This time the shot was full-length, and showed black and red shoes with stiletto heels. The third shot was totally different. Sarah was wearing a cream, full-length wedding dress and holding a bouquet of pastel-pink flowers. Her make-up, though, looked identical to that in the earlier shots. Rae closed down the photos and looked at the dates. They all bore the date 11 June, two years earlier. Rae was aware that this was not conclusive proof of when they'd been taken; it could be the date on which they'd been copied to the laptop, but it was interesting nonetheless. She went to Sophie's office and told her about the three "glamour" shots.

Sophie looked at the images in silence. 'And there are no more?' she asked finally.

'No. I've finished checking every file on the machine. This is it, ma'am. These three are the only ones that look out of place. All the other files are pretty mundane, even the other photos. I'm just wondering, ma'am, whether computer forensics did a deep check on the hard drive? I think they've just listed the files that are there now. What if others have been deleted?'

'Maybe we didn't make it clear enough that we wanted the full works. These three photos make it all the more important to get a full scan.'

'I could drive up with it if you want me to, ma'am. It'll mean they get it this afternoon and can make a start. Then maybe we'll get it back before the weekend.'

Sophie frowned. 'Okay, you take it and I'll phone through so that they know what to do once you arrive. Bloody hell, why on earth didn't they do the full job when they had it? I thought it came back rather too quickly.'

'But it does mean that Jimmy's been able to start on the email checks, ma'am.'

'Okay, you've calmed me down. Jimmy's only just started on Derek's laptop, so wait until he's ready and take them both together. While you're waiting can you check round and see if anyone's got any further with tracing Brian Shapiro? I can't believe we haven't managed to find out anything about him yet. If nothing's happened by tomorrow, I'm going to have to rethink how we go about finding him.'

Sophie walked over to speak to Marsh.

'What check did we expect on Sarah's laptop, Barry?'

'Just a quick one, ma'am. We didn't think it would be of much significance. Why?'

'I thought we'd requested a detailed examination.'

'That's probably my fault. You left the decision with me, and I went for speed. We could send it back for a more detailed check if you're suspicious.'

'Rae's just about to set out with it. There were three odd photos but no other images at all. And they were in a folder labelled recipes, stored along with exactly that. Why would that be? Here, take a look.'

Sophie plugged the flash drive into Barry's computer and they looked at the images.

'Does that wedding dress picture look like a genuine wedding?' asked Marsh.

'Difficult to say,' Sophie replied. 'It's a very plain background, so she could just have been modelling the outfit. But it's the kind of picture often taken before the ceremony. Look at the filename: SarahWedding1. That number could suggest that there are other wedding photos of her, taken later. But why aren't the others anywhere on her laptop?'

'Maybe they were emailed to her, just these three.' Marsh looked at the other two photos. 'Phew. These are quite something. Not your average wedding photos, are they?'

'They tie in with what we've learned about her, though, don't they? Rae spotted that the date is the same on all three. If there has been no touching up or re-saving then they were taken on the same day. The wedding dress shot was taken in the early afternoon and the other two in the evening. And the times do make sense, don't you think? She's sitting on a man's lap in this photo, but there's not enough of him for us to even hazard a guess about who he was.'

'It can't be Derek, ma'am. Even though the height would be about right, Derek didn't have a tattoo on his wrist. Whoever it is, he's been in the sun a lot. And these two glamour shots are totally unwedding-like. How do they fit in?'

'Barry, you're too much of an innocent. The corset would be covered up by the wedding dress. And many women do wear very sexy lingerie for their wedding nights. Trust me, I know. She's put on black stockings and different shoes, but the rest is perfectly feasible.' She looked at the photo again. 'In fact the dress is so long it would hide her legs and shoes, so she could be wearing the same stockings and shoes underneath. So the key question is whether the scene is genuine or not. Was she just modelling a wedding dress or was she acting out some type of fantasy? Rosemary hasn't mentioned anything like this.'

'I don't think Rosemary knew the real Sarah Sheldon at all. I think Sarah only gave her a very few details. She seems to have led a very complicated life.' Marsh paused. 'I'm sorry if I made the wrong call on the laptop check, ma'am.'

'Don't worry. We haven't really lost any time. But I'm still puzzled about why these photos are stored in her recipes folder.'

'Probably just a mistake, ma'am. Imagine if someone had just sent her a recipe and then these photos arrived in the next message. If she was in a hurry she might just have clicked on save. So they've ended up in the same folder as the attachments from the previous message.'

'That's why I decided on a full hard-drive scan. I want to see if there's a lot of stuff that might have been wiped, particularly photos. Her pictures folder was empty, which is a bit suspicious, and there was nothing on her work machine.' She looked at her watch. 'I've got to phone Pamela Derek and arrange a time to collect her and her sons and take them to Dorchester for the identification. Do you want to be there? It could be useful. The two boys might open up to a man where they wouldn't to a woman.'

He nodded. 'By the way, Peter Shakespeare, Sarah's son by Hugh, should be arriving from the States late this evening. His dad is collecting him and will call me to confirm his arrival. If he's agreeable, shall we arrange the formal identification for tomorrow?'

'Absolutely. We'll pencil in tomorrow late morning, and we'll take him for a quick lunch afterwards and pick his brains.'

'The father wants to be there as well.'

'That's understandable. I think I'd feel the same.' Sophie took the flash drive out of the computer. 'Show these three images to Jimmy. It might help him see what he's looking for.'

* * *

Lydia picked up her bag, collected her coat and made her way out into the fresh air. She walked over to a bench and sat down facing the river, its grey surface rippled by the chilly breeze. The swans ruffled their feathers when a small child ran towards them but settled as he threw some pieces of bread in their direction. Someone sat down on the bench beside Lydia. She jumped, then turned and smiled at the tall young man.

'Hello, Ian. I'm so glad you could make it. Where shall we go for lunch?'

They set off along the riverside walkway, and she slipped her arm through his. She was already feeling more cheerful.

Their lunch in a local café was full of animated talk. It was followed by a slow walk back along the river to the area where they both worked. Lydia gave Ian a hug and a peck on the cheek as they parted.

'Can we do this again? she asked. 'Maybe without the work discussion? I've really enjoyed it.'

The young man gave her a shy smile. 'That would be great. Or why not an evening?'

Lydia gave him another hug. Then she ran up the steps to her office. Life was suddenly looking a whole lot better. Her office was still quiet, so she sat down at her desk and logged on to her computer. She spent several minutes composing an email to Sophie, outlining some of the ideas Ian had suggested. When the unit leader returned in the mid-afternoon, Lydia was deep in cross-checking some financial records.

'Boss? I think I've uncovered something interesting.' It was the first time in several weeks she'd shown such enthusiasm.

* * *

Jimmy Melsom was examining the first batch of documents belonging to Paul Derek. Nothing had come to light on the company network, but they'd reported some relevant emails and images on his work laptop and Jimmy was inspecting these. Although some were relevant to the case, they threw no new light on events or motives. The emails consisted of mild flirtations between Derek and Sarah, and the photos showed the two of them at various pubs and clubs. None bore any resemblance to the three racy photos that had turned up on Sarah's laptop. Melsom switched his attention to Derek's home laptop. Sophie had decided that one of her team should give it a quick examination before it was sent away for full forensic examination. This would gain time if any useful files were found. Jimmy spent half an hour digging through the folders and then hit gold. Hidden deep within a documents folder called "Us" were a number of photos and short videos.

Jimmy opened the first image. It was a shot of the couple naked on a bed, having sex. The other fourteen images were similar, all showing Sarah and Paul in various stages of undress and arousal.

Jimmy was glad his bosses had left the incident room. It was one thing having a laugh over lewd photos with his male colleagues, but he knew he'd feel awkward and embarrassed showing them to Sophie or even Rae. This way he could just copy them onto a flash drive, report his findings and hand it over. He looked at the video clips and his eyes widened. The five film sequences were between five and fifteen minutes long, and showed the couple having sex on the same bed as in the photos. Sarah was very much taking the lead. Jimmy looked carefully at the room in the films. It matched the forensic photos of the bedroom in her flat. The video clips showed clearly that Sarah had been the one making all the running in the relationship. Derek appeared to be going along with her in a slightly bemused way, although he obviously enjoyed what she was initiating.

Jimmy switched off the laptop, sealed it in a labelled forensic bag and took off his latex gloves. He took the equipment across to Rae's desk and added it to the pile.

CHAPTER 13: OBSESSED

Thursday morning

'Where are we with the search for Brian Shapiro?'

Not long after eight that morning the team were seated in the incident room. Sophie stood beside the incident board. It now contained plenty of information about the two victims, Sarah Sheldon and Paul Derek, and about the two main witnesses, Rosemary Corrigan and Ed Wilton, but the area around the name Brian Shapiro was noticeably bare. She looked at her team of detectives and uniformed officers.

'He's our prime suspect. We have detailed descriptions of him from Rosemary and Ed. There are statements from other witnesses who saw him on Friday evening. We know what he looks like, we know what he was wearing, we even know something about his personality. We know how he talks, how he walks, how he drums his fingers on the table when he's irritated. But not only can we not find him, we are not making any progress in finding anything about what he's been doing for the past four years. I find that strange. He's become even more important following the post-mortem on Paul Derek. It showed that, at the time of his death Derek was drugged with a strong sedative. This means we're thinking murder rather than suicide or an accidental fall. It's imperative that we find Shapiro. I've asked Rae to summarise what we've discovered so far. Please go ahead, Rae.'

Rae stood up. 'I managed to speak to all of you at some time yesterday, and I've put together what little we know. So here goes. We think he's in his early fifties, is a little shorter than average, has blue eyes and mousey-coloured hair. He was a uniformed constable in Southampton but he left under a cloud. Apparently there were rumours about him abusing vulnerable women. It came to a head in Portsmouth and he was sacked four years ago. There hasn't been much trace of him since, although there are some reports of him being seen on the fringes of the underworld. We think he was divorced about eight years ago and we're trying to trace his ex-wife. But we can't find a woman in either Portsmouth or Southampton with an age and a name that corresponds. That might indicate that she's married again. There's a large family of Shapiros who run a couple of Italian restaurants in Southampton, but they say he's not one of them. Are they being truthful or have they cut all ties because of his behaviour? It's impossible to say at the moment, but I think it needs further investigation, ma'am. The other Brian Shapiros that we've traced don't seem to correspond to our man. There are two in Bournemouth, one in Poole and a few others spread across the Southampton area. There was one in Weymouth until two months ago, and that led us astray for a while because he was the right age. But yesterday Jen discovered that he died in a car crash two months ago. So it's back to square one. Can I give you my hunch, ma'am?'

'Yes, go ahead,' Sophie replied.

'I think he's one of the Southampton restaurant Shapiros, even though they say he's not. I phoned a couple of them. I spoke to two different people from each of the branches of the family since they run two separate restaurants. They gave answers that were almost identical, practically word for word.

I suppose it could have been coincidence, but it made me suspect that they'd talked to each other and agreed on what to say. I know that would be a normal thing to do — they were brothers — but it went beyond what I'd expect just from a chat. That's all I have, ma'am.'

Sophie nodded. 'Very interesting, Rae. Thanks. Good stuff.'

Rae sat down. She was conscious of the others all looking at her. How had she done? It was the first time she'd had to talk to a large group, and she was aware that her voice might betray her masculine origins. She looked at them but the others had already transferred their attention back to Sophie. Only Barry Marsh was still looking at her, and he nodded and smiled. Jen Allbright looked at the floor, frowning, and then back at Rae. Had she guessed? Well, so what if she had? Rae thought. She was who she was, and they would all have to accept it. All she could do was work hard, do all that was expected of her and trust in the judgement of her two superiors. She took some deep breaths and tried to concentrate on what the boss was saying.

'I think we'll go with Rae's instinct and dig a bit deeper into the Shapiro family. Rae, you take charge of it. Jimmy can help you once he's finished with the computers. But you must be tactful with the Shapiros. They're not criminals and shouldn't be treated as such, not unless we find they really have been hiding something from us. Even then, check with me before you confront them. Use any type of record you think might be useful to cross-check them, but it has to be legitimate. And if you do find something, try to get it verified. The other angle that we're trying to follow up is John Renton, the man who went missing from the hotel. That's reached an impasse as well. Apparently he's serving a tour of duty in Afghanistan, so it can't have been him at the hotel. Yet the booking was made from his credit card. Someone might be masquerading as him. His photofit hasn't helped much. There's been some vaguely positive responses from people in the pubs, but nothing definite. Please keep an open mind and if anything does crop up, let one of us know.' She looked at Jen Allbright. 'Jen, you spend a bit more time summarising the information we have on John Renton. But don't waste time on it. Once you've joined up all the dots, and if nothing else occurs to you, give up on it and lend Rae a hand. Barry and I are going to see Sarah Sheldon's son so we'll be out for most of the morning. He's flown in from the States and is due to formally identify his mother's body. Then this afternoon we've got Paul Derek's eldest son identifying his body. Jen, later this morning could you collect the Derek family from their home in Portsmouth and drive them across to Dorchester for the identification? Barry and I can take over then, since we'll already be there. You can give me a rundown on any progress that's been made. I may be paying another visit to Bath tomorrow. Lydia's contacted me with a list of the hotels that the jazz festival promoters included in the information pack sent out to people who've booked into recent festivals. It seems a good idea to check them out, but that's for tomorrow. There is one further bit of news, but I don't think it helps the investigation much. The roadie who had the argument with Shapiro and Derek in the pub on Friday night claimed he'd seen Shapiro before somewhere. He had, but it was a couple of years ago at the Bath jazz festival. We already know that Shapiro was there, from Brenda Plant's evidence. Nevertheless, it's useful corroboration.' She looked around. 'Everyone clear on what to do today? Let's get busy.'

* * *

'Jimmy said you've got a degree in engineering, Rae. Is that right?' Jen Allbright asked as she followed Rae back to her desk.

'Yes,' Rae replied. 'Marine engineering.'

'What? Ships and things? What made you join the police rather than looking for a job with ships?'

'As I told Jimmy, I found out I actually didn't like ships very much. But I do like people. And solving crime puzzles.'

'You haven't been in the Dorset force very long. I looked. Where were you before?'

Rae sighed. 'I haven't got time to chat, Jen. Can we leave this till later? I'm not trying to dodge your questions, but I'm new so the boss has her eye on me.' She glanced round. 'She's watching us now.'

Jen Allbright returned to her own desk somewhat reluctantly. She still had a puzzled frown on her face. Rae was perturbed by Jen Allbright's interest in her. Had she guessed? If so, would it be the start of the trouble the boss and Barry had warned her about? Well, she couldn't do anything except wait and see what would happen next.

* * *

As they walked out to the car, Sophie was talking to Marsh about the same incident.

'I think that Jen Allbright has guessed about Rae, Barry. I watched her face as Rae was giving her summary. We need to be prepared in case it goes further, or she decides to start stirring.'

'I thought it would be more likely to be one of the men, ma'am. Shows how good my judgement is.'

'Men are less observant. They only look at the obvious. Legs, bum and tits. Facial features to some extent, but only so far as they compare to the media images. Rae's face is actually quite attractive, and she also has a good figure. I'd guess that Jen had already picked up some slight anomalies, and Rae's voice confirmed her suspicions. Rae can control it when she's speaking quietly in a one-to-one situation, but reporting to the group was a different matter. Maybe it was wrong of me to ask her to do it, but I was just treating her the same as everyone else. That's what she wants. The other thing to remember is that Rae's situation is more of a challenge to women than men, particularly if they've got prejudices. Some might

146

object to their toilet being used by an "interloper." They feel threatened by the presence of someone they think is not one of them. It can get really bizarre, Barry. So if you hear anything more, let me know. I'll stamp on it before it goes any further. One thing I won't tolerate is mindless prejudice. Given half a chance Rae will be a good detective, and I won't allow her development to be put at risk.'

'I've known Jen for some years, ma'am, ever since she joined us. She's got a very understanding personality. I don't think she'll give us any problems.'

'Let's hope you're right.'

* * *

Sarah Sheldon and Hugh Shakespeare's son, Peter, was dark-haired and brown-eyed like his mother and tall, like his father. He looked tanned and fit, although his eyes showed signs of strain. He stood slightly hunched as the two detectives approached.

Sophie spoke gently. 'I'm sorry to have to meet you in such awful circumstances, Mr Shakespeare. It must have come as a terrible shock to hear the news of your mother's tragic death. I can only try to imagine how you're feeling.'

'Thank you,' the young man replied. 'Dad has helped. He's been very understanding. I still can't take it all in. Are you getting close to finding who did it?'

'We're making progress, but that's all I can say. The case is complicated and your mother wasn't the only victim.'

'Do you mean there were other women killed like her?' Peter asked.

'No, not killed. But other women have been assaulted in a similar way in the past, at least one at a music festival, although not murdered. But that wasn't what I meant. We found the body of one of the men we believe was involved in your mother's death, and we suspect that he too was murdered.'

'Christ.' Hugh Shakespeare looked stunned.

After a moment Peter broke the shocked silence. 'So the killers might be killing each other? Is that what you're saying?'

'It's possible. We're still awaiting full forensic results, so please don't talk about it to anyone else at the moment.' She paused. 'Now, are you okay to go ahead with this straight away or would you like a coffee first? If you feel up to it, I thought we could talk more over lunch, but it's entirely up to you.'

Peter turned to his father. 'Let's get it over with, okay, Dad? And lunch will be fine if it's just something light.' He turned back to Sophie. 'I suppose you want to know stuff about Mum?'

Sophie nodded. 'It would help us complete the picture of her life. There are some things about her that just don't add up, and you might be able to help. I know a lovely café in the town centre that's ideal for a quiet chat. But I do want some time alone with you, Peter.' Hugh stiffened when he heard this. 'Please don't be offended, Mr Shakespeare. I have to do this. There was clearly a serious breakdown between you and Sarah, so I need your son's account of things.'

Hugh didn't reply.

'Okay. Let's get it over with,' said Peter.

The four of them made their way to the viewing room.

* * *

Sophie had always liked Dorchester. The market town was full of interesting buildings, and the pubs and cafés were cheerful. She'd again settled on the Oak Room, where she'd taken Rae earlier in the week. They sat in a panelled room upstairs to eat their lunch. She and Barry Marsh gave Hugh and Peter a short summary of the investigation so far, and the two men seemed satisfied enough. After lunch, Marsh took Hugh out for a walk through the town centre, leaving Sophie and Peter behind.

'So what do you want to know, Chief Inspector?'

'Your father is pretty hard on your mother, Peter. He was obviously deeply hurt by her. I'd like to hear your view of things.'

Peter thought for a while. 'I loved my mother. She was always caring and warm-hearted to me. Growing up, I was always aware of her lively personality. She loved the company of other people. But, to me, that made her all the more special. I don't know how much sense it makes, but I felt closer to her than my friends were to their mothers. It's as if there was a special bond between us. There was a kind of link that meant we were together even when we were apart.'

'Were you still in regular contact, even though you lived in New York?'

'Yes, we talked on the phone every few weeks, and we emailed each other.'

'Did you get birthday cards or presents, Christmas cards and the like?'

'Yes. She hardly ever forgot, although some of her recent choices were a bit off-the-wall. And I did my best not to forget her birthday because I knew how much she appreciated the presents I sent, especially after I went to New York.'

Sophie thought for a while. 'Your father implied that your move to New York was partly to get away from your mother. That doesn't square with what you've just told me.'

'No. They were fighting with each other, Chief Inspector. It was pretty awful. I desperately wanted to stay on good terms with both of them, so I suppose I told him what he wanted to hear.'

'And what did you tell your mother?'

'I didn't need to tell her anything. She always knew what I felt. She knew I needed a break from both of them.' He paused. 'She visited me in New York a couple of times, but Dad doesn't know that.'

'This is a difficult question, Peter. If you'd prefer not to answer it, I'll understand. Okay?' She waited for his nod of agreement. 'Your father told us that your mother had numerous affairs and that was the cause of their split. Was that your understanding also?'

Peter thought for a long while, and his answer was slow and hesitant. 'The fact that she had a couple of affairs didn't surprise me. They really were like chalk and cheese. Is that the right expression?'

Sophie nodded.

'She loved people. She loved parties, dancing. Dad is nothing like that, so it led to friction. It's no surprise that she looked for those things somewhere else. I expect he felt betrayed, though he was always tight-lipped about it, particularly when I was a teenager. He thought I should be protected. I guess I just wanted Mum to be happy. And she wasn't, she really wasn't. But if he used the word numerous that was his bitterness coming out. It makes her sound as if she was completely flighty. He really did love her you see, especially when I was young. When it all started going wrong I think he was angry for a while, but then accepted that separation was the best option. After they divorced he met Francoise and she's very different to Mum. They seem to be devoted to each other. Maybe that comes with maturity. The thing is, I saw the vulnerable side of Mum. Maybe no one else ever did. She had this party-girl facade, I know. I saw it. But she was really thoughtful and caring towards me. When the two of us were together it was just the best thing, you know? I had a good relationship with Dad, but it wasn't the same.' He shook his head slowly.

'There is this other thing, Peter.'

He looked her in the eye. 'What other thing?'

'We have some evidence that recently she was involved in group sex activities. I'm sorry if this is a shock to you, and I wish I didn't have to mention it, but it will come out in court when we catch the killer and put him on trial. You may as well know now rather than finding out then.'

He was silent for almost a minute. 'I expect she was looking for something, something to fill the emptiness. Cheap thrills, Chief Inspector. That's all it was. I guess she got herself hooked on those thrills.'

'We found a photo on your mum's laptop that shows her in a wedding dress. It could have been taken just a couple of years ago. The dress was cream. Does it ring a bell?'

'No! How bizarre. When she married Dad she wore white.' Peter looked astounded.

'You don't think she could have married again some time, in secret? Much more recently?'

'If she did, then it would destroy everything I thought about our relationship. To get married and not invite me? That would be so hurtful.' He shook his head. 'I think she went on an exotic cruise two and a half years ago. I got several postcards from places in the Caribbean.' He paused. 'The trouble was, she was very mercurial. She had a habit of doing things on the spur of the moment, then regretting them later.'

'So you're not saying the idea is totally ridiculous?'

He bit his lip. 'No. It's conceivable, even if I hate the thought of her having done it.'

'You've shown the most astonishing maturity and understanding, Peter. What do you do for a living?'

'I took a degree in Psychology and Human Behaviour. I'm a clinical psychotherapist. Quite apt, given the circumstances, don't you think?' He sighed. 'I think I may need some therapy myself now. I've lost the single most important person in my life. And I don't know how to cope with it.'

CHAPTER 14: FAMILY CONTRASTS

Thursday afternoon

Two sets of families, each come to identify the body of a loved one. It was interesting to observe the contrast between them. Soon after the Shakespeares left Dorchester, Pamela Derek arrived with her two sons, Andy and Kenny. Sophie and Marsh had returned to the pathology department and were waiting in reception when Jen Allbright arrived with the family. The two boys, both in their late teens, were quiet and damp-eyed and, despite her earlier protestations, Pamela was sobbing. Sophie was glad that the two Shakespeare men had departed a good while earlier: a meeting of the two families could have been catastrophic, given the tragic circumstances. She sent Marsh on ahead to double-check that the two bodies had been correctly exchanged.

All three family members entered the viewing room, with Andy, the elder son, at the front. Barry Marsh lowered the sheet covering the corpse's head and the young man sighed, then nodded.

'Yes,' he whispered. 'That's Dad.'

He turned and put his arms around his mother and his younger brother.

The small group went to the hospital café for some tea.

'Were you close to your father, Andy?' Marsh asked.

'Suppose we were, sort of a bit. But Kenny saw him more than me, didn't you Kenny?'

The younger teenager nodded. He looked utterly miserable. He had red, swollen eyes and a streaming nose. Sophie reached across the table and put her hand on his.

'It's alright to show your feelings, Kenny. It's a mistake to think that you have to keep them hidden from other people, particularly from Sergeant Marsh and me. Our job means that we've seen far too much tragic loss. The worse thing is when people bottle it up and hide it away, thinking that's the right thing to do. You loved your Dad and you feel as if a huge chunk of you has gone missing now that he's dead. It's not wrong to feel devastated by that.' She waited. 'You're frightened of a future without him, aren't you?'

'Sort of. I dunno what to think. Not now. Everything's gone wrong. I feel wrong. I just want him back.'

'Of course, Kenny. We're human beings and that's what we feel when someone we love is taken from us.' She paused. 'Kenny, Sergeant Marsh has a few questions for you, and for Andy as well. I'm going to stay here with your mother while he takes you outside. The fresh air will probably do you good.' Pamela looked as if she was about to protest. 'We have to, Pamela. I have to get to the bottom of this awful crime. I need to know the facts, and they rarely come from any one person, however honest he or she is trying to be. We pick up snippets from talking to everyone. If we're lucky, we can begin to get a picture of the real situation. Andy will be with Kenny, and Barry will be careful.'

Pamela slumped in her chair.

* * *

Marsh and the boys walked out to a grassy area just outside the café windows. There they stood, watching some birds pecking at the damp turf.

'How are you feeling about all this, Andy?' Barry asked. 'You're older, but you probably feel the pressure just as much as Kenny. You might not want to show it, though.'

'Yeah. It's been like that ever since Dad left. I felt hassled after that, as if I was in charge or summat. I never asked for it. Just got landed with it. I worried about both of 'em. And Kenny. I worried about him. But I didn't have no one to talk to. It's like now. It's fine for Kenny to cry, but I can't, cos I'm the eldest.' His voice was choked.

'What do you remember about your parents' breakup?' Barry asked.

'I felt sick about it.' Andy's voice was little more than a whisper. 'What was wrong with them? Why couldn't they patch things up? I was sick every morning before I went to school. And I had to put on this pretend show so my mates didn't know. Stay tough. And all the time I wanted to crawl away and die. I would have done if it hadn't been for Kenny. He needed me. Mum was useless for a long time. She drank. We saw Dad most weekends and it was like a different world. He still gave us money. He lived in a flat, and he was like he always had been, and I could pretend we were back to normal. But then we'd go home on Sunday and see the state Mum was in.'

'And this was about two years ago?'

Andy nodded. 'It took her months to get over it. She still isn't, really. But she's cut back on drinking, and it's tidier at home.'

'Do you know why they split up?'

'It was another woman. That one who's dead. It was the first time we've seen Mum laugh, I mean a proper laugh. When she found out that that woman was dead. *That Sheldon bitch* was how she referred to her.'

'Did you ever meet her?'

The young man nodded. 'She came into Dad's flat a couple of times when we were there.'

'What did you think of her?'

The younger son suddenly broke in. 'Fucking bitch. She stole our Dad. She deserved what she got. Serves her right.'

Marsh put his hand on Kenny's shoulder. 'I can understand how you feel, Kenny. It was her that changed everything, wasn't it?'

Kenny nodded miserably.

'I liked her,' Andy said quietly. 'And that made it all worse. She talked to me about her son. She knew how I felt. And she was pretty, even though she was older than our mum. And there was something about her. I didn't know what it was then, but I do now.'

'What?' Barry asked.

'She was kind of sexy. Dad was obsessed with her. I can see it now.'

* * *

It was a cold, bright afternoon, with the sun already beginning to dip in the sky. Jimmy Melsom and Rae Gregson set out for Portsmouth in order to look more thoroughly at Paul Derek's flat. Marsh had tried to find out more about the two boys' weekend stays with their father. Then he phoned through to the incident room with instructions for the two detective constables. They parked behind the block of flats and walked towards the entrance.

'How could he afford it?' asked Melsom. 'The divorce wasn't amicable. The wife kept the house and he probably had to pay for the boys' upkeep. He couldn't have been earning that much, surely? So how did he manage to buy this?'

'Barry found out that his parents left him some money,' Rae replied. 'Pamela kept the house. She has to fund the last few years of the mortgage, but the monthly payments aren't that much by today's standards. They bought it twenty years ago. He only needed a small mortgage to buy this place. Pamela took the split badly, but he made sure she and the boys were alright by transferring the house title over to the three of them. That's according to what Barry told me on the phone. He said that Derek wasn't a complete rogue.'

They took the lift to the first floor of the four storey block and made their way along a short corridor.

'The boss made a quick visit yesterday while I was left at his workplace, but she only had a few minutes because of the post-mortem. A local forensic team is supposed to meet us here.'

They slid into their nylon overalls, opened the door and entered a small hallway. The layout of the flat was fairly standard: a kitchen-diner, a lounge, two bedrooms and a bathroom. One of the bedrooms had an en-suite shower room.

'Not bad,' Melsom said. 'It's got everything you'd need.'

'The view isn't much, though,' Rae replied, looking through the window. 'The front windows look out over the car park, and the others across that strip of grass to the next block of flats.'

'You're too picky. It'd be fine for me. I suppose the boys slept in the second bedroom when they were here. Shall we start? I'll take the kitchen and lounge and you do the bedrooms? Okay?'

They set to work. Some of the furniture was worn and faded, although everything was clean and tidy. Rae started in the main bedroom. She began with the cupboards. Work clothes, a few suits, jackets and trousers, were separated from more informal clothes. A tie rack was fitted to the inside of the wardrobe door, holding some brightly-coloured ties in different colours. These contrasted with the black and grey of the trousers and suits. His boxers were all patterned, in reds and bright blues. Most of his shirts were coloured. Rae went through the contents of the bedside table. Tissues, spiced massage oils, condoms. There were a couple of erotic paperbacks with storylines about group sex. Rae took them out and sealed them in a bag. The bottom drawer contained several items of lingerie. The size suggested they might be Sarah's. There was a nightdress in soft gold; a bra, panty and suspender belt set, all in deep red; several pairs of sheer, black stockings; a black and purple corset. Rae carefully removed these and sealed them into evidence bags.

The en suite contained the usual: shaving gear, soap, shower gels and shampoos. Two towels hung from the rail.

She moved to the smaller second bedroom. There, the twin beds took up most of the available space. The cupboard was largely empty, containing a few items that obviously belonged to the boys. There was nothing else of interest, so she walked through to the lounge to see how Jimmy was getting on.

Fairly normal stuff, really,' he said. 'Maybe a few unusual books on the shelf, but apart from that it's pretty standard.'

Rae looked at the bookshelves.

'What do you mean by unusual, Jimmy?'

'Dickens and stuff. That's a bit unusual, isn't it?'

Rae snorted. 'Jimmy, most people think that having a few books by Dickens and Jane Austen is a sign of good taste. Either that or the homeowner's put them there to impress people.'

'Whatever. Doesn't impress me.'

'What have you got on your bookshelves then? Top Gear annuals? Football book of the year?' She walked across to the DVD collection. 'Have you looked through these, Jimmy?'

'Yeah, but nothing caught my eye.'

Rae noticed that several cases stuck out and she removed them to see what lay behind. She found a case behind them. 'Not even Fun With Your Boyfriend?'

'Why that one?' Jimmy said in a bored voice as he moved about the room.

'Jimmy, you really are a young innocent. It's a very unusual sex film. I'm not going to embarrass myself by describing it to you. But we should take it, and we'll have to go through these films again in case there are others you've missed. Remember what the boss said. Anything out of the ordinary that can help her build a picture of the man and his life.'

Between them, the two detectives pulled out another two half-hidden DVDs with a sex theme.

'How did you miss them, Jimmy?'

He shrugged and looked glum. 'I just didn't spot the fact that some were hidden behind. I looked at the titles on the spines and none of them mentioned sex, as far as I could see. Should we watch a bit from a couple of them, just to check you're right?'

'No, no, no. Absolutely not. If you think I want to be caught watching sex films with you when the forensic team arrives, you've got another think coming. These won't be soft, romantic sex films either. Five minutes of these and you'd want to run a mile.'

'Bit of an expert, aren't you? For a woman, I mean?'

'Please don't turn it back on me like that, Jimmy. I know my stuff, but from my job. Why are you looking at me like that?'

'Jen said there was something odd about you, something a bit weird. Is that what she meant? And how did she know?'

'She doesn't know anything about me. Look, Jimmy, just forget it. The boss and Barry know everything about me, and they still took me on, so they must have been happy with me, mustn't they? Just trust their judgement, will you?'

To Rae's relief the forensic team arrived. Shaking slightly she finished bagging up the films and told them what they wanted analysed and fingerprinted. She and Melsom then started on the long job of interviewing the neighbours.

CHAPTER 15: A VERY TROUBLED WOMAN

Thursday evening

Rosemary and Ed were enjoying a meal out in one of Wareham's pubs. Her mobile phone rang. She looked at the caller and mouthed 'Police' to Ed. She told the caller where they were.

'We're having company,' Rosemary said. 'She's joining us in twenty minutes. Apparently she only lives a short distance away. She's walking over cos she needs the fresh air and a drink. Well, that's what she said.'

'So much for our romantic evening out,' Wilton replied.

Rosemary squeezed his hand. 'Ed, we have plenty of time together. And in a strange kind of way, I rather like her company. She's intelligent, but she doesn't talk down to you. And don't you think she's a bit of a looker? I realised it when I was describing Sarah to her. She really knows how to dress too. Don't tell me you hadn't noticed?'

He laughed. 'Yes. That first day I was quite taken aback. It was in the evening, when she called in for the long interviews. She must have had a heck of a frantic day, but she looked almost immaculate. And then her sergeant asked all the questions. She just watched and listened — and made me feel nervous. Psychology, I suppose. All planned.'

The two lovers were still talking when Sophie arrived. Rosemary noticed her two-piece, close-fitting skirt suit in mottled grey and the mid-heeled black shoes. 'I like your outfit,' she said.

'Oh, thanks. Can I get you a drink?' Sophie asked.

They shook their heads, indicating the unfinished bottle of wine on the table. Sophie went to the bar, quickly returning with a pint glass of ale, full to the brim. Rosemary watched in astonishment as Sophie swallowed half of its contents.

'Ah. I have a thing about quality beer,' said Sophie. 'I'm a regular at the local branch of the real ale society and we visit this pub quite often. But don't worry. You won't have to carry me home.'

'It's a bit unusual, isn't it? Sorry, I don't mean to be rude or anything, but I always have this vision of beer drinkers as big guys with fat bellies and beer-stained shirts. They usually have beards,' said Rosemary.

'I shaved mine off this morning,' Sophie laughed. 'I know. Lots of people have that image of ale enthusiasts. But it's not the case nowadays. The secretary, another woman, is a friend of mine. She talked me into joining when she found out that I've always enjoyed a pint or two, and we go along together. And we dress up for it too.'

'What do you mean?' Rosemary asked.

'Smart casual usually. You know, like what you wear to the blues gigs. Skinny jeans, ankle boots and a leather jacket. A sparkly top. It had an instant effect on most of the men too. When I first started going many of them were dressed rather like you've described, but they'd smartened themselves up no end by the next meeting. And for last year's Christmas evening we both wore sequined dresses, without telling the others in advance. So there we were, knocking back pints in the town's best pub, perched on bar stools, glammed up to the gills. The men were buzzing round us like bees around a honeypot, particularly towards the end of the evening. There were a few long faces when our husbands arrived for the last hour.'

'Do they know you're a senior police officer?'

'I told them I was a nightclub singer at first but they soon realised it wasn't true.' She laughed again. 'So I owned up and they still seemed to accept me.' She grew more serious. 'It's my way of coping. I need to escape occasionally. From the pressures, I mean. I love my job, but sometimes what I deal with can get a bit much, and I have to let go a bit. Martin understands. He's wonderful.' She looked at her empty glass. 'I'll get another before we talk. I promise to drink it more slowly. Do you want anything?'

'Maybe a glass of what you're having,' Rosemary answered. 'A small one, please.'

Ed shook his head. They both watched the slim figure of Sophie make her way to the bar.

'Do you believe that?' asked Ed.

'You know, I think I do. She probably exercises a lot and watches her diet. And her explanation makes sense. I've been reading about some of the cases she's worked on. They've been horrific. And I found out some other stuff about her too. I'll tell you later.'

Sophie deposited the drinks on the table.

'Rosemary, I need to ask you another question about Sarah, as I'm sure you've guessed. We've had a tentative report from one of her neighbours that she might have married again some time in the past three years. Did she ever give any hint of it to you?'

'No. I'd have told you if she had. Is it true?'

'We're still checking, which is why I'm here talking to you. What about a wedding ring? Did she ever wear one?'

'Well, the second time we met, when we went out for a meal together, she was wearing a ring. When she saw me looking she took it off. I asked her about it and she said something about trying it on to see if it still fitted. I assumed it was from her failed marriage.'

Sophie shook her head. 'Peter, her son, kept both his parents' wedding rings when they divorced and he still has them. He's adamant about it. Did it look genuine, or could it have been a bit of costume jewellery?'

'Well I only caught a glimpse of it so I can't be certain, but it looked real enough to me. And if it was false why would she have reacted like she did when I noticed? She'd have just laughed it off. She never seemed to take anything particularly seriously.'

'She took her son very seriously, so he says. Did you pick up on that?'

Rosemary took a tentative sip of beer. 'Yes, she did. We only talked about children once because I guess she was sensitive about my own situation. But it was clear she had strong feelings for him. She said she missed him. He was her rock, and after he moved to New York she felt bereft. Something like that. I can't remember her exact words.'

Sophie thought for a while. 'You said she was sensitive to your situation. Are you sure? Couldn't you be reading too much into what she said and how she acted?'

'No. That's why I liked her. She truly was a nice person, Chief Inspector. I wouldn't have had such a close friendship with her otherwise.' Ed Wilton took her hand. 'I still can't make sense of all the other stuff she was involved in. It's all too weird for me, but that's my problem not hers, if you know what I mean. She was who she was. I've never met anyone else quite like her. I never got to the bottom of her personality, and what motivated her, and I won't ever now, will I? Such a tragic waste of a lovely person.' She straightened up in her chair and took another sip of her beer. 'You're right, this is rather nice. I've had lager before, but this is entirely different, isn't it?'

Sophie nodded. 'It's local, brewed in Dorchester. It's named after Dorset's Jurassic coastline, a world heritage site. It's one of my favourite beers. When you told me where you were, that did it. I had to have one. But there's something else I need to ask you. The festivals you went to with Sarah, they were always blues music, right?'

Rosemary nodded.

'Did she ever mention going to jazz events at all?'

'No, I'm pretty sure she didn't. I don't think she liked jazz very much.' Rosemary paused. 'But Derek and Brian had been to at least one jazz weekend. Derek started talking about it soon after we first met up. That was before we came back to where you were, Ed. It was a bit strange. Brian didn't look at all pleased that Derek had mentioned it. I saw him glare at Derek and almost shush him. That was partly why I didn't take to him. It seemed odd, why get angry when a friend starts talking about an event you've both been to? I'm really sorry I didn't mention it before. It's only just come back to me.'

'Did he say where this was, Rosemary?'

'Bath, I think. It was when Derek said Bath that Brian got angry. It was really peculiar.' She took another sip of beer.

'Think for a bit longer. Does anything else they said seem unusual now?'

Rosemary shook her head. Sophie drained her glass and stood up. 'I'd better be on my way. My sixteen-year-old daughter's cooking tonight so I daren't be late.'

'Will you be alright? Isn't someone collecting you or anything?'

Sophie stared at Ed. She suddenly looked angry.

'That's patronising. You may have meant well, but even so. Would you have said the same thing to a man?'

'No. I'm sorry,' he said.

'There's less chance of a woman being assaulted of an evening than a man of the same age. You wouldn't dream of saying something like that to a bloke, would you? Most of the people here know me. They'd need to be mad to try anything, and if they did they'd soon be sorry, even with a couple of pints inside me.' She smiled and gave a small bow. 'Sophie Allen, lethal weapon, at your service,' she said. She turned on her heel and walked out.

'Christ.'

'Well, you've been well and truly told off, haven't you?' Rosemary giggled. 'She's a woman and a half. But you did

163

walk into it, didn't you? Couldn't you have been a little more subtle?'

'Honestly, I meant well. I had no idea she'd take it like that.'

'But that's why she was so angry, Ed. You were patronising her without even realising it. She knew you had the best of intentions, and that's what made her angry. That's what women have to put up with all the time. It's not just the deliberate or openly sexist remarks that upset us. It's the assumption, however well meant, that we need to be looked after, as if we're incapable of dealing with life's little problems by ourselves. You know, the pat on the head and the "there, there, calm down dear," attitude.'

Ed looked miserable, and Rosemary squeezed his hand. 'She's already forgiven you. That's what she meant with that last remark. But please try not to patronise me, Ed. I couldn't bear it.'

'But if I don't know, how do I control it?'

'It's not difficult. I'm my own person, just as I would be if I were a man. Treat me like a close male relative. Except for the love. And the affection. And the sex. And remind me occasionally how beautiful I am.' Rosemary laughed.

'If you say so. Shall we have dessert?'

As they walked back to the house the moon was so clear in the night sky that some of its craters were visible.

'You were going to tell me some stuff you'd found out about our Chief Inspector friend,' Ed said.

'Apparently her last two major cases in this area have been multiple murders. The one last winter must have been particularly horrific. They found the remains of a couple of young women buried in a field. She solved it but was on sick leave for a long time afterwards. I wonder if she had some kind of nervous breakdown.'

'Surely that means she isn't right for the job if the crimes affect her that much?'

'Ah, but one press report went a bit further. Apparently one of the criminals had murdered her father when she was a child, but had never been found. She was the one who discovered it and made the arrest. Imagine what scars that could leave, if it's true. I wonder if, underneath, she's a very troubled woman. Look at the way she knocked back those two beers. That's not normal, is it?'

CHAPTER 16: CRUEL COINCIDENCE

Friday morning

Sophie Allen and Barry Marsh were having a quick chat in her office before the early morning briefing. Rae had told Marsh that she thought people suspected her of being a transsexual. But so far, no direct questions had been asked and no one had made any pointed comments, apart from Melsom's rather vague ones.

'I'm still not convinced that anyone's rumbled her, ma'am. When Jimmy attempted to make a date with her, Rae hinted that she was a lesbian. Maybe that's all it is. Jimmy isn't the world's most perceptive man. He probably took it literally and has been gossiping to Jen Allbright. This is a small town. It runs on gossip and scandal. When I split with Sammie, everyone knew within a couple of days. Suddenly women I hardly knew were making a beeline for me. And it wasn't just evenings in the pubs, either. I mean, even when I was doing the shopping in the supermarket some of them would stop to chat.'

Sophie laughed. 'Told you last year what women like in a man. You must have been paying attention. So you think we should leave it for now?'

'Well, I could have a quiet word with Jimmy, if you think it'd be a good idea.'

'Okay. I'll do the same with Jen Allbright. But if they do suspect she's a TS, then we'll have to change our approach. They must treat her like anyone else. No compromises, okay? We'll do it just after briefing. I'll take Rae when I go across to Bath this morning. She seems to have an uncanny ability to unearth relevant details even if they're hidden in a mass of information. That's just what I need if we're going through hotel booking records. You and Jimmy can call in on the two Shapiro families in Southampton. See what you make of them. If Rae's right, they're hiding something. And as for the other thing Rae picked up, I don't know what to make of it. It might be a complete misunderstanding on the part of the neighbour, but we have to double-check. Rosemary couldn't confirm it when I spoke to her yesterday evening, but couldn't discount it either. Shall we put Jen onto it? Could she cope with searching through registry records?'

'Probably. But it's a bit strange. I mean, why haven't we picked it up from anyone else? Surely she'd have talked about it to someone — at work or to Rosemary Corrigan? Or even to her ex, Hugh Shakespeare?'

'Rosemary did see Sarah fiddling with what looked like a wedding ring on one occasion. That's what she told me, although apparently Sarah wouldn't talk about it,' Sophie replied.

'Hugh seemed genuinely shocked to hear about our discovery of the second body,' Marsh added. 'He knew another body had been found, but he seemed really taken aback when I told him who we thought it was. That was while you were talking to Peter. I asked him to keep it to himself. He didn't seem to be listening to me, so I had to repeat what I'd said.'

* * *

Sophie and Rae walked to the first hotel on their list. A young Asian woman was waiting outside. She stepped forward as they approached, looking hesitantly at Sophie.

'Rae, this is Lydia, your predecessor. I managed to winkle her out of her normal duties to give us some local knowledge. I'm guessing that analysing account sheets all day long can get a bit much, can't it, Lydia? I thought you'd be glad of a day out.'

Rae extended her hand, but Lydia gave her a quick hug.

'I don't know how you did it, ma'am,' Lydia said. 'He's never let anyone else have time away before. "Positive liaison with our Dorset colleagues," was how he put it.'

'Unfair use of influence, Lydia. Benny Goodall says my fame has spread far and wide. Too far and too wide, as far as I'm concerned. I had a request from the Home Office last week to head up some official inquiry or other.'

'You turned it down of course?' Lydia said.

'Hah. You're wrong. I haven't answered yet,' Sophie laughed.

They entered the ornate lobby of the hotel and asked to see the manager.

'Thank God for computers,' Sophie murmured. 'This would take forever without them.'

Rae and Lydia spent a tedious morning going through hotel records. Sophie talked to the various managers. They were in the fourth hotel on their list when they found it. Rae sat up with a jerk and choked on her coffee, trying to speak and swallow at the same time.

'Derek Paul,' she squeaked. 'Here. Booked in for the same weekend as the jazz festival. A single room for two nights, the Friday and Saturday. His name, but reversed.'

Sophie thought for a while. 'Brenda Plant identified Shapiro as the one who paired up with her at the bar and took her back to his room. He'd booked into the hotel under the name Brian Nelson, which we know was false. So this appears to confirm that our two were the ones involved in the rape. But we're still missing the third name. Sorry, but we need to keep looking, for the name Renton.'

The search went on. Late in the morning, in a quiet hotel away from the city centre, they found the next name.

'It can't be!' gasped Sophie. But there it was, stated clearly in the computer records for the same weekend. Ed Wilton.

She immediately phoned through to Matt Silver, her boss at Dorset police headquarters.

'Do we keep looking, ma'am?' Rae asked.

'Yes. I'm not making any assumptions here. We finish with this hotel's records and continue with the others on the list. We need to see if Renton was here as well.'

Nothing else was found.

Lydia spoke. 'We've only looked at the hotels, ma'am. A lot of people coming for a music festival stay in a bed and breakfast or a guest house. And there are dozens and dozens of them. It would take too long to visit them all. Why don't you leave it with me? I'll do some phoning around this afternoon and the next day or two. I'll clear it with my boss, or maybe you could have a word. If I have a list of names of everyone linked to the case, there's a good chance I'll spot something. If I do I can easily pay a visit to check.'

'That would be great.' Sophie looked into Lydia's eyes. 'I'm very grateful for your help, Lydia. But don't prejudice your own future here in Bath by helping me more than your current boss has agreed to. I think I can guess how you are feeling at the moment. I imagine you're missing the intensity of these investigations. But the move here was good for you. I had a word with your boss yesterday, and he holds you in high regard. Don't let the low-level admin work get you down. We all have to go through it. It will come good, believe me.' She paused. 'I'm a bit shell-shocked by this discovery of Ed Wilton's name. I really thought he wasn't involved.'

'He might not be, ma'am,' said Rae. 'It was a jazz festival, and he's a musician. It could just be a coincidence.'

* * *

'What is this all about? Why did someone come to collect Rosemary? Why am I being kept in the dark?'

169

Sophie stood in the hallway of the police safe house in Wareham and looked at Ed Wilton. A local plain-clothes officer stood to one side.

'Can we sit down, please?' Sophie said. She didn't wait for a reply, walking into the lounge with Rae behind her. Ed came after them and sat down facing Sophie. Rae remained standing by the door, beside the local detective.

'Two years ago in September. You were in Bath for a weekend. Can you tell me why?'

He frowned and scratched his forehead. 'There was a jazz festival. I'd composed a short suite of songs to be performed by a really talented singer from Bristol. I certainly wasn't going to miss the première.'

Sophie nodded her head slightly. 'Can someone verify that, Mr Wilton?'

'Of course. The musicians could, the festival organisers, and Ella was there with me. With us, I should say. It was the last music weekend that Lizzie could get to before the cancer began to cripple her. Maybe even someone from the hotel we stayed in will remember us. I've still got the festival programme if you want to see it, though it's at my house in London.'

'Would the programme still be available online, Mr Wilton?' asked Rae.

'I suppose it could be.' He opened up his laptop and typed into a search engine.

'There we are,' he said.

The two detectives read the details, which corroborated his story. He'd written a five-song cycle for voice and piano, performed in public for the first time at the event in Bath.

'Could you give me Ella's mobile number please? I'd just like to check with her.'

Ed took his phone out, and held it across for Sophie to see. She took a notebook out of her bag and compared numbers.

'What? You already had it?' He smiled grimly. 'You're too devious for words.'

Sophie left the room.

'She verified it, of course?' said Wilton when she returned.

170

'Yes, but I don't think you fully understand, Mr Wilton. She's just verified the fact that you were in Bath the very weekend a woman was sexually assaulted in the same way as Sarah Sheldon. Although, luckily, the woman from Bath survived. The assault took place late on the Friday night, roughly the same time as last weekend's attack. Ella has just told me that she didn't arrive until the Saturday morning because the premiere of your music was on the Saturday evening.'

'But Lizzie and I were at a gig on the Friday. We returned to our hotel room. She was tired and ill, so we went to bed. I sat reading for a while.'

'Unfortunately we can't verify that, given the tragic death of your wife.' She sat looking at Ed Wilton. 'I had to move Rosemary out. She's gone to another location.'

Wilton looked distraught. 'Oh, for God's sake. You could see last night what we feel for each other. She's in no danger. I'd never hurt her. I've never hurt anybody.'

'Whatever you say is irrelevant to me, Mr Wilton. The victim in Bath has recently identified Derek and Shapiro from photographs. She wasn't able to identify a possible third man because she didn't get a clear view of him. Think about it. How could I possibly leave her with you? How could I gamble with her life in that way? Step out of yourself for a moment. Could I, as the senior investigating officer in a murder investigation, even consider leaving her in the care of someone who admits to being in the vicinity of a previous set of assaults?'

'Why don't you leave her here, under protection? I can go back to my flat in Swanage.'

'No. I'm moving her somewhere you don't know about. And I still have to protect you too. When a situation reaches such a critical point, I don't believe or disbelieve what any individual says, Mr Wilton. It goes beyond that. I do what logic dictates is the only possible course of action. So there'll be no contact of any kind between the two of you until I say so. I want your promise that you won't phone her, otherwise I'll insist on taking your mobile phone from you. If you want to write her a letter, then that will be fine, but I will need to check it first. I'll get it delivered by hand later today.'

Ed put his head in his hands.

'This will only be for a few days, I hope. Once I'm satisfied that you weren't involved with the Bath assault, I'll relax the conditions and maybe you can see her again. I don't enjoy this, whatever you may think, but I can't gamble with either of your lives. We've had two murders and a very serious multiple rape, and I don't think it's over yet. Rosemary's safety is paramount, but I also have to plan for your own protection since the possible perpetrators are still at large. We'll visit Rosemary as soon as we've left you, so get that note written now, if you want me to take it with me.'

Wilton sighed. 'I can see your problem. Just look after her, will you? Make sure she's safe? That's all I want.'

He took the offered pen and started writing on a sheet of paper that Rae handed him. When Wilton had finished, Sophie took the page and read it.

Darling Rosemary,

I am trying hard to convince myself that our friendly, beer-swallowing police person has your best interests at heart. My head tells me that this is the case, but my heart feels as if it's tearing itself apart. I can only hope that she gets to the truth quickly, so that we can be together again. I will turn to the one thing that offers me escape at times of agony like this: my music. Something good will come out of the next few days of enforced separation. The first piece is already starting to form in my head.

Do what she says. She is right to be concerned.

Of course, my presence in Bath was for the music. That, and to give my Lizzie one final experience of my own music performed live. It was a composition dedicated to her. Everything else about that weekend is just cruel coincidence.

All my love,

Ed

'I'm truly sorry to be doing this, Mr Wilton. I'll see what I can do to make things easier for you both. Meanwhile, don't go out without your escort, and clear it with me first.' She paused and added, 'I may see you this evening.'

* * *

Barry Marsh and Jimmy Melsom were still in Southampton. They had spent much of the day speaking to various members of the two branches of the Shapiro family — and trying to decode their answers. The two brothers ran a restaurant each, and it quickly became apparent that there was little love lost between them. The younger brother seemed open and honest, but Marsh sensed that even he was choosing his words carefully. The older brother was surly and impatient, and he gave little away. While they talked, Marsh examined a rather faded family photo on a shelf in the older brother's office. He suddenly realised that there was a third brother, who looked suspiciously like the man they were seeking.

'Why didn't you tell us?' he asked. All he got in reply was a shrug. The older brother said his sibling had returned to Italy some years before.

On leaving the office Marsh spoke to a younger family member, who was busy unloading stores from a delivery van. The young man told Marsh that Uncle Briano still visited them at Christmas. Then he spotted his father watching from the window and refused to say any more.

* * *

'There was a distinct similarity to our man,' Marsh reported to Sophie back in Swanage. 'Neither of the brothers really wanted to talk about him. It was lucky I bumped into the son while we were coming out, otherwise we'd be nowhere. I'm convinced they're hiding something. If it is him, he might well be back in Italy by now, and that'll make things difficult for us.'

'Let's put someone onto it. If his proper name is Briano rather than Brian it might explain why we haven't been able to find him. By the way, how did you get on with Jimmy this morning? Has he twigged anything about Rae?'

'No, not as far as I can tell. He just thinks she's a lesbian. I think he's suffering from a bruised ego after she turned him down.'

'Allbright has guessed. I've told her to treat Rae the same as any other woman officer. I took a low-key approach, and I think she'll toe the line. I hope you're right, and Jen really is as understanding as she appears. The trouble is, appearances can be deceptive in these situations. Apparently fair-minded people can turn bloody-minded and people you think are bigoted can be as wise as Solomon . . . I'm off to visit Rosemary with a note from our Mr Wilton. His story does seem to ring true, so it looks as though I'm in for a part as a go-between.'

'Doesn't sound much like fun,' said Marsh.

'Hmm. I'm going to invite them to my house for a meal, and try my hand at cooking. It's something I rarely do. Martin and Jade are such good cooks. There won't be any opportunities for hanky-panky between them, not with Jade on the case. She's enough to intimidate anyone, believe me. But then you've met her, haven't you?'

'Yes, at your father's funeral and, before that, at last December's charity do. She sat opposite us at the meal. It was about then that Sammie and I realised that maybe we weren't meant for each other.'

'Probably not a coincidence, knowing my daughter the way I do, although I have to say that she is mellowing slightly as she gets older.'

'Just slightly?'

'Do you want to come along as well and see the sparks fly? That's if you aren't already booked this evening?' There was a pause. 'Bring Gwen as well. It's a long time since I last saw her, and you weren't a couple then. The more the merrier, though I'll only be doing a fish pasta bake.'

'Thanks, ma'am. I'm sure Gwen will enjoy watching.'

'Could you collect Ed Wilton on your way? We can give the duty man the evening off.'

174

CHAPTER 17: ROUND MIDNIGHT

Friday evening

Barry Marsh hurried his two passengers across the pathway. They huddled together in the porch of the old cottage, trying to shelter from a sudden downpour. Jade Allen opened the front door and welcomed them into the warm interior. Jade seemed to have grown another inch or two since Marsh had last seen her. She was now an attractive young woman, taller and slimmer. She was dressed in deep red and black. She smiled at Marsh.

'I remember you, Barry. So this must be Gwen, and you,' she wagged her finger, 'must be Ed Wilton, the composer. I've heard of you from your music. Come in out of the rain, and I'll take your coats. Mum's in the kitchen burning the dinner. Dad's in the lounge chatting up a blonde.' She ushered them into the hallway and hung their coats up. 'I get so fed up with blondes, don't you, Gwen? Acting as if they own the world, simpering over any man who happens to be around? Doesn't it make you want to weep? Really!'

Gwen Davis laughed. 'My feelings exactly. I think that we brunettes should unite, don't you? Once women get full equality and the feminist movement isn't needed any more, we should start a pro-brunette campaign.'

'I'm glad you came,' Jade added. 'I was feeling outnumbered, being the only brunette. Not that I can't hold my own against them, you understand. They're a bit of a lightweight species really. But I'd have had to hold back out of common courtesy and that's quite hard for me to do.'

'Sorry, but who are we talking about here?' asked Marsh. 'Men or blondes?'

'Blondes of course,' Jade replied. 'Men don't even count. Though I suppose they must have their uses.'

'Hmm. What does your father say to that?'

'He's a supporter of feminism, so we get along. Anyway, dear guests, follow me into the lounge. I will endeavour to make you comfortable while Mum continues to ruin the fish I carefully chose for this evening's meal. Please ignore the smell of charred food that permeates the air. She does try, really.'

Marsh smiled. He had always avoided talking to Jade because she made him feel so uneasy. He couldn't quite keep up. No change there, he thought. He took Gwen's hand and Ed Wilton followed them into the lounge. He didn't follow for long. As soon as he saw Rosemary Corrigan sitting on a couch he stepped towards her. At the same moment she rose, her hand to her mouth.

'Ed! I didn't know.' She fell into his arms, nearly knocking him over.

'Young love,' said Jade, sardonically.

Gwen tried to suppress a giggle and choked, at which point Martin Allen appeared with a tray of drinks. 'Looks like these are needed,' he said. 'Chilled bubbly. One for you, too, Jade.' He stopped and looked at the newly arrived guests in surprise, Rosemary was sobbing into Ed's shoulder, and Gwen was coughing into Barry's. 'What on earth has Jade been saying now?'

'Oh, right. Blame it all on me, Dad. As if my mere presence can set off hysteria and oxygen starvation. Even my personality isn't that powerful.'

'Jade, just cut out the theatricals and help pass the drinks round, will you?'

176

By now Gwen had stopped coughing. 'She gave us all a lovely welcome, Mr Allen. I love your home, by the way.' She looked around at the low-ceilinged room and its slightly uneven walls and timbers.

'Thanks, I'll take you all on a tour in a minute. And please call me Martin. I have enough of being called Mr Allen at work every day.'

He and Jade handed round the drinks. Rosemary and Ed peeled themselves apart. They held hands and Martin ushered them all into the hallway.

The visitors greeted a rather flustered-looking Sophie as they passed through the kitchen. Marsh had visited before, but he'd never seen the rest of the house. It consisted of two adjoining cottages converted into a single spacious home, and had a very welcoming feel. Despite the dark brown timbers, the house was open and airy. The group ended up in a large study, which contained a baby grand piano. Ed sat down at once and tinkered on the keys.

'Who plays?' he asked.

'Dad,' Jade answered. 'He's pretty good. And me too.'

Ed leafed through the sheet music in front of him.

'Challenging stuff,' he said. 'Beethoven, Mozart, Chopin. Not for the faint-hearted. Who plays Chopin?'

'Both of us,' Martin replied. 'But Jade is better. When I play, it all sounds a bit mechanical, but she has a much more fluid technique.'

'How about a tune?' Ed asked, looking up at Jade.

Jade stood still for a moment, looking at Ed. She moved to the piano, extracted a sheet of music from a folder and began to play. It was a jazz piece, and the notes tumbled through the air like a waterfall. The music lasted for about three minutes, then ended abruptly. The group applauded but Jade was looking at Ed Wilton.

'Well?' she asked.

'Thelonious Monk. *Round Midnight*,' he answered. 'And perfect.'

She broke into a broad smile. 'Oh yes. You're my man.'

'I hope you've considered turning pro. It would be a waste not to.'

She shook her head, and her long, shiny hair swayed. 'No. I want to be a doctor. But I'll always play. It won't go to waste. I'm in a small band at the moment, but it's not serious.'

'What kind of music?'

'A sort of mishmash of jazz, blues and funk. We've done a couple of gigs in the local pubs and earned peanuts. But we all enjoy it. Clouds on Venus, that's what we call ourselves.'

'What subjects do you take at school?' Marsh asked.

'Chemistry, physics, maths, biology. And music, of course.'

'That's a pretty heavy load,' Gwen added. 'Five A levels?'

'That's what people keep telling me. But it's all okay. I think I've inherited my parents' brains, so they've been of some use.' She smiled tentatively at her father. 'Sorry, Dad. Only joking.'

'I know.' In the light from the table lamps it was easy to see that the two of them were father and daughter. But Jade has inherited the colour and shape of her eyes from her mother, thought Marsh. Sophie walked into the room.

'I think that's the food ready, so please come through to the dining room. I'm afraid the only music there comes from the hi-fi, but we'll let Jade choose.'

'Chopin,' she answered without hesitation. She stood up and walked away from the piano. She was tall, striking, and clearly fashion-conscious.

Marsh couldn't help feeling overawed. Was the entire Allen family like this? He remembered being deeply moved by the poems that Jade and her elder sister, Hannah, had read at their grandfather's funeral the previous winter. How many sixteen-year-olds could have carried that off? No wonder she seemed so mature. She'd found out all those things about her family background and then had to nurse her mother through a nervous breakdown. Marsh suddenly realised that Jade was watching him and he smiled nervously. She took his arm and whispered in his ear.

'You'll look after Mum for us, won't you? We're all trusting you with her. She's still a bit fragile, you know.'

'I'll do my best.'

Had she been reading his mind?

***

The visitors soon realised that Jade's comments about her mother's cooking had been entirely mischievous. Sophie served up a simple yet delicious meal. The conversation flowed freely. Jade and Ed talked about the process of composition.

'I'm not much of a pianist,' he said. 'I'm competent, but that's all. I'm nowhere near as good as you. And I don't write classical music or even complex jazz, just songs. It's only a matter of creating a melody and matching it up with some lyrics. I suppose it's a mood thing. It depends on the state I'm in. I was a bit nervous about the song suite I told your mother about. It was the first time I'd ever composed anything outside of my comfort zone, and I knew I had to get it right. With jazz, there's more expectation and the audience is more discerning, though I might have imagined that.'

'You said that you're writing at the moment, Ed. Did you get anywhere after I left? What have you started on?' Sophie asked.

'It's a short song cycle called "Songs for Rosemary."' He stroked Rosemary's fingers. 'It's just a few ideas at the moment, but I'll start to flesh them out over the weekend. The sequence at Bath is the only jazz I've ever had performed. The problem is that jazz doesn't bring in the kind of money that mainstream music does, so it's a sideline really. I have to rely on the ordinary stuff for my income, both writing and producing.'

'How did you first get into the music business?' Jade asked.

'In my younger days I was in a band, playing keyboard. We had a few hits and did some touring, but I could see that it wasn't going to last. I started writing songs for the band, then tried my hand at studio work, production stuff. And I liked doing it, better than the touring and performing. That was all a bit wild.'

'Sex and Drugs and Rock 'n' Roll?' Jade suggested.

Ed laughed. 'That just about sums it up.'

'Wow. Now I've actually met someone who did all that. You've made my day. Well, nearly.'

Ed raised his eyebrows.

'The day's not over yet. I'm going out clubbing tonight,' she said. 'Not that I've got any plans to indulge in those three unmentionables. Not tonight, anyway.' She looked at her mother. 'So . . . Rosemary, Mum says that you're a woman of style. I need some advice on my outfit. What do you think? Okay for clubbing?' She stood up and twirled round.

Rosemary nodded. 'I should think so. Yes, I think I'd let you out of the house. But I'm not sure I'm the right person to ask, Jade. I'm a bit old and I don't have any daughters, so I'm really out of touch. I think you should wear what you're comfortable with. What do you think, Gwen? You probably see lots of young women out and about in a university city like Southampton.'

'Black and red. Good colours for a brunette, Jade. What more can I say? Seriously, I approve. It's much better than the skimpy outfits some girls wear out on the town . . . Oh. I think I may have said the wrong thing. I can guess what you're thinking,' Gwen said to Jade.

'That we should be able to wear whatever we like? Absolutely. That no dress, however flimsy or short, is an invitation to assault or rape? Yes, totally. That men should stop seeing a woman's appearance as an invitation to animal behaviour? Dead right. And I think that the police and the courts should change their attitude.'

'I totally agree with you. I've been fighting the system from the inside for a long time now, as I'm sure your mother has. But it all takes time, and my advice to you is the same as I'd give to any young woman friend or family member. And it isn't that different from my advice to young men, either. Out on the town at weekends, be cautious. Be sensitive to social dangers. Statistics show that you're in less danger of being attacked than young men of your age, although it's a different kind of assault. Find ways of deflecting possible dangers and, for a young woman, choice of clothing is one of those ways. I'm sorry, but that's just how it is.'

'Jade is her own person and we let her make her own decisions,' said Sophie. 'And we respect them. To be fair to our guests, Jade, you did ask for an opinion, so you can't complain if they tell you what they think. Anyway, who am I to advise anyone? When I was a schoolgirl I used to make myself up and sneak into university dances and my mother hit the roof when she found out. At least you don't lie to me, and I hope you never do. Now, maybe we should move through to the lounge? I'll get the coffee ready.'

Jade, Ed and Rosemary returned to the piano and Jade asked to hear some of Ed's compositions. She stood enthralled as he played and sang some of his songs.

'I had no idea you wrote those,' Rosemary said. 'They're so well known.'

'The glory always goes to the singers and performers and to be fair, many of my songs are a joint effort with someone else. But I've had a great career. The music business has been very good to me. It would be nice if I could play the piano as well as Jade, though. I'm envious.'

'I've got a brilliant idea,' Jade said. 'Let's do some duets. Have you ever done duets? Dad and I often do. It's great fun. Just give me a moment and I'll get some music.' From a folder by the piano she took a booklet of Lennon and McCartney songs.

'I'll play, we'll both sing,' she said.

As the sounds drifted through the house, the others came in. At first they listened and then they joined in. As they sang, one of Ed's musical ideas began to crystallise: a jazz ballad for piano and solo alto voice.

When they returned to the living room, Rosemary asked, 'Do we still have to stay separate?'

'Yes,' was Sophie's immediate response. 'And it will stay that way until I can rule Ed out of the running entirely, and with enough verification to convince a court of law. It doesn't matter what I think or don't think. It's a matter of adhering to standard procedures. I hope you understand that. That's why I wanted to have you both here this evening. Barry and I agree, and I've checked it with my boss at HQ. I'm not doing this out of some weird sadistic streak . . . At least I don't think so.' She laughed. 'We never really know what's going on in our subconscious minds, do we?'

'You're the psychologist, sweetheart,' said Martin. He looked around at the others.

'Okay, I'll shut up. But if you get bored, Rosemary, let me or Barry know. We might be able to arrange an outing occasionally, if it fits in with what one of us is doing. Otherwise I'm afraid that it's just a question of watching TV, reading, listening to music or whatever you can find to keep yourself amused. Feel free to borrow any of our books if you want to. I have something here for you, although I'm sure it's highly illegal.'

She took a small mp3 player from a shelf and handed it to Rosemary, who looked a little bemused.

'It's a pirated copy of the performance of Ed's song suite from the Bath jazz festival two years ago. I got it from the organiser, who recorded most of the performances without telling anyone. I had to swear solemnly that I'd never drop a hint to the composer that I'd been given this copy. I had to convince him that it was necessary for the investigation.' She looked at Ed. 'So you don't know about it, okay, Ed?'

'Hmm. Right. Aren't you meant to uphold the law in all its forms, including copyright?' he said.

'Oh yes. I take it very seriously. I can advise you who to contact should you wish to pursue the matter further and make out a complaint against me. Would you like a brandy, by the way? You're not driving tonight, remember.'

'Very neat sidestep. And yes, please.'

'So how long have you two been together?' Rosemary asked Barry Marsh and Gwen.

'About a month, I suppose,' said Marsh.

'A bit longer, actually,' Gwen added. 'And it would have started a lot earlier if he'd taken any of my hints. I really started worrying that I'd lost my touch, because I didn't seem to be getting anywhere. I ended up asking him out, and a lot of men think that's going a step too far. Though I don't see why.' She laughed.

'I did understand,' replied Marsh. 'I just didn't know what I wanted. I was still a bit shaken by what my last girl-friend did, and I wasn't sure I was ready.'

'What was that? Can you tell us?' Rosemary asked.

'She went abroad for a month, for her job. I found out that she'd had a series of one-night stands while she was away. She told me that she couldn't cope for any length of time without a relationship, so she found a couple of short-term substitutes. I saw it as cheating on me, because that's what it was. But to be honest I also realised that I hadn't missed her as much as I should have done. So maybe we just weren't meant for each other.'

'Isn't absence meant to make or break a relationship?' Rosemary said.

'Well, it certainly broke ours.'

Gwen was squeezing his hand. He glanced at his boss, realising that he'd never talked about his private life this way before. But Sophie seemed to be miles away, deep in thought. Then her mobile rang.

'Hello? Hello? Who's speaking? Is that you, Rae? Are you there?' A pause. 'Where are you?' she asked. 'Okay. Stay there. Put a security chain across the door if there is one. If not, wedge a chair under the handle. I'll call the local station and get a squad across to you, and we'll be with you as soon as we can. Stay on the phone if possible.'

Her look at Marsh was full of concern. 'That's Rae. She's at Paul Derek's flat in Portsmouth. There's been an intruder and she thinks he's still around somewhere. I'm afraid we have to go. There's something terribly wrong.'

CHAPTER 18: VOMIT AND BLOOD

Friday night

Rae slid out of her car and looked up at the misty drizzle. She took an umbrella and started to walk over to the block of flats that she and Jimmy had visited the previous afternoon.

Earlier that evening she'd suddenly realised what had been niggling away in the back of her mind. She'd been putting up a framed family portrait in her new home when it occurred to her that one of the portraits hanging in Paul Derek's lounge might have been in the wrong place. She remembered that it hadn't quite filled the shadowy mark on the wall behind it. It was probably not important, but to make sure she checked the photos that she'd taken inside the flat. There it was, just as she remembered. A mismatch. And neither she nor Jimmy had thought to check the picture. It was probably nothing, but still. Rae sat thinking for a few moments. Had that picture been a portrait of Sarah Sheldon? Sarah, in a colourful silk camisole, with a smile on her lips. Rae looked again at the photo on her camera and zoomed in, trying to make out the detail on the wall portrait. It looked like a dark-haired woman but was too fuzzy to make out clearly. She searched for her mobile phone in order to call DCI Allen but realised with alarm that she'd left it on her desk in the incident room in Swanage. She was still waiting for a landline to be connected in her flat. She made a quick decision, got into her car and drove out to the dead man's flat.

Now, an hour and a half later, she was in Portsmouth. Rae was surprised at how quiet the area was. She recalled that many of the occupants were elderly people. Maybe most were securely locked inside their homes this late in the evening, watching television, or perhaps already tucked up in bed. She had begun to shiver. A fine layer of tiny droplets of rain covered her hair and clothes because, in the end, she hadn't bothered to raise the umbrella. The outer door had been left unlocked, despite the notice in the lobby requesting that it should always be kept secured. How careless people were.

She pressed the button for the lift and waited. Was that cigarette smoke? A bit strange, she thought. Surely it would be banned inside the apartment block? The lift door slid open and she entered and pressed the button for the first floor. Why hadn't she just taken the stairs? They were right beside Paul Derek's flat, so she'd probably have been there by now. But it was late on a Friday evening, and she was exhausted from the long hours she'd been working all week. She had wondered about paying a quick visit to the local pub, but in the end had decided against it. And, of course, there was the other factor. Her body still hadn't entirely adapted to the hormones that she was taking each day. Maybe in another year she'd feel less tired. The lift slowed and the door opened. Expecting silence, she just caught the sound of a door slamming shut ahead of her followed by running feet. A figure was just turning into the stairwell. She broke into a trot and reached the door in a few seconds. It was closed but not locked. She quickly locked the door then headed for the stairs in pursuit.

'Stop,' she called. 'Police! Stop!'

The footsteps ahead of her indicated that her quarry had increased his pace. She tried to run faster, hampered only slightly by the skirt she was wearing. It was short, though the heels on her ankle boots were a hindrance. She soon realised that she was gaining on whoever was ahead. She turned at the bottom of the stairs and caught sight of a jacketed, hooded figure turning a corner which led towards the entrance. Rae ran faster. With luck she'd catch up with the figure in the car park. There it was again, a faint hint of cigarette smoke in the air. She slowed as she approached the entrance, and was about to shout again when a second figure ran out of the lift recess and cannoned into her. She went down headfirst and rolled several times, trying to control her slide across the floor. Her head and left upper body struck the wall with a force that knocked the breath out of her. She was trying to manoeuvre into an upright position when the figure ran past her. She just had time to push her umbrella forward and catch him at ankle level. He tripped, collided with the wall but remained upright. He staggered through the door and disappeared into the darkness outside.

Rae pulled herself up and limped to the door, holding her side and gasping for breath. As she opened the door she heard a car starting up, and she watched helplessly as a small, dark red car accelerated away. Her vision was blurred and she couldn't even make out the registration number. She sank to the ground, panting, drawing in gulps of cold air. Something was wrong. As it turned away, the car's passenger side had been closest to her, yet she hadn't seen anyone in that seat. Only the driver had been visible, an indistinct blob behind the steering wheel. Either the second person was hunched forward and hidden from view, or he was lying down on the rear seat. Or? Supporting herself against the wall, she groped her way back inside. She held her chest where she'd taken part of the impact. Blood was trickling steadily down her face. Why was she feeling so dizzy? She pushed her way through the double doors, dropped the catch on the lock, found her umbrella and pushed it through the door handles as an extra security measure. Then she looked up. It seemed quiet enough. Her vision began to clear and she peered through the glass panes of the doors. Was that a movement, just on the edge of her vision? She looked for a switch in order to turn off the lobby lights, then realised that they must be automatic. She stood still, leaning against the wall on one side of the doorway. It could have only been a minute or two but it seemed an age before the internal lights went out. She cursed when the exterior light remained on, illuminating the outer porch and doorway area. Of course, it would stay on all night. She kept watching. There it was again, the faintest flicker of movement in the shadows at the edge of the car park. She needed to be at an upstairs window, looking down. Paul Derek's flat would be ideal, its bedrooms overlooked the car park.

Rae limped to the lift. The bright corridor lights snapped on the moment she moved. She looked back as she reached the lift, noting the streak of blood smeared against the wall from her head injury and the trail of bloodstains along the carpet. No wonder her head throbbed so badly. She'd hit the wall on a protruding corner and the top of her skull had taken the full force of the impact. How much blood was she losing? She passed her hand over the back of her head and felt a mass of soggy hair clumped around the point where she'd hit the wall. The lift door opened. She lurched inside and leant against the button for the first floor. All she wanted to do was curl up in the corner and go to sleep. The lift stopped, the doors opening onto a silent corridor. She groped her way towards the apartment. It wasn't the near darkness, she needed the wall for support. Her head felt as if it was about to break open, and the side of her chest ached badly from her crash against the wall. She stepped carefully inside, listening for any sounds of movement. There were none. She went to the main bedroom and looked out of the window. This was a much better view. She could see her own car and a vacant slot at the end of the row. What had occupied that slot? Rae shut her eyes and tried to visualise the cars that had been there when she'd arrived. No good. Her mind was still whirling. She opened her eyes and saw him. There, below. A dark-clad, hooded figure moving in the shadows towards the entrance. She couldn't make out his features in the dim light. She moved away from the window and back to the hallway, where a telephone sat on a shelf. She needed to phone the boss. Good job she'd made the effort to memorise the DCI's mobile number. She prayed that her umbrella would hold the entrance doors secure for a little longer and began to press buttons on the phone's keypad. But the numbers jumped before her eyes. She sank to the floor, with the handset still in her hand. She could hear a voice talking in her ear. It sounded familiar and reassuring. She tried to speak but her mind went blank.

Time passed. Rae sat on the floor in the hallway, leaning against the wall. She could hear a banging in the distance. What was it? What had the voice said? She struggled to her feet, then suddenly doubled over and vomited. She looked at the mess. Leave it, she thought. It's not important. She had to do what the boss had told her. Her mind seemed to have cleared a little. Supporting herself against the wall, she made her way through to the kitchen and took hold of a chair, leaning against its back as she struggled for breath. Why was she so weak? Leaning against the wall with one shoulder, she tugged the chair through to the hallway, moving only a few feet at a time, gasping with the effort. She coughed and spat up a mouthful of blood. Now there was a double stain on the hall carpet. Would she have to pay for the cleaning bill? How much would it cost? She had her own rent to find and she really needed a new car. Everything was so expensive. How would she cope . . ? She started to sob. She heard a faint voice coming from somewhere nearby. It took her some time to realise that it was the phone, still lying on the floor. Ah, yes. The door needed the chair to keep it shut. She pushed it forward and managed to get its back propped under the handle. She sank down to the stained carpet and tried to grasp the phone, but it seemed to slip out of her hand. She put her face down to the floor and tried to speak into it.

'Okay,' she whispered. 'It's okay. I've done it. But I've been sick on the carpet and got blood on it. I can't clean it up, not by myself.'

'Rae, I want you to keep talking to me,' the voice said. 'Did you lock the door? Is it propped shut?'

'Yes,' she murmured. 'He can't get in. I'm alright, really.' She vomited again, noisily.

'Hold on, Rae. There'll be an ambulance and a local squad car with you in a few minutes. Keep listening to me and answer my questions.'

Rae watched the door handle turn silently.

'He's outside,' she said. 'But it's okay.'

There was a slight sound as a key slid into the lock and rotated. The door was pushed from the outside but the chair wedged under the handle held it firm.

'What's happening, Rae?' asked the telephone voice. 'Talk to me.'

'He's here,' Rae whispered. 'It's okay.'

Sirens wailed in the distance. Rae watched the door, listened to the voice on the phone, but nothing made sense anymore. She slumped back against the wall.

CHAPTER 19: QUESTIONS

Saturday morning

In the intensive care unit lights and dials blinked and murmured in the silence. Sophie sat beside Rae's bed holding her hand and watching her face. Rae's eyes flickered open, dark against her pallor.

'I fucked up, didn't I?' she whispered. 'All I ever wanted. To be a woman, to be in the police, and I've ruined it all.'

'No, you certainly haven't. The exact opposite. We've got him. Shapiro. We've got him under lock and key. And we wouldn't have done that without what you did last night.'

'But what I did was wrong. It was nuts. I shouldn't have gone.'

'Well, maybe what you did was a bit foolhardy but it also showed great initiative and courage. You've passed my test with flying colours. By the way, I told the staff in A and E last night that you were transgender and that you'd be on hormones. I thought they'd need to know. Was that okay?'

'Of course. It was the right thing to do. They've been in touch with my GP to see what I'm on, and they've all been fine about it.'

'Good. So how are you feeling this morning?'

Rae paused as if testing to make sure. 'I'm okay.'

'That's common police terminology for "I feel like shit." You can't fool me, Rae.'

'Do I look that bad?' she asked. 'It really was stupid of me ma'am, and I can't even remember much of it. I can vaguely recall getting in the lift to go back up, but that's as far as it goes. What happened after that?'

'Somehow you managed to get into the flat and phoned me. I told you to prop a chair under the door for extra security and you must have been listening because the officers from the first squad car had to shove it out of the way. You were on the floor, unconscious, and I was still burbling away on the telephone. Barry drove like a mad thing to get there, but it still took us an hour and you were in A and E by the time we arrived. You were badly concussed, that's why you were losing consciousness and being sick. Shapiro tried to escape down the stairs and ran straight into the guys from the second car.'

Rae yawned and sighed. 'What's he like? Shapiro?'

'We'll be questioning him this afternoon. He was in here last night for a while, getting treatment for bruising. He's got some injuries to his nose and mouth where he hit the wall. I've just spoken to the local forensic chief and she's fairly clear about what happened from the bloodstains and your injuries. But to answer your question, he's got a mean temper. He'd obviously been trying to kick the door down and even when he was caught they had to haul him off, cursing. A bit aggressive, you might say. Even the staff who treated him last night commented on it.'

'Why did he come back? Why didn't he just run?'

Sophie shook her head. 'God knows. I can only guess that there was something in that flat he needed to find. You must have disturbed him when you first arrived. Maybe it was the same thing you went looking for.'

Rae seemed to struggle with her memory. 'But it wasn't him in the flat. Not when I first arrived. He must have been waiting downstairs, keeping a lookout. He must have warned whoever was inside that I was coming up.'

'What?'

'There was someone else in the flat. The person I chased. I was faster and would have caught them up, but this second man, Shapiro, came out at me. The other one drove off in a car. I only got a quick look.' Rae closed her eyes. 'I've been thinking about it. It might not have been a man at all. The face was just a vague flash, but she looked at me as she drove past.'

Sophie could see that the effort of remembering was exhausting Rae, but they needed a complete picture of what had happened before questioning Shapiro.

'Rae, I need you to tell me what happened. Take it slowly and tell me if it's getting too much. But if there was someone else, we have to find out who it could have been. Everything you can remember is going to be vital. Are you okay to do this?'

Rae nodded weakly and pressed Sophie's hand.

***

Later that morning Sophie and Marsh questioned Brian Shapiro at Portsmouth's police headquarters.

He snarled at the two officers as they entered and sat down. 'I don't know why I'm being held. Christ. Anyone would think I was the guilty party. Just look at the state of my face. It'll take weeks for the bruises to go.'

'So the person you slammed into a wall, and who's currently in intensive care by the way, she's the one we should be charging, is she?' asked Marsh.

'She's one of my officers, Mr Shapiro,' Sophie broke in. 'Maybe you didn't realise that. She was on a routine visit when she stumbled across you. Now, let me introduce myself. I'm Detective Chief Inspector Sophie Allen from Dorset police, and this is Detective Sergeant Barry Marsh. We're currently investigating two murders that have recently occurred on our patch and we have reason to believe that you can tell us a lot about those deaths. In fact, as I'm sure you're aware, we've been looking for you for the past week. And then when we do find you, you end up assaulting one of my officers for no apparent reason. So what's going on, Mr Shapiro? Please enlighten me. The floor is all yours, as they say, but whatever you say had better be convincing. I don't like having my time wasted, especially not by people who stand in the shadows, only to come out and seriously injure one of my team. I'm sure you can imagine how I feel about that, with you being ex-police yourself.'

She looked at the man who faced her. Rosemary's description had been very accurate. He had mousey hair and blue eyes that bulged slightly. And his nose did, indeed, turn up at the tip. Doesn't look very Italian, she thought. He was wearing grey denim trousers and a blue, zipped jacket. His feet were bare. His shoes had been removed for forensic examination.

'I need protection,' Shapiro finally said. 'He'll be after me, too. And that woman? I didn't know she was a copper.'

Sophie looked at him with distaste. 'She called out that she was a police officer. All officers are trained to identify themselves in a chase situation as you well know, and she confirmed that she did.'

'How could I have known? She was by herself with no walkie-talkie, no phone, nothing. She certainly wasn't dressed for work. She's not police, that's what I thought. I thought she was just shouting that to scare somebody. She's okay then? I mean, if she spoke to you?'

'It looks as if she'll recover. Luckily for you. Otherwise you'd have been facing something a bit more serious than an assault charge.' Sophie paused. 'So who did you think she was?'

'I panicked. I thought she was with the bastard that killed those two across your way. That's what I thought. I thought he'd caught up with us. He must be a fucking psychopath. For all I knew, he was out there as well, waiting for me.'

She looked at him with renewed interest. 'Who are you talking about, Mr Shapiro?'

'I don't fucking know. I haven't a clue who he is. I just know he'll be after me. And I'll end up going the same way as bloody Derek and Sarah. Tipped off a cliff or stuck with a knife in my back or brained with a lump of rock.'

Sophie looked sideways at Barry and nodded.

'Why were you there last night, Mr Shapiro? What were you looking for?' asked Marsh.

Shapiro shrugged. He said nothing.

'If you had nothing to be guilty about, why did you resist when the police arrived last night?'

'Look, I wasn't going to try and escape. But I panicked when I realised how it would look. If I'd really wanted to get away I could've done. And I did want to see how she was. I knew she was hurt and how it would look if I left her. I was scared. Whoever killed those two last week is still out there, and he'll be looking for me. And if he finds me I'm a goner. I'm safer with you lot.'

'Do you expect us to believe all this, Mr Shapiro?' said Marsh. 'It sounds very improbable to me. Two people you were with were murdered last weekend and you immediately vanished. Why would you go into hiding if you weren't involved in their deaths? And then when one of my colleagues does stumble across you, you assault her, leaving her seriously injured. And you haven't even asked about her injuries. Concussion, a fractured skull and two broken ribs. You obviously don't feel any remorse about it. I mean, come on. What do you take us for? The way you reacted last night is exactly how someone guilty of two murders would react. Violently. And who was the other person with you?'

Shapiro was silent.

'Well if you're not going to even tell us why you were there and who was with you, how do you expect us to believe you about the other stuff? I think you'll find that we've got plenty of evidence against you. As far as I'm concerned, you're the only psychopath in this case.'

'What happened last weekend, Mr Shapiro?' said Sophie. 'On the Friday evening of the Blues Festival? How did you get there?'

'We came by car. Derek's. We arrived early evening and checked in to the B and B. We dumped our stuff then went out for some food and a drink in one of the pubs. That was where we met the two women. Derek hit it off with the brunette, Sarah. I wasn't so lucky with the other one. They talked us into going to another pub, the White Swan, I think it was called. That was later in the evening. I still wasn't getting anywhere with the blonde. She was more interested in some other guy. When the band finished we walked back to their hotel. Derek was doing okay. Sarah did a deal with the blonde so she and Derek had the room for the night. The blonde left with the other guy, and I went my own way.'

'Did you go back to your room at the guesthouse?'

'No. You know I didn't.'

'So where did you go?'

It was some time before he replied. 'I walked around a bit, then came back into the hotel by the garden entrance. I knew what room they were in. I checked it was all quiet, knocked on the door and went in.'

'It was unlocked?'

'Yes. I knew it would be. It was prearranged.'

'What was prearranged, Mr Shapiro?' Sophie asked. Her voice was sharp and she leaned forward. 'I want to know exactly what had been agreed, who was involved and what was supposed to happen.'

Shapiro stared at her. 'Yeah, I'm sure you do. But explaining it to an outsider . . . it's difficult. You wouldn't understand.'

'Try us.'

'Me and Derek. Sarah. And anyone else who joins in. We're into group sex. It had all been set up beforehand. The only trouble was, the blonde wouldn't play ball. It wasn't even worth trying to talk her into it. Sarah had already decided she was a dead loss. We could tell from the uptight way she acted.'

'So it was just the three of you? Derek, you and Sarah. Is that right?'

He nodded. 'And Sarah was fine when I left. A bit tired, we all were. But they were both okay. I swear it.'

'Where did you go then?'

'I took the car and came back to Portsmouth.'

'But it was Mr Derek's car, wasn't it?'

'I had the keys. We'd agreed he would stay on a few more days with Sarah — a kind of holiday. I was always going to take the car back with me. I just went earlier than planned.'

'Why? Why would you do that? Why leave in the early hours of the morning? You had a room booked at the Hawthorns. Your bag and spare clothes were there. Why did you leave in the middle of the night?'

'I was just pissed off at the way things had gone. I knew things were just going to get worse and worse cos I'd be on my own. Derek was going to call in at the B and B the next day to pick up his stuff. I decided to cut my losses and come back home early.' Shapiro glanced at Marsh. 'I get depressed. I'm on medication for it and I forgot to bring my pills with me. So I decided to go home.'

'Why are you still refusing to tell us the truth, Mr Shapiro?' Sophie's look was cold. 'You've put your story together very carefully, haven't you? Enough truth to correspond with what you've guessed we know. But the thing is, you can't be sure. How much do we know?' She looked at Marsh.

'We know there were at least three people in that room with Sarah, not two,' said Marsh. 'So who else was there, Mr Shapiro? And why are you trying to protect them? Were they with you last night?'

'What we did had nothing to do with what happened to those two. They were fine when we left.'

'We? You said we? So you admit there was someone else?'

'I've said all I'm going to say.'

'But it casts doubt on your whole story. Can't you see that? Why should we believe you?' Marsh said.

Shapiro didn't answer.

'Why were you at Derek's flat last night, Mr Shapiro? Tell us that.'

Silence.

Marsh cleared his throat. 'Brian Shapiro, I am arresting you on suspicion of murder. You do not have to say anything. But it may harm your defence if you do not mention when questioned something which you later rely on in court. Anything you do say may be given in evidence.'

CHAPTER 20: DOUBTS

Saturday afternoon

'What do you think, Barry? Really?'

Sophie Allen and Barry Marsh were leaning on the parapet of the bridge over the Swan Brook, watching a pair of ducks splashing in the reeds. They'd returned from Portsmouth half an hour earlier and had just finished a quick lunch in a café.

'Everything seems to fit. He admits he returned to the hotel. He admits he had sex with her. He admits that he left in the middle of the night. All good reasons for us to consider him as our prime suspect. But it just doesn't ring true. He's obviously hiding something, but what? I can't see the motive. Okay, he could be a psychopath who killed Sarah because of some argument they had. But to then wait a couple of days and kill Derek as well? It doesn't fit. Paul Derek's murder is a real problem. If he was killed at the same time as Sarah it would have made some kind of sense. But a day or two later? To me that means Derek was involved in her death, helped dispose of the body and then there was some later disagreement. I just can't get my head round it. Maybe I'm making it too rational. You've always said that many murders are ruled by emotion and passion rather than logic. But aren't they the ones that get solved really quickly because the killer isn't careful enough?'

Sophie nodded. 'Usually, yes. And I agree with you. Maybe things will become clearer if Benny can narrow down the day of Derek's death. But something just doesn't seem right, and catching Shapiro has brought it to a head. He could easily have got clean away last night. They had what they came for, so why did he come back to the flat? He says it was to check on Rae. If that's true it paints a different picture of him.' She sighed loudly. 'He isn't a nice person, that's obvious. But a double killer? I have my doubts. The problem is, where does that leave us? We've spent all week looking for the son of a bitch, thinking that when we've got him it'll be case over, and now we've found him we're not sure.'

'Remember there was someone else with him.'

'Yes. A scared-looking, pale-faced woman, according to Rae. And she couldn't run very fast. So let's assume she's a girlfriend. He's in his mid-fifties, isn't wealthy and doesn't have knock-'em-dead good looks. So what is that likely to tell us about her? Also middle-aged? Rae says that she was fairly short and slightly built. Hardly the description of a ruthless double killer. Paul Derek was tall and fit, from what the post-mortem has told us. He worked out in a gym, so his work colleagues say. Even Shapiro might have struggled to overcome Derek. He's obviously a heavy smoker and looks flabby. Of the three we know were in the room, the two victims ought to have been able to defend themselves easily. They were the fit, healthy, strong ones, both of them taller than Shapiro. It just doesn't make sense. And my number one rule is, if it doesn't make sense, start looking elsewhere.'

'It's been a week now and we're not much further forward. Is that what you're saying, ma'am? But who else could it be?'

She looked down at the ducks. 'It's got to be one of those on our list, Barry, including Hugh and Peter Shakespeare.'

She put her hands in her coat pockets. 'Let's go back in. I'm getting cold.'

As they were about to enter the police station, Sophie put her hand on Marsh's arm. 'We must trace this John Renton character, if only to remove him from the list of suspects. Or whoever was pretending to be John Renton, since he's supposed to be in Afghanistan. Why haven't we managed to find out anything about him? We also need to get the story behind that photo of Sarah in a wedding dress. But let's not write Shapiro out of the equation yet. I don't trust what he's told us one little bit. We have to remember that he was involved in the probable rape of Brenda Plant two years ago, along with Paul Derek and with Sarah Sheldon as a possible accessory. That's what I meant when I said he's not a nice person. In fact, not one of them was nice. Yet people who knew Sarah and Paul Derek have said what great people they were. Human behaviour is such a complex thing.' She sighed. 'Let's get the rest of the team involved with filling in Shapiro's background and trying to trace this woman that Rae saw. Maybe you can switch to the Renton business and I'll back you up as necessary. Keep in mind the description we have from the hotel. Our friend Mr Brodie thought someone was watching Derek and Shapiro in the pub early on Friday evening. It could easily be the same man. With Rae in hospital we're an officer short, but Jack Holly has agreed to do a stint this afternoon. I'll ask for someone else to be sent down from HQ next week if it's necessary, but we'll leave it until Monday to decide.' She paused. 'At this stage we don't let anyone else know about our doubts. We still need the background on Shapiro to be filled in, so that's what they can do. Happy about all this?'

'Of course, ma'am,' he replied. 'And I haven't said thanks for yesterday evening. We were really enjoying it up until the time you got Rae's phone call.'

Sophie smiled. 'You were lucky. My cooking worked out well for once.'

* * *

Jimmy Melsom looked worried. 'Do you really need to take it over, boss? I've done my best, but there's really not much to go on.'

'We're not criticising you, Jimmy,' said Marsh. 'The DCI thinks there might be more to this Renton business than meets the eye. She wants someone on it full-time. Most Whitehall departments will be pretty empty at weekends and they're probably trying to delay us until Monday. She wants me to push them hard. If you can give me everything you've got on Renton, I'll get started. Stay here, because she's got something important for you to follow up. She'll explain it better than me.'

It didn't take Marsh long to read through the thin folder. The hotel staff's description of Renton, the photofit image, a printout of the hotel booking record, some pages of credit card statements, and several sheets of information from the MoD. Renton's unit was currently stationed in Afghanistan and wasn't due to return to Britain for another three months. Melsom had compared the purchases from the credit card against times when the regiment had been in the UK. There were several discrepancies, including the hotel booking the previous weekend. Some of the purchases listed on the bank statement could have been made over the internet, but in several cases the purchaser would have had to be present in the UK. It was puzzling. He tried to call the MoD in Whitehall. It took him well over an hour to find someone who could provide him with the information he wanted.

Meanwhile Sophie was briefing PC Jack Holly, temporarily standing in for Rae Gregson.

'We need to fill in all the background on Shapiro, so you and Jen Allbright will concentrate on that. Read what we've got so far, spot the gaps and fill them. We need to know everything about him and it all needs to go in here.' She placed the file on the desk. 'And I want to say thank you for the work you've done so far. I'll make sure we finish before five. You've both got homes to go to and lives to lead.'

She walked over to Melsom's desk. He looked at her apprehensively and she laughed. 'It's not the end of the world, Jimmy. I'm just reorganising the tasks. Okay? It's a bit of a shot in the dark, but I want you to work through the companies running cruises to tropical or semi-tropical destinations. Start with the Caribbean. Try to build up a list, then contact them one by one looking for a booking for Sarah Sheldon. If that doesn't work, we'll try the Mediterranean and Aegean, then other places further afield. She may not have made the booking herself, but she should be on a passenger list. We think it was between one and three years ago. Let me know right away if something crops up. Okay?'

He nodded. Sophie left him to the job and returned to her office in order to think. Barry had been right. Nothing seemed to add up or make sense. She needed to look at the problem from a different perspective. She dialled Hugh Shakespeare's number.

'Mr Shakespeare? It's DCI Allen. I wonder if you can do me a favour. I need the names and contact numbers of whoever would have been Sarah's superiors when she was still at the bank in Portsmouth. My problem is that it's a Saturday afternoon. I can't go through normal channels, which is why I'm phoning you.' She listened. 'Fine. Can you call me on this number? I know it's a bit of a long shot, but it's worth a try. Thanks.'

Sophie sat looking at the photo of Sarah in the cream wedding dress. The flowers Sarah was holding were tropical, the sunshine looked strong. Sarah was tanned and the sand underfoot was pale, almost white. Where had the photo been taken? What did it signify? If only the Sarah in the picture could talk. The whole case would be wrapped up in a few minutes, she was sure. Sophie sighed and went to get herself a coffee while she waited for Hugh Shakespeare's return call.

* * *

Late in the afternoon the group reassembled in the incident room.

'I think I might be getting somewhere, ma'am,' said Jimmy Melsom, first to report back. 'But it was only a few minutes ago so there are no details yet. I need to phone them again on Monday morning to get the full picture. Someone called Sarah Sheldon was on a cruise in the summer of 2010, in July. She made the booking, so that's why it was easy for them to trace it. But any more information than that will have to wait.'

'Where was it?' Sophie asked.

'The Caribbean, like you thought. Antigua, Barbados and a few other islands. She booked a double room on the cruise ship. That's all they could find . . . Is that okay, ma'am?'

Sophie smiled at his anxious expression. 'Of course, Jimmy. Well done. It's just that you mentioned Barbados. It's one of those places where you can get married with just two days' notice. Couples have a romantic cruise, call in there and get themselves hitched on the spur of the moment. Interesting, don't you think?' There was a silence. 'Fine. Follow it up first thing Monday. Get to the bottom of it, Jimmy. Don't let them give you the run-around. Take tomorrow off and have a break.'

She looked at Jack Holly and Jen Allbright. 'Anything else to add at the moment?'

'Not much, ma'am,' Allbright replied. 'Rae and Jimmy did a good job and had already got all the information from when Shapiro was in the police in Portsmouth. The only thing we've managed to add is that he worked at a petrol station for a few months after getting sacked. He then helped out at one of his brothers' restaurants and recently had a job with a Portsmouth security firm. He's still on their books. They act as a kind of agency and send people out to different jobs, so they don't actually employ him. Like Jimmy, we'll need to wait until Monday to get details from the people who hired him.'

'Good. You too should take a break tomorrow so you're fresh on Monday.' She turned to Marsh. 'Anything useful from the MoD, Barry?'

'Yes, and it's quite definite. John Renton serves with an armoured unit which has been in Afghanistan for five months.

And there's a stunning piece of luck for us. He's coming home this weekend to attend a family funeral. He's due to arrive at Brize Norton tomorrow morning. What do you think?'

'What do I think?' she said. 'What do you think I think? We need to be there to greet him. We'll go and have a look-see, as my American cousins put it.'

'Did you discover anything useful, ma'am?' Marsh asked. 'From the bank people, I mean?'

'Like you, I'll get more on Monday morning. I did get through to one man who was her boss before she left last year. He was happy with her work but couldn't tell me her reasons for leaving because apparently she didn't want to talk about it. But he did say that she hadn't been her normal self for some months. She seemed uneasy at times. He also told me something else, but couldn't confirm it. Typical man, really.'

'What? You can't just leave it there, ma'am.' Barry sounded put out.

'Can't I? Oh well. He said that he'd had a one-to-one, target-setting meeting with her a couple of years ago. He was sitting across the table from her the whole time. He let her go at the end without noticing anything different about her. When his secretary came in just after the meeting was over, she asked if he'd noticed the new ring on Sarah's wedding finger. He hadn't of course. She'd spotted it in thirty seconds and he hadn't clocked it at all, despite being with her for an hour. Incredible, isn't it? What was he looking at all that time? Don't answer that, anyone. I'll hit you if you give me the obvious answer. Anyway, the ring didn't appear again, but he says that his secretary swears she saw it. A thin, plain gold band. It can't have been the ring from her marriage to Hugh, because Peter, the son, has had that ever since his parents divorced. So was it of any significance? Maybe not on its own, but coupled with that photo of her in a wedding dress and the cruise to the Caribbean, it could be significant. And Rosemary reported seeing her wear a similar ring on one occasion, though she can't be sure it was a wedding ring.

Jimmy, first thing Monday morning I want you to get onto the registrar's office in Barbados and get them to track back through the marriage records. If she did marry again, it puts a completely new slant on things. What I can't understand is, if she did so why keep it from her son, Peter? He claimed that they were very close.'

Marsh was looking thoughtful. 'Peter also said that she often acted on the spur of the moment. What if it was just that? A sudden impulse while on holiday? Maybe she regretted it, or never found the right way of explaining it to Peter without upsetting him, so she never told him.'

'Human nature is a strange thing, Barry.'

She was interrupted by a tap on the door. Rae's head appeared round the corner, still heavily bandaged.

Sophie looked horrified.

'What on earth are you doing here? For goodness' sake, Rae, are you mad? You need another couple of days at least to recuperate.'

'No I don't, ma'am. I look worse than I feel. I was discharged an hour ago, and the doctor said I'd probably be fit for light work by tomorrow. So here I am. I'll be fine to be here for an hour or two, really. It'll stop me from getting bored and I'm sure there's something you can find for me to do.'

CHAPTER 21: BRIZE NORTON

Sunday morning

The three detectives were waiting in a customs room at the Air Force's principal transport hub. It was a Sunday and Brize Norton was quieter than normal, but there were still passengers making their way through the building to be embraced by family members. Through a window they watched the groups of uniformed personnel at the customs desk, wondering which one of them was John Renton. Marsh had managed to contact Brize Norton the previous evening and had arranged with the duty officer to speak to Renton. He would be brought into the inner office as soon as he appeared at the check-in desks. Renton was returning for a brief spell of compassionate leave, giving the detectives the opportunity to question him in person. They'd reluctantly brought Rae with them because she was familiar with the layout of the complex. She'd visited Brize Norton several times to collect her father when he'd returned from an overseas posting.

The customs officer entered, accompanied by a middle-aged man in plain clothes. He was wearing blue chino trousers and a dark grey leather jacket. He walked briskly across the floor and extended his hand.

'John Renton. I understand you wanted to see me?' He had a soft Hampshire accent. He was just under six feet tall, with dark hair beginning to go grey at the sides, and a smooth, olive complexion. He looked wary despite his confident, authoritative manner. Sophie stepped forward and shook his hand.

'I'm DCI Sophie Allen from Dorset police. This is DS Barry Marsh. We'd like to speak to you for a few minutes. If you wouldn't mind sitting down?'

'This will be about Sarah, I expect,' Renton said, seating himself and stretching out his long legs.

Hiding her surprise, Sophie nodded to the customs officer, who went out.

'Yes. If you don't mind me asking, why exactly have you returned?'

'To help Peter with the funeral arrangements. He contacted me a few days ago, so I made the necessary arrangements and took the first available transport back here.'

Sophie was struggling to keep up with all this.

'Peter Shakespeare has contacted you? Why? Do you know him?'

'He's my nephew. Sarah was my half-sister, although I'm quite a few years younger than her.'

'We didn't know. . No one in the family has mentioned you. Even so, I can't believe we missed it.' Sophie shook her head.

'I'm not really surprised. Sarah and I were never close. We fought constantly when we were children, and didn't have a lot to do with each other after we grew up, partly because of the age difference. And I haven't been in contact with Hugh for years. But I got on well with Peter when he was young, and when he contacted me with the news of her death, I thought I should come over and give him some support. I used to take him to football matches when I was home on leave, and we had some good talks. I was midway between his age and his parents', so maybe that made it easier for him to open up to me . . . So if you didn't know who I was, why were you waiting for me?'

Sophie sighed audibly. 'That's a long story, and maybe it should wait until we have a chance to speak further. What is your role in the army, Mr Renton?'

'I'm an RSM with an artillery and armoured brigade. At the moment I'm training a unit of the Afghan army in mortar use. I'm due to leave the army soon. Since Sarah's death I've been thinking a lot about my future. Everything depends on how Peter is. He's the real reason I've come back. I think he'll welcome my support. At least I hope he does.'

Sophie smiled weakly at Renton. She felt like holding her head in her hands.

'Can we give you a lift anywhere, Mr Renton? We're heading back to Dorset, but we could easily divert to Portsmouth.'

'That's very kind of you, Chief Inspector, but no thanks. I've travelled back from Germany with a friend and we've hired a car. And call me John. Please.'

'I'd prefer to keep things on a more formal footing, but don't take offence. So you didn't fly directly from Afghanistan?'

'No. I've been in Germany for over a week. As I said, I'm due to leave the army in a few months and I plan to train as a church minister. The army organises short courses to help ease people into civilian jobs when they leave. I've been on one for servicemen who want to enter the caring professions. It's being run jointly with other NATO personnel at Bielefeld, our headquarters in Germany.'

'Exactly how long were you there?'

'Ten days. The course finished yesterday. Patrick Adams, the friend I'm travelling with, is one of the facilitators. I've known him for years.'

'Well, if you're not returning to Portsmouth with us, it means that we'll need to talk a bit longer here. Do you fancy a bite to eat or a coffee? We could visit the café.' She looked around her. 'This room isn't exactly pleasant.'

'A coffee would be fine. I'll have to start watching my weight now I'm moving into less active work. Can Patrick join us?'

Sophie nodded.

* * *

In the cafeteria Marsh joined the queue at the counter with Renton's friend, Patrick Adams. Sophie began to question Renton more closely, while Rae took notes.

'I think you noticed our surprise when you told us. We had no idea of the connection between you and Sarah. You must be wondering why we came all this way to meet your flight.'

Tapping his fingers on the table, Renton nodded.

'You'll know by now that Sarah's death was no accident, that she was murdered. You may also know that a couple of days after we discovered her body, the man she was with was also found dead some forty miles further along the coast. They were in Swanage attending the local blues festival and spent the first part of the night together in a hotel. One of the other rooms in the hotel was booked on the same night in the name of a John Renton. He checked in during the early part of the evening, but was not seen again. He vanished that night and didn't return.'

'But there must be dozens of John Rentons in the country.'

'The room was booked using your credit card details. Your bank gave us access to your statements. Your card was used to book that room, although the bill was paid in cash.'

'And this was last weekend? But I was in Germany then,' he protested.

'I will need precise details of your location, and people who can corroborate that. The hotel room was booked over the internet some weeks earlier. If it wasn't you, then some-one has used your card details fraudulently. That's obvious. But until now we had no idea you were a member of Sarah's family. So, if it wasn't you, then who knows your card details? Who booked that room? And who used that room for the first part of the night on Friday, nine days ago? Do you have any ideas?'

'No, absolutely not, but I can assure you it wasn't me.' Renton shook his head. 'For goodness' sake. I fly in, expecting to be helping support Peter, only to find I'm a suspect in his mother's murder. This is all too absurd.' He looked up as Marsh returned carrying a tray of coffees and biscuits, followed by Renton's friend. 'Pat, where was I on Friday night last week? What was I doing?'

Renton's friend frowned. He was tall, older than Renton but handsome in spite of his grey-streaked, stubbly beard. He was tanned, and carried himself with assurance. As he stretched across to pick up a biscuit, Sophie noticed a sticking plaster on the inside of one wrist.

'You were three days into the course.' Adams spoke with a soft but authoritative voice. His spectacles reflected the sunlight in the room. 'We'd completed the induction material by then, and we'd moved on to the individual assignments. We gave you all the briefings on Thursday, so you were either in the library or working in your own study.'

'Can you vouch for Mr Renton's presence for the duration of the weekend?'

'Of course.' He took a sip of coffee. 'I need a while to get my head around the exact details, but he was there, I know it.' He frowned again.

'Have you ever been to Barbados, Mr Renton?' said Sophie suddenly.

'Barbados? No, not recently. Though I was there a long time ago. I used to play a lot of cricket for an army team and we did a tour of the West Indies some twenty years or so back. That's how I met Patrick. He was one of the team coaches and we've remained friends ever since, even after he quit the army. Barbados was one of the places we played in, wasn't it, Pat?'

Adams nodded. 'I'd forgotten about that. It was a long time ago.'

'Does that count?' Renton added.

'No. Nothing more recent? Anywhere else in the Caribbean?' Sophie asked.

'I was on a cruise there about five years ago, along with a girlfriend, but we missed Barbados because of a storm.' He finished his coffee in several large mouthfuls. 'That was one of the best times of my life,' he added, somewhat bitterly.

'But you were never there with Sarah?'

'No. Whatever gave you that idea?'

Sophie paused for a while. 'Are you married, Mr Renton?'

He shook his head. 'No. I never have been, but it wasn't a conscious decision. If I'd met the right woman, who knows? But it's not easy, being in the army and moving around all the time.' He scratched his arm. 'Like Sue, the girlfriend I was with on that cruise. She just couldn't cope with me being away for months at a time on long tours of duty.'

Sophie nodded. 'I can understand the difficulties. But what about now? Presumably you'll be much more settled from now on? Is she still a part of your life?'

He shook his head. 'If she wasn't willing to settle for me in the difficult times, how could I ever be sure about her? She couldn't have really loved me, could she? Maybe things will be different now, easier for a woman to cope with but with her, there'd always be that doubt in my mind.'

Sophie sat back in her chair. How should she broach the next set of questions?

'You say you weren't close to Sarah at all, Mr Renton. Did you know anything about her private life and her recent relationships?'

'Not really. I knew the reason for the breakup of her marriage to Hugh, and his claim that she kept having affairs. I took much of what he said with a pinch of salt, and we haven't really spoken since. I tried to talk to her about it, to find out the truth, but she made it clear that her private life wasn't up for discussion. Certainly not with me, anyway. Peter was still a teenager at the time and she knew we were close. I think she saw how important my relationship with him was, and didn't want to spoil it. That might have happened if she confirmed Hugh's claims. As for more recently, I've been away for so long that I'm out of touch.'

'Was there ever any hint from anyone that Sarah had married again? Maybe secretly?'

'No, never. That's really a shocker. Good grief. Where have you picked that up from?'

'It could just be rumour, but we have to check it out. So there was never any indication?'

'No. But anyway, I'd be the last to know. It would have only come to me via Peter or Hugh, and presumably they haven't been able to confirm it?'

Sophie shook her head. She turned to the other man. 'So, Mr Adams, have you had time to think about last weekend? Can you vouch for Mr Renton from Friday through to Sunday?'

'He was there all the time, I know it. We had breakfast together on Friday morning. He was in the lounge late on Saturday afternoon, because we watched the football results together. I was in the administration offices for most of Friday, dealing with completely unrelated issues, so I wasn't present at the course venue. What I can do is give you the names of the other course participants and the other tutor. The librarian on duty will be able to help as well.'

'I didn't use the library.' Renton began to look worried. 'You know that, Pat. I used the web to research my assignment because the topic I was given was unusual. I was in my study for most of the day and only joined the others for a quick snack.' He paused. 'In fact, I didn't even go out with you all on the Friday evening. I was feeling very off-colour, I remember now, and stayed in. I went to bed early that night and slept for a long time.'

'I'm sorry, John. I didn't mean to land you in it. I feel a complete bastard now,' said his friend.

'We'd have found out anyway,' said Sophie. 'This is a double murder investigation, so we have to cross-check everything and follow up every single lead, every alibi and every statement. People think the police do their work by hunches, second-guessing suspects' possible motives, but that all comes from television drama, not real-life policing. In reality a lot of it is based on fact-checking, looking for discrepancies.' She sat up straighter. 'So we need a list of all the course participants and their contact details, all staff members and anyone else who might have seen Mr Renton during those key hours.'

'Where will you be staying while you're here, Mr Renton?' asked Marsh.

'We're staying in my Portsmouth home for a couple of nights, to give us time to see Peter and his father and check on the arrangements. I'm staying until after the funeral. Pat has to return to Germany in a few days.'

'We'll need your full contact details and you need to inform us if you decide to go anywhere else. I hope you understand.'

Renton nodded. 'As for the other stuff, witnesses who can vouch that I was on the course, I'm sure we can give you most of the names here and now. Pat helped to organise the course, after all.'

His friend nodded reassuringly. 'It'll be fine, John.' Sophie rested her chin on her hands, looking across the table at this man who had been so difficult to track down. 'I'll also need your passport, Mr Renton. I can't afford to leave you the opportunity to get out of the country before I've had a chance to eliminate you from my enquiries. It will remain safely in my possession and I'll return it to you as soon as I can.' She looked at him steadily. He returned her stare, sighed and handed his passport over. 'Thank you for your co-operation,' she said.

* * *

On their way back to the car Barry's phone rang. He spoke very little, merely listening carefully. Finally he turned to Sophie.

'That was the station. Apparently reception took three odd phone calls this morning, all from the same number. In the first two the caller hung up without speaking. In the last one a woman spoke and said she was in trouble and that she knew Sarah. She was crying and sounded terrified, but she hung up before they could ask her any more.'

'They'll be tracing the call?' Sophie asked.

He nodded. 'Should know by tomorrow morning.'

CHAPTER 22: MESSED UP LIVES

Monday morning

What was going on? Barry Marsh ran his fingers through his ginger hair as he spoke into the phone.

'No, no one from this unit was asking those questions last month.' He was getting more than a little annoyed at the belligerent tone of the man on the other end of the line. 'We're not psychic. We only start to investigate a murder once it's happened, not before. Since we're talking about a death that occurred last weekend, why would we have contacted you before then, before it happened? It wasn't us, and I don't know who it could have been . . . The call was about three weeks ago? Did you get a name? That's great. And did he say where he was from? Okay. Leave it with me. So is it possible to answer my original question now? Can you confirm that Sarah Sheldon booked a twin room for the spring blues festival at your holiday complex?' He listened. 'And the other names? Shapiro, Derek or Paul? Yes? Great. Thanks for your help. We may well be back in touch.'

He replaced the handset and sat looking at it for a few seconds. Then he picked it up and dialled a Gloucester number.

* * *

'Something interesting, ma'am.' Barry poked his head around the open door to Sophie's small office.

'You too? Okay, you go first.'

'Someone else has been asking exactly the same questions as us about Sarah Sheldon's room bookings at the two music festivals. We already knew about her reservations, but I contacted the Hayling Island one to see if Shapiro had booked a room. They couldn't confirm it when I spoke to them last week. The manager got quite angry. He said he was fed up with having his time wasted by people asking him the same questions. He was definite that someone claiming to be from the police had asked for that very information a few weeks ago. I double-checked with the hotel at Gloucester where Sarah and Rosemary stayed in the summer, and exactly the same thing happened. One of the receptionists remembers a call from a policeman requesting the exact information I was looking for. Both calls would have been made at the beginning of September, about five weeks ago. The Hayling Island manager even remembered a name, a DS George Smith from Portsmouth. But there's no such officer.'

'And whoever it was asked about the men too, not just the women?' asked Sophie.

'Exactly. So someone knew of their existence weeks before the festival here. And if whoever it was knew that much, he must also have known what Sarah was getting up to. Don't you think?'

'You're right,' Sophie said. 'It is very odd and the implications are worrying. By the way, Rae has managed to trace where those odd calls came from yesterday. Someone called Lily Dalton. She lives in Poole, so we're just about to pay her a visit. Can you hold the fort here? We'll talk more when I get back.'

* * *

'Was it that easy? To find me, I mean. I thought it would take ages.' Lily looked at Sophie with a weak smile.

216

Lily was like a china doll. She had small, elfin features, a strawberry-blonde bob and she was wearing a neat skirt and top. She can only be about five foot two, Sophie thought. She probably fits into children's clothes.

'You're on all kinds of lists, everyone is. Voters roll, council tax, the phone book. It's not difficult for anyone to trace where you live, even if they aren't police. And that's the problem. If you really are in danger, then it would be all too easy for them to find you. I think it took Rae here less than ten minutes.' Sophie paused. 'Why were you in Paul Derek's flat, Lily?'

'Brian remembered the photo on the wall, so we went to get it. Brian was in the background of the shot, and Paul had written his phone numbers and his address on the back. I was the one in the flat and I panicked when Brian phoned up from the lobby to say that someone was coming up.' Lily looked at Rae. 'He didn't mean to hurt you. It was an accident. That's why he didn't come back with me in the car. He went back to see how you were and when he saw all the blood he was worried about you. I took the car out of the car park and was waiting along the road. He texted me to let me know he was going back up to the flat to check up on you. Then I saw the police cars arriving but I couldn't get through to him in time to warn him. He left it too late to get away so you caught him.'

Lily looked at Rae and bit her lip. Rae still had a dressing covering one side of her head and her face sported several colourful bruises.

'She doesn't look well. I'm really sorry about what happened. Brian didn't mean to hurt her, I know he didn't. He went through a bad time a few years ago when he lost his job with the police in Portsmouth, but he's been a lot calmer for the last couple of years. I didn't like him much then, but he's okay now, though I'm still not sure he's my type.'

'Why didn't you tell us more when you phoned us?'

Lily sighed. 'I can't cope on the phone. I get tense and I go to pieces, and when I get really worried and anxious my voice keeps giving out. And I haven't slept more than a few hours since Friday, so I'm even worse than normal. I don't think straight at the best of times and now my brain is one big, fuzzy mess. I wondered about getting away from here, maybe going to London. That way I could really disappear and hide for a while. If I'd been on the phone longer, they'd have talked me into staying, I know they would.'

'But you have stayed,' Sophie replied.

'Yes, but it was my choice. I have to plan things by myself. Other people always walk all over me if I give them a chance. So I don't give them the chance any more. That's how I've learned to keep at least some control over my life.' She looked again at Rae. 'Are you really alright? Shouldn't you be in hospital or something?'

'I'm well enough to be at work. I just have to be careful, that's all.'

Lily paused. 'You're a transsexual, aren't you?' she asked hesitantly. 'I thought it when you first came in, and your voice has kind of confirmed it.'

Sophie became angry. 'That's totally irrelevant. DC Gregson is an officer in my unit and you, Ms Dalton, need to stick to what we're here for.'

'She's quite protective, isn't she?' said Lily. 'That's good. I bet not everyone has been as supportive as her. You are very good, though. I can only tell cos I've met lots over the years — at parties though, not when they're at work. I know the signs. It's like a sixth sense with me.'

Sophie was ready with another rebuke, but Rae interjected. 'It's okay, ma'am really. I don't mind.' She turned back to Lily. 'Yes, you're right. And the DCI has been totally supportive. I love my job with her. That's why I'm back today, even though I could have swung another few days off.'

'You're really lucky, you know. To have a boss who looks after you so well. I'm jealous in a way, cos I never did. I suppose that's why I ended up in the mess I'm in.'

'I still don't fully understand how you're involved, Lily,' Sophie said.

The reply was sharp. 'No, you wouldn't, would you? I expect people do exactly what you say. If I tell people what to do they laugh at me. It's easier for me just to lie back and enjoy life the best I can. That's how I met all these people. I just gave up trying to lead a respectable life, as my parents would have called it. What was the point? I'd tried to do everything right, please people just like a good girl should, but my life got into one big mess. So I started seeing men for sex. And I liked it. Not just anyone, though. It was always through people I met, at parties. It was just after that when I met Brian. He knew people who organised these parties and he got me onto their lists. That was when I lived in Portsmouth. He was a kind of protector for me. It was all good for a couple of years but then it went wrong when he got the sack from the police. That really shocked him and he got difficult, really moody and he drank too much. But we stayed in touch, even after I moved to Poole.'

'Why Poole?'

'It's got a good party scene and I was picking up lots of invitations. I'd make it clear that I expected something for taking part in a threesome or foursome, and I was usually treated really well. I decided that I could tap into things a bit better if I was local, so I moved here.'

'So how were you involved with what happened on Friday night?'

'Brian texted me mid-evening on Friday to see if I was free to come down to Swanage for the night, but I was seeing another man at the time and couldn't make it until after midnight. I drove down and picked him up. He seemed to be a bit down. I parked the car in the lane at the back of the hotel and we went in through the grounds. Brian seemed to know where he was going. I knew Paul and Sarah, but I didn't realise they were an item until then. I'd met her a couple of times at parties. She was a bit of a live wire, always pushing the boundaries. Derek was quieter but good fun. So the four of us had a good time for a few hours, then Brian and I left

219

at about two. Brian collected the car from the car park and followed me back to Poole and stayed for a few more days. We were shocked when we heard the news about Sarah. Neither of us knew what to do. Then we found out that Paul's body had been found too, and that shook us, it really did. I mean, what was going on? So Brian stayed on while we talked things over. He was with me until Friday night. It wasn't us that harmed either of them, Sarah or Paul. Please believe me. They were fine when we left them.' Lily broke off at a muffled sound outside the door of the flat. She made to stand up, but Sophie gestured for her to remain seated.

'Were you expecting anyone, Lily? It sounded as if someone stumbled against the door.'

'No. I hardly ever get visitors midweek mornings and I don't think any of the neighbours are in. They'll all be out at work.' Lily looked frightened.

Sophie went to the door, followed closely by Rae, but there was nobody there. Sophie told Rae to remain in the flat, and hurried along the corridor to the stairs. Was that the faint sound of footsteps coming from the stairwell? She heard a door bang, so she ran down the stairs two at a time. All was silent on the ground floor. She raced to the entrance doors. She heard a car starting up. Sophie ran outside and into the car park in time to see a dark blue Ford moving rapidly out of the entrance into the road. Its number plate was partly obscured. She halted, panting.

'Blast,' she said. 'Fuck, bugger and blast.'

When her breathing had slowed, she made her way back up to Lily's flat. Rae was standing at the window.

'Did you see the car?' Sophie asked.

Rae nodded. 'A completely nondescript blue Ford. Could be a rental. But it was too far away to get the licence plate.' There was concern on her face. 'I had an awful feeling of déjà vu. Was it the right thing to do? Go after him?'

'Possibly not, but I didn't join the police force to be cautious about everything. Same as you.' She turned to Lily. 'We need to get you out of here, Lily. Can you pack enough clothes to keep you going for a few days? We'll stay with you until a team arrives to move you to a safe house.' Sophie nodded to Rae and left the room to arrange safe accommodation for Lily. When she returned, Sophie took a photo of John Renton out of her bag. Rae had taken it surreptitiously with a hidden camera at their meeting at Brize Norton. 'Have you ever seen this man before, Lily?'

Lily studied the picture closely, her brow furrowed. Finally she shook her head. 'No. I'm pretty sure I haven't. Problem is, I've known so many men. But this one? He doesn't ring any bells. Sorry.'

Sophie didn't know whether to feel disappointment or relief. 'It's not a problem,' she said. 'It's just someone who cropped up during our investigations. So he wasn't a friend of Brian or Derek's? Not as far as you know? And you haven't met him on your own?'

'I had big gaps of time away from Brian, so I wouldn't know all his friends. But if you're asking whether I've ever had sex with this man, then the answer's no.' Lily's voice was choked. 'I'm not a common prostitute, you know. I don't sell myself for sex. How could you think that? I do parties and sometimes I've seen men, women and couples that I've met at the parties. That's it.'

'I didn't mean to offend you, Lily. And I wasn't implying that I thought you were a prostitute. I don't judge people like that. I'm investigating two murders, and I have to be absolutely sure about everything. I would be failing in my job if I did any less.'

Lily regained her composure, her face once again like a china doll.

'Do you have a job at the moment, Lily?'

'No. I was waitressing at a café near the quayside, but it closed at the end of September. I don't know if it's going to open again at Easter for the summer season. The only other job I really liked was when I worked behind the counter in a cake shop. I could chat to people and have a laugh. I loved it there. But it closed when the owner moved away, and I went back to my old ways. It's easy, you see. I've been married twice and they both failed. Maybe I pick the wrong type of man to marry. The right type of man doesn't want to marry me anyway. He just wants to have me for fun.'

Lily blew her nose loudly.

'I noticed a few days ago that there's a job vacancy in a café in Wareham. They sell pies and cakes,' Sophie said. 'Your other café experience would be useful. Why don't you apply for it? It's near the quayside. You'd need to drive in or get the bus. I don't know how convenient that would be.'

Lily looked at her suspiciously. 'Why are you telling me this? What's in it for you?'

'I need a spy on the inside to give me advance warning of any expected cream cake deliveries.' Sophie laughed at the puzzled expression on Lily's face. 'Do I have to have a reason, Lily? Can't you just accept it as a favour that doesn't have a hidden motive? Anyway, it's entirely up to you. Take it or leave it.' She glanced at her watch, then at Rae. 'We'll wait until your nanny arrives to take you somewhere safe. Then we must be off.'

CHAPTER 23: A HUNTED LOOK

How did you get on, Barry? Any progress?' Sophie had brought back a selection of sandwiches and snacks, and the team were huddled around the central table in the incident room for a working lunch.

'I've double-checked, and there's no doubt someone else has been doing some digging, but it all stopped two weeks ago,' he said.

'Just before the murders,' Rae added.

'Exactly. And it was a man, sounding confident, who was convincing as a police officer. He gave the impression of being middle-aged.'

'Could it have been Shapiro?' Jimmy suggested.

'I had another talk with him and he denies it. He's still happy to be here, by the way. Well, maybe not exactly happy, but he told me that at least he feels safe here. He's not pushing to get out, and I can understand that. Maybe I'd feel the same if I was him and I thought there was someone out there wanting me dead.'

'Did you believe him?' Sophie asked.

'Yes, I did.' Barry shrugged. 'I think he's genuinely scared. I didn't mention anything about Lily Dalton by the way. Several times he looked as though he was on the verge of telling me something, but then held back. How did you get on with Lily, ma'am?'

Sophie thought for a moment. 'She's not as innocent as she makes out. I don't mean that she had anything to do with the murders, just in her attitudes and opinions, particularly where Shapiro's concerned. She kept making out that he isn't as bad as we think and that he went back into the flats on Saturday to see how Rae was. But that doesn't square with what the squad car crew said about the way he behaved. I think she sees people through the proverbial rose-tinted glasses.'

Sophie finished her sandwich. 'We'll put him out of his misery this afternoon. Maybe once he knows that we know about Lily, he'll open up a bit more. Eat up, everybody and let's get back to work.'

* * *

Sophie could see exactly what Barry meant. Even though he was safely in custody, Brian Shapiro had a hunted look about him. His eyes were rimmed with dark shadows and he looked around as if demons were lurking in shadowy corners, waiting to jump out at him.

'Good afternoon, Mr Shapiro.' Sophie tried to sound breezier than she felt. 'How are you? Sergeant Marsh here still thinks that you're holding back on a great deal of information that might be important to us. Is he right?'

Shapiro grunted.

'We know about Lily Dalton, by the way. So would you like to expand on your account of last weekend?'

'How did you find out about her?'

'We'll have an exchange of information, shall we? You tell me something and I'll tell you something back. How does that sound?'

Shapiro stared at her and then nodded.

'She phoned, worried about you and about her own safety. Once we had her number it didn't take us long to find her address. Now it's your turn.'

'Is she safe? Is she alright?' Shapiro sounded anxious.

'Yes. We saw her this morning and she was moved to a safe house an hour ago. Now tell me something.'

'Lily was with us on that Friday night. She picked me up and we joined Derek and Sarah in the hotel room.'

'Yes but what I meant was, tell me something I don't already know. We've had a full account of Friday night from Lily. I'm trying to solve two murders here, Mr Shapiro. Tell me something I can use, for God's sake.'

He shook his head. 'That's just it. I don't know anything. I don't know why it happened. I don't know who it was. If I knew anything I'd tell you.'

Sophie leant across the table and stared into his eyes. 'Now let me tell you something, you miserable little toad. You refused to tell us about Lily when we gave you every opportunity on Saturday. You could have said that she was in danger, you could have given us her address, but you didn't. We only just got to her in time this morning. Someone came calling while we were there. If she hadn't called us, if the person on the phone here hadn't been so concerned, if I hadn't decided to follow up on it, if we'd have been delayed getting to her, she'd probably be lying sprawled and bloody on her kitchen floor right now. And all because of you. I need information. I need to know two things. Was Sarah secretly married again? And was there someone watching you and Derek on Friday evening?'

'What? Married again? If she did, she never told me, and Derek never mentioned it, so he didn't know.' He wiped his forehead with the back of his hand. 'Watching us? You mean, apart from that creep Ed something or other?'

'Yes, I do mean apart from him. Earlier, before you met the two women. Just after you had the argument with the roadie who was trying to bring kit in to the pub.'

Shapiro shut his eyes. 'There was a guy near the bar. He was scanning every bloke in the place. Derek reckoned he was gay.'

'We know about him. Anyone else?'

Shapiro shook his head. 'No. I didn't see anyone else, but Derek muttered something about someone in the corner, well away from us. He said the guy looked our way a couple of times. I couldn't see because of a fat woman in front of me. By the time she moved, he'd gone. I just forgot about it.'

'Did Derek say anything about what he looked like?'

'I don't remember him saying anything.'

'Did he say anything at any other time? About spotting someone looking at you both, I mean?'

'No, never. Except for gay blokes, like the one that evening.'

'So the fact that he mentioned it might have meant something. This man wasn't just someone looking around him vaguely, like people do in pubs. Don't you agree?'

Shapiro shrugged.

'Come on, Mr Shapiro, you know how this works. You're an ex-cop. Am I on the right track here?'

'Okay, you might be right. It had never happened before, so I guess there must have been a reason for Derek to mention him. But the guy didn't stick around. One minute he was there, the next he was gone.' He paused, scratching at a hand. 'Do you think it might have been him? But why?'

'Your guess is as good as mine. But there must have been a reason for it. It was too carefully planned to be otherwise. But I really don't think I want to share any more of my thoughts with you, Mr Shapiro, not if you've got nothing else for me. I've been doing some digging into your past, and I don't like what I've found. Maybe Lily thinks you're a changed character but I doubt it. Manipulating lonely and vulnerable women into drinking too much and then forcing them into group sex is multiple rape in my book, so don't think you're getting out of here scot free. I despise men like you. Women need the criminal justice system to protect them from the likes of you, and I intend to ensure they get that protection. Do you understand me? So don't get your hopes up that I've seen some kind of light as far as your possible guilt or innocence is concerned. When this murder inquiry is over, I'll be throwing the book

226

at you for the other stuff, all the things that have messed up other women's lives. You're an ex-cop so you should know the difference between right and wrong.' She rose from her seat. 'You did know, of course. You just chose to manipulate them anyway, for your own sick ends. And that's despicable.'

Sophie walked out of the room.

CHAPTER 24: AN INTRICATE WEB

Monday afternoon

So who was the man who'd been masquerading as George Smith from Portsmouth's police force? Whoever he was, he had used a pay-as-you-go mobile phone with an unregistered SIM card. All of the calls had been made from the Portsmouth area. The GPS data from the signals showed them to have originated in the town centre. Whoever it was might have used a café or bar as a base while he made his calls. They were almost impossible to trace. It had all been planned very carefully indeed.

Marsh sat back in his chair, his hands behind his head, and pondered. Could it have been Shapiro? He had insider knowledge of police procedures, after all. But Shapiro just didn't seem bright enough. And why would he have needed to ask these questions anyway? He was a close friend of Sarah's lover. He would have known about the other weekend festivals from Derek. He might even have been present at them. No, there would have been no real need for him to have checked the bookings in this way. So it had been someone else, possibly someone with an intense hatred of the murdered couple. Either that or someone looking to gain from their deaths.

He suddenly stood up and tapped on the door of Sophie's office. She'd been reading through another set of forensic reports, looking for any clue they might have missed. She looked up.

'What if we've been going about this the wrong way, ma'am? What if we've made the wrong assumption?'

She leant back in her chair. 'Explain please, Barry.'

'We've assumed Sarah was the main target and that Paul Derek was only killed because he knew too much, or saw something that might have identified her killer. But what if it was the other way round? What if he was the intended victim and Sarah was killed to silence her?'

Sophie thought for a while. 'Is there a motive, though? I can't think why he would have been the prime target. Any ideas?'

'It could be his work, ma'am. He was the senior IT manager. What if he'd spotted something going on? Serious fraud or something like that. And he wasn't careful enough with his suspicions. Wouldn't that be a good enough motive? And killing his girlfriend would naturally shift our focus onto her rather than him. The thing that made me wonder is the sheer amount of effort that's gone in to cover the killer's tracks. It isn't just a crime of passion, is it? It's got to be something else, surely?'

Sophie frowned. 'The problem is, technical forensics have gone through all the data on the company system with a fine tooth comb and haven't found anything. There's no indication that Derek had any enemies, other than his wife. Everyone else has always said what a nice guy he was. I don't see his wife being capable of killing two people and then covering it up so neatly. Other than Pamela Derek and her family, we're the only ones who know about his other, darker activities. Oh, and possibly some of his group-sex victims. But none have turned up other than Brenda Plant, and I don't for a moment think it was her. A wronged husband? It would have to have been someone with a deep resentment combined with top-notch planning abilities. But if Derek was the main target, why kill Sarah as well? Few people knew about their relationship, not even their closest workmates. We're looking for the same kind of individual whichever of the pair we think was the main victim. Someone out to avenge a perceived injustice or personal insult. It's a revenge killing, Barry. That's what I think. And that makes it more likely to be a man. It has to be a man who feels deeply wronged, enraged and insulted by something Sarah did to them. But I do take your point. It's conceivable that a husband of one of Derek's willing or unwilling sex partners found out and took revenge. Maybe we should double-check everything we have on Paul Derek in case we've missed something.'

Jimmy Melsom, in the main incident room, gave a sudden whoop. They hurried to his desk.

* * *

'Say that again, Jimmy. Maybe I didn't hear you right.'

Sophie dropped into the nearest chair. Melsom swallowed hard and repeated his words, reading from notes scribbled on his pad.

'The Barbados authorities have been on the phone. They confirm that Sarah Sheldon arranged a civil wedding two and a half years ago, while she was on a cruise. The ceremony took place because there are records of the wedding and a party afterwards in one of the beachside hotels. But the relevant page from the civil records has been torn out. They had a break-in last month, but hadn't noticed anything stolen or damaged. It means they can't tell us who she married.' He looked up sheepishly. 'Sorry, ma'am.'

'For pity's sake. What in God's name is going on here?' She looked at Marsh. He shook his head. Sophie took a deep breath. 'Okay, let's assume there really was a break-in and that the record was taken. It must have been planned. Which means someone probably flew out from Britain. Barry, you check all flights from around that date, looking for the name of anyone on our list. Jimmy, get back to the cruise company and get a list of the other passengers. Someone on that boat must remember who she married, surely? I want them all contacted, and I want their memories prodded so you can get me that name . . . And the crew, the ones who might have mixed with the passengers socially. You know, bar staff, stewards, even the captain. One thing about this news, Barry. It confirms that Sarah's murder was no sudden crime of passion. Someone had been planning it for a long time.'

Marsh spoke quietly. 'I can't see it being Shapiro, ma'am. He hasn't been out of the country for years. There's no evidence that he has the money to fly off to Barbados, and I just feel that this level of planning would be beyond him.'

Sophie nodded. 'We'll keep him in, though. He's happier downstairs in the cells than out on the streets. He's convinced he'll be next on the list. And maybe the food's better here.' She gave a tight smile. 'Rae. Time to contact our Bath colleagues, I think. They ought to be told that we have one of the men who probably raped Brenda Plant in custody. Can I leave that with you? Once you've done that, give these two a hand. Help whoever's looking most under pressure — Jimmy, I expect.' She looked quickly at Marsh.

* * *

Was that a sly wink? Marsh asked himself. She's managed to calm herself pretty fast, quicker than me. She got herself organised in a few seconds. Could I do that? I've got a lot of learning to do if I'm going to cope full-time with the way she works. He walked across to his desk and began. Airports and airlines — he hated them. Why couldn't people slow down a bit, enjoy their travel and go by train and ship? But at least it made his job easier. Thank goodness for flight records. He drew up a list of organisations and started to phone. An hour later, there it was. John Renton had taken a weekend return flight to Barbados early in September. And how had the ticket been paid for? That very same credit card. Jimmy had been looking into it. Why hadn't he mentioned it an hour earlier when they'd been talking about Barbados? He'd gone through all of the credit card statements earlier in the week, matching them up against dates. Hadn't he checked the most recent transactions? It hadn't been in the file. Barry was more certain than ever. The boss was right. Jimmy was a competent enough detective for routine work, but didn't have the extra insight for a complex murder investigation like this. She'd spotted it the previous winter during the Charlie Duff case, when Jimmy had needed so much supervision. There had been a huge difference between him and Lydia, and the same was now true where Rae was concerned. She got on and did things, used her initiative and found things out. Jimmy? He always had to double-check with a superior, seek approval. He didn't have the drive of the two young women. He hadn't spotted the fact that the most recent purchases on that credit card could be key to their investigation, and he hadn't asked the bank to send them.

Marsh put his mind to his task. If there was a flight booking as the ticket system had shown, then there should also be a record of passport use. Maybe that would be the next logical item to check. He looked up to see Rae standing beside his desk.

'I've been doing a search on the blue Ford we saw at Lily's place this morning, Sarge. I know we only got part of the registration, but I thought it was worth a try. And guess what? One of the Portsmouth rental companies hired a Ford out to a John Renton early today, and its registration matches what the boss saw.'

Barry only just restrained himself from hugging her. The thoughts he'd been having about Melsom were completely justified. Rae had jumped ahead of the game and had come up trumps. They hurried in together to see the DCI.

'John Renton? In both cases? The flight to Barbados and the car hire? That's wonderful news. But how did he manage it if he was in Afghanistan, as the MoD tell us? The murders were so carefully planned, you'd think he'd put a similar effort into covering his tracks.'

'It was the same with the hotel booking, ma'am,' Marsh added. 'He didn't try to hide that under a false name either.'

'No. Maybe we're just overestimating him. It puzzles me, all the same. Why would he fly out to Barbados, break into the registrar's office in order to remove an incriminating page from a log of marriages, but leave his name for us to find on a flight passenger list? What kind of incompetent planning is that?' She paused. 'I wonder if he inherits something from Sarah's death? You know, considering that they're half-siblings. There's got to be a motive, after all. We need to go into the family background, Barry. Find out if they inherited something. It could be property, money, shares. Anything that could have caused a dispute between them. He told us yesterday that there was never any love lost between him and Sarah while they were growing up. Maybe that animosity lasted through into their adult lives and her murder is a result. We won't move on him just yet, though. I want a clear motive before we bring him in. He didn't seem particularly unnerved when we turned up at Brize Norton yesterday, so he must be feeling confident. Let's get our facts right before we confront him.'

CHAPTER 25: BLOOD ON THE STEPS

Monday evening

It was very dark, but at least the weather was dry. Sophie switched her torch on again: nine thirty-five. Barry had said he needed five minutes to work his way around to the back of the house, look through the French windows, and return to where she was waiting on the front porch. Eight minutes had now passed. A twig snapped, and Marsh's face followed the dim light from his torch.

He whispered, 'there's a light on in a back room, but there's no sound. It could just be a security light. There's also a small window open in one of the upper floor rooms. I'm guessing it's a bathroom. All the rear doors are locked.'

Sophie was puzzled. 'If there is someone in, why aren't they answering? And if the place is empty, why has that window been left open? He doesn't seem like the kind of person who'd go out leaving his house unsecured. All these bushes and shrubs in the garden — the place is too tempting for thieves.'

'And what a place. How does an NCO in the army afford a house like this? How much do you think it's worth, ma'am?'

'Four hundred thousand? And it was the parents' house, Barry. Rae did some more background checks on him. He bought out Sarah's share when their mother died. It's all totally genuine, as far as she could tell. It corresponds to the time when Sarah bought her flat. She didn't need a mortgage for it because she'd just sold her share of this house to her half-brother. She paid cash.' Sophie looked around. 'Did you see anything else interesting on your little walk?'

'There's a garage with a car in it. I could see it through the window. I might be wrong but it doesn't look as though it's been moved for some time. But that would fit, wouldn't it? He's been in Afghanistan for a good length of time and didn't he say they were going to hire a car? Maybe this one needs a service if it's been sitting for months.'

Sophie stepped back and stumbled slightly as her heel caught in a groove between the paving stones. She grabbed Barry's arm to steady herself, then drew her hand back. The skin on her fingers was damp and sticky. She shone her torch on her hand, then onto Marsh's jacket.

'Barry, why is there blood on your sleeve?'

He looked down at the damp stain with a grimace and started to wipe it off. Sophie grabbed his arm.

'Don't. Leave it.' She radioed through to the uniformed snatch squad waiting in a van parked in the road outside. The vehicle turned into the driveway and came to a halt, disgorging several officers in black.

'Okay, Greg,' she said to the tall, burly squad leader. 'Do your thing.'

He nodded happily, swung his arms back and hurled the heavy-duty ram at the front door lock. It bounced open with a crash and the team spilled into the hallway. The first officer through the entrance turned on the lights. Nothing seemed amiss in the rooms at the front of the house, but there was a pool of blood on the kitchen floor. A bloody trail led to some French windows set in the rear wall of the lounge. They could see streaks across the timber decking towards the lawn, as if someone had crawled out through the doors and into the garden. Sophie tried the doors but they were fastened, the key still in the lock. She put on a pair of thin, latex gloves and opened the door. She peered out into the dark. Barry noticed a switch on the wall behind the curtains. A set of floodlights illuminated the back garden, but nothing moved. Sophie ordered the squad to spread out and search the dense, shadowy mass of shrubs and bushes surrounding the lawn. Minutes later one of the team called out to her. She shone her torch down at a figure lying prostrate under a dense patch of bushes. It was John Renton, with blood smeared over his apparently lifeless features. She reached down and felt gingerly for traces of life at his neck.

'There's a faint pulse,' she said. 'Get an ambulance here as quick as you can. Tell them we're dealing with severe blood loss, probably due to a stabbing.' She turned to the sergeant. 'Greg, do you keep one of those foil space-blankets in your van? Can you get it? Judging by the amount of blood around, he's lost far too much and we need to keep him alive.' She looked down at the white face of the man who had been their prime suspect. What did this latest twist mean? She took off her coat and laid it gently across Renton. She took his wrist to pull his arm down under the coat. And then she stopped. She suddenly realised with icy certainty who Renton's assailant had been, and who had murdered Sarah Sheldon and Paul Derek. Oh, God. Why hadn't she seen it earlier? Now it would be a race to catch up with him before he could flee the country. She glanced at her watch again. Still not ten o'clock. Maybe they wouldn't be too late. Sophie's mobile phone vibrated in her pocket. She took it out and looked at the caller display.

* * *

The only officer still at work in the incident room, Rae had been doggedly cross-checking the information they'd accumulated during the previous two days, looking for a link that might bring it all together. Surely, if she kept probing, something would give? She found some large sheets of paper and drew a series of interlinked diagrams of the victims and suspects and all their acquaintances that the police knew about. When she started it looked like the simple chart on the incident board, but as she worked it grew into an intricate web.

The office phone rang. It was an official at Passport Security, responding to a request from Barry. Apparently she too was working late, double-checking John Renton's passport. Rae opened the original passport.

'So you can confirm that the passport in question is in the name of John Renton and that it's genuine? . . . And you say that the town of birth matches? Portsmouth? And the date of birth matches the one DS Marsh gave you?' She listened to the replies. 'Fine. Can you give me the number? Can you read it out again? Are you sure?'

Rae paused. What did it mean?

'Look, we're really grateful for the time you've given us, but I really don't understand. The number you've just given me doesn't correspond to the number the airline has recorded. Could you check the number they gave us? I'd be really grateful.' She read out the passport number that had taken so long to obtain from the airline. She waited. When the response came, Rae almost stood up in shock.

'What? But it can't be a mistake, surely? If it was a typo it would be one character wrong, two at the most. But the whole number? So you're saying it doesn't exist? Yes, I can wait. Of course I can.'

Rae drummed her fingers on her desk. Ah. Finally. 'And there's no doubt? It is on that list of suspected fake passports? So the man on that flight could have been anyone, even someone posing as John Renton?' She listened. 'Well, that's fantastic. I'm so grateful for your help, and I know that DS Marsh will be too.' She replaced the phone and sat thinking before writing down the new findings in her notepad. It made sense. Earlier that evening she'd managed to make direct contact with Renton's immediate superior, and he'd been adamant that Renton had been in Afghanistan throughout August and much of September. He hadn't left for Europe until two weeks previously, so he couldn't have made that flight to Barbados. And he couldn't have used his credit card in the places logged on the bank's records. Was the credit card a forgery too? She thought for a while. Should she phone the boss immediately? Rae looked at her diagrams. There were only two witnesses who claimed to have seen the supposed John Renton in Swanage on the evening of Sarah's murder. One was the young man who thought he'd seen someone watching Shapiro and Derek. Timothy Brodie. He'd been interviewed before she joined the team, but she remembered her colleagues' story about him. But the receptionist at the Ballard View Hotel who had checked this person in was a different matter. She'd have been face-to-face with him. According to the boss, she'd been upset and very anxious when she was interviewed. Could she have overlooked something? Rae phoned the hotel, hoping that Maria was on duty. Her luck was in.

'Maria, it's DC Rae Gregson from DCI Allen's team. Do you have the time to answer a couple of questions? You do? Good. I'd like you to think back to that Friday afternoon when you checked John Renton in. I want you to take me through the few minutes he was there. Describe each step in detail. Is that okay? Start from the first moment you saw him. Where was he, and what were you doing?' Rae listened intently. 'Stop for a moment. Was there anyone else at the desk or in the reception area? No? So what did you say? What did you ask and how did he respond?' She waited. Maria described a man obviously intent on saying as little as possible. 'What about his face, Maria? What was he wearing? Tell me your impression of him.' She listened again. 'Well we all form instant judgements of the people we meet, Maria. We can't help doing it. What thoughts went through your head when he was so uncommunicative?'

Maria recounted her impressions during the brief encounter. As she continued, she recalled new details. Rae noted everything down.

'So. He was across the desk from you, Maria. You asked him to sign the check-in form. How did he do that? Did he use his own pen or did you offer him one?' She waited. 'So he must have reached across to take the pen from your hand. Which hand did he use? Can you remember?'

Rae heard a gasp and listened to the words that followed. After a few more questions she ended the call.

The man Maria had checked in had a small tattoo of a heart on his left wrist. She had completely forgotten about it until she spoke to Rae. Rae checked with the post-mortem report on Sarah Sheldon. Yes! There it was. A small heart-shaped tattoo on her right wrist. In a wedding ceremony, those two tattoos would have touched when the couple held hands. The boss had been right all along. That wedding photo had been the key to it all. And she, Rae, knew who that man was. It all made sense. She reached for the phone but then hesitated. There was one more check she could make. Jimmy Melsom had left the phone number of a couple who had occupied the cabin next to Sarah Sheldon's on the cruise. Melsom hadn't been able to get an answer earlier in the evening. Rae dialled the number. It was answered almost immediately. Rae explained her reason for calling. She asked five questions: had Sarah Sheldon married on the cruise? Had it been in Barbados? Did they recall any photos being taken? Could they remember the name of the groom? Did he have a tattoo of a heart on his wrist that matched hers? Yes, yes, yes, yes and yes. She should have spotted it at the beginning. Why would someone wear spectacles with plain lenses? It could only be part of a disguise. Rae pumped the air. Got it!

Now she was ready to call the boss.

CHAPTER 26: FLOPPY HAT AND SUNGLASSES

Tuesday morning

From her vantage point, Sophie looked around at the various members of the team, all trying to blend in with the crowd at Gatwick's busy terminal. They'd worked until just after midnight checking details and formulating a plan to snare their quarry. None of them had slept much. Sophie glanced down anxiously at the distant figure of Rae, hoping that the young detective would last the morning. She'd insisted on being present at the arrest, almost shedding tears of exasperation when Barry had suggested that she take the day off. Rae deserved to be present. It was her first big case. She had made an enormous contribution to it, and she was being asked to miss the climax? She had to be there. Now Rae was sitting on a plastic seat in the general waiting area. She wore an out-of-season sun hat to cover her bandages, an enormous pair of heart-shaped sunglasses perched on her nose and she was reading a magazine. Sophie smiled. That floppy hat, those sunglasses and the iPod earphones dangling from her neck gave her exactly the right look. She was nothing but a young woman leaving the chilly weather for a holiday in the sun. Amazing to think that Rae had only joined the team a week before. The first day or two, Sophie had had serious misgivings. And now? She'd have to thank Sandie Blake. The head of HR had turned up a true gem. Rae had brought real flair to the team. And she had been through such a difficult time. Just look at her down there, thought Sophie. Who here could possibly guess her background? People criss-crossed the concourse with luggage, shopping bags, snacks, or cartons of drinks, and no one gave Rae a second glance. Sophie could see the person sitting next to Rae make some brief comment, then return to her book. Rae was a natural. And she must have gone through such torment in her previous life as a man. One thing was certain: after her efforts of the previous evening, her place in the team was secure for as long as the young DC wanted to stay. Sophie recalled the pride and excitement in Rae's voice when she called them the previous evening. Sophie had sensed her triumph as she'd said, 'I know who it is, ma'am.' Rae had reasoned it all out without any help. Rae's conclusions had matched her own perfectly, but the advantage of extra corroborating evidence was with the younger woman. Those other details had clinched it.

Her mobile beeped. It was a text message from Jen Allbright, stationed outside. "He's here." Sophie glanced at tall, burly Greg Buller, and nodded. He spoke briefly into his phone, turned back and nodded at Sophie. They were off.

Nothing seemed to happen for several minutes. Then she became aware that the team members she could see were all advancing unobtrusively in the same direction. Greg Buller was moving down an escalator, towards the centre of the check-in area. Sophie caught her first glimpse of their quarry, making his way through the clusters of people gathered in the vast concourse. She could just make out several members of the team, closing in on him slowly.

Then things went badly wrong. A group of people, obviously a choir, suddenly stood up and broke into song at one side of the concourse. A second group, some yards away, also stood up, singing a response. Naturally, people's heads turned towards the sudden musical distraction and several started to clap along with the unexpected entertainment. From where she stood, Sophie could clearly see what happened next. Their man slowed and looked around uneasily. He must have seen that a number of people had not switched their attention to the singing. They were all straining to keep him in view as they made their way through the surging crowd. He'd seen that he was being watched.

The reaction was instant. He turned and ducked away, bending his tall frame so that he could be seen less easily. He headed into the thickest part of the crowd, now gathered around one of the singing groups. Then he doubled back towards the nearest exit. Even Sophie was having trouble keeping him in sight.

* * *

Down on the concourse Rae realised instantly what was happening. She could see their quarry pause. She guessed he must have realised that there were security officers and police personnel in the concourse, all looking out for him. She slowly rose from her seat and moved diagonally across the open area towards him, all the time pretending to read her magazine while she surreptitiously undid the clasp of her shoulder bag and fumbled inside it. So, when it happened, she was in the right place and fully prepared.

* * *

Sophie was beginning to feel panic herself. She knew there were officers outside who would prevent his escape, but the whole idea had been to detain him quickly and efficiently when he wasn't expecting it. He now knew. What would he do? Would he attempt to escape by himself, or grab a nearby person as a hostage? A hostage situation was every officer's worst nightmare. So much depended on the reaction of the hostage taken. It was impossible to plan for every eventuality. Who knew how a terrified member of the public would react to being held against their will? She looked again. What was Rae doing? She seemed to be wandering towards their man, her eyes on the magazine held in front of her. And then Sophie understood. Rae was putting herself forward as a potential hostage. Her disguise was perfect. She was just a slightly dozy tourist, who happened to be in the wrong place at the wrong time. And it worked.

* * *

An arm snaked round Rae's neck, pulling her in close. She gasped and then relaxed into his movements, giving no resistance. He pulled her back towards an exit doorway.

As the police and security team closed in he shouted, 'I've got a knife at her back!'

They stopped. Greg Buller was closest. His fists clenched and unclenched in helpless anger. Barry Marsh stood still beside him.

'Do what I say or I'll use it. Clear a path to the door and let us through.'

He started to move backwards towards the exit, one arm around Rae's neck. She gasped. Then she saw his feet. Soft suede shoes. Rae was wearing high, wedge-soled sandals with a small, hard heel. It was now or never. She stamped down hard onto the front of one foot, grinding her heel into the toes. She felt his body stiffen but, before he had time to react, she jabbed her elbow into his midriff with all the force she could muster. Then she spun around and kicked him hard in the groin. He crumpled to the ground. Rae kicked out again, knocking the knife from his grasp. She pulled a can of incapacitant spray from her bag and pointed it at his face.

'Just don't,' she panted. 'Don't make me use it.'

By now Marsh and Buller were beside them. They turned him over and fitted the handcuffs. Rae replaced the unused canister into her bag, just as Sophie arrived. Rae's boss looked down at the figure with grim satisfaction, then across to Rae, still panting hard from her exertions.

'You do it, Rae. You deserve it.'

Rae looked around her at her fellow officers, the crowds of gaping people, and finally at her new boss who had given her the chance to show what she could do. Rae, still breathing rapidly, looked back at her and nodded. She calmed herself for a moment before speaking.

'Patrick Adams, I am arresting you on suspicion of murder. You do not have to say anything. But it may harm your defence if you do not mention, when questioned, something which you later rely on in court. Anything you do say may be given in evidence.'

Rae turned to Sophie and gave a broad smile. Greg Buller gave her a bow. Barry Marsh shook her hand. The crowd, silent until now, broke into spontaneous applause. Rae had never felt happier in her life. It couldn't get any better than this. She walked across to Sophie Allen and gave her a hug before breaking into tears, her head buried in the older woman's shoulder.

* * *

Talking to Adams was like trying to communicate with a serpent. Gone was the carefully-controlled, moderate manner of Sunday morning. His eyes burned, smouldering with pure hatred.

'Why?' Sophie asked. 'Why did you do it? What was the point of it, for goodness' sake?'

His lip curled, but no words came out, just a slight hiss.

'You know why you're here, Mr Adams. There are two people dead, another is hanging onto life by a mere thread. We don't even need to question you, not really. We have all the evidence a court will ever need, with more due over the next few days. We have your fingerprints all over John

Renton's house, even in the bloodstains on the knife you used to stab him. All I want to know is why. How did it come to this? How did you, an educated, apparently rational man allow yourself to reach this state? Why did you have to take such a barbaric course of action?' She shook her head.

His eyes glittered. He didn't speak.

'And last night? Did John finally work out who'd been masquerading as him? How did it happen? Were there a few questions? Some half-baked explanations on your part? Gradual realisation? And then a knife in the gut as a reward. Stabbed by the man he considered a close friend, but in reality his sister's killer.' She stared back across the table at him. 'You don't intimidate me, you perverted creep.'

She spoke to Marsh. 'Let's get him back to Dorset, get the duty solicitor in and charge him.' She turned to Adams. 'You're looking at thirty years at least. How old will you be when you get out? Eighty? Eighty-five? Ninety? Is it likely, really, that you'll ever get out?' She let her words sink in. Was any of it worth it? When you stand back from it all, Mr Adams, and consider what you've done, you have to ask yourself that question. Was it worth it?'

CHAPTER 27: BARBECUE

Saturday afternoon

It was one of those warm, mid-October days that seem to be sent from heaven. It was now mid-afternoon. All the heavy morning dew had disappeared from the lawn. The flowers and shrubs were well past their best, but were making a valiant effort to recapture a little of their summer glory. One of the apple trees still bore its crop, a late variety whose fruit glowed in the sunlight.

On the patio, Martin Allen sipped at his glass of beer while tending the barbecue. Hannah, his and Sophie's elder daughter, was pouring a glass of ale for her boyfriend. Jade was trying to sip from a small glass of beer while keeping hold of her companion, who was clearly nervous at being in her parents' company for the first time. He didn't seem to be sure whether he ought to be holding hands with Jade. Barry Marsh smiled and wondered if he should be feeling pity for this young man. Did he know just what he was letting himself in for? Jade was certainly very attractive, but so far this afternoon Marsh had managed to steer clear of her. He never knew what she was going to say and how he should respond to it. Best to avoid her. Gwen put her hand on his arm.

'Let's go and chat to Jade,' she said. 'She's such a lovely young woman.'

'Hello, Barry,' Jade said. 'I saw you watching me. I don't bite, you know.'

How had she seen him watching her? It had only been a couple of surreptitious glances, for goodness' sake. Before he could speak, Gwen burst into laughter.

'She's joking, Barry,' she giggled. 'She's teasing you. Don't take it so seriously. If you could just see how worried you look!'

Jade took Barry by the arm, pulling him away from Gwen towards a bench seat on the lawn. 'Sit down,' she ordered. He did. She sat down beside him, then leant towards him and spoke quietly. 'Barry, I want you to know how much I appreciate how you've looked after Mum at work. How much we all do, really. It's great to know that you'll be there most of the time now. It means we can all rest a bit easier. I don't think anyone realises how worried we were about her over the past few months. Things are going to be so much easier now we know that you'll be there to keep an eye on her. You'll do that for us, won't you? Keep looking after her, I mean?'

'Of course,' he replied. 'I mean, I'll do my best to.' He couldn't think of anything else to say. Jade kissed his cheek, then pulled him to his feet and took him back to Gwen and the nervous boyfriend.

'Why does she do these things?' he said to Gwen, once the young couple had moved away. 'I never know how to react.'

'I think she likes you,' Gwen replied. 'I don't blame her. I like you too. In fact I like you rather a lot. What was the kiss for?'

'I think she was thanking me, but I'm a bit confused by it.'

The two of them walked over to have a chat with Benny Goodall, the county's senior pathologist. He was standing quietly to one side, glass of wine in hand, admiring a bed of late-flowering dahlias. He looked up as they approached.

'I'm glad you got it solved quickly,' he said. 'She's still not fully fit, as I'm sure you've guessed. I would have worried if the case had dragged on too long.'

Barry nodded. 'We were lucky. That, coupled with some determined work from the team, saw us through.'

'Do you have the whole picture yet?'

'Almost. All the major bits and pieces, anyway. John Renton, Sarah's half-brother, regained consciousness a couple of days ago. He's been able to fill in a few of the gaps. And we found a lot of stuff at Adams's house that helped us complete the picture. He'd been seeing Sarah for a long time, since before she split with her first husband. He originally met her through Renton, though Renton didn't know that they'd become lovers. Apparently they kept the relationship secret because he was in a messy divorce at the time. He was due to inherit some money and didn't want to put it at risk. Adams had always been besotted with her, but it got a lot more serious when they went on a cruise together and got married on a whim, on a Barbados beach. We don't know why she did it, not really, since she should have known it would restrict her activities. Maybe she didn't take it seriously, but Adams certainly did. We think that she regretted the wedding almost straight away, that's why she didn't tell anyone. Maybe he got too controlling. But it clearly preyed upon his mind. We think she treated him like just another casual lover even though, legally, they were married. Seeing him when it suited her, refusing to move in with him, keeping her own flat. It was a recipe for disaster.'

'But why now? Why wait this long? And why resort to such extreme violence?'

Marsh ran his fingers through his hair. 'That was always our problem. We couldn't see the motive for why it happened a couple of weeks ago, rather than when they first split. But apparently he didn't know about the group sex. He just thought she was having occasional affairs, particularly because he was away with the NATO training team a lot. Then he saw a video of her on the internet, performing with two men — Shapiro and Paul Derek. And he felt totally humiliated. He would have seen it as a complete betrayal. He realised that the wedding had just been a bit of a laugh as far as she was concerned, and the resentment built up. He went after all three of them. Shapiro is lucky to still be alive. We still don't know the sequence of events that Friday night, after Shapiro and Lily Dalton left. We suspect that Adams drugged Renton with some rohypnol on the Friday afternoon in Germany, which is why he went to his room for the rest of the day and slept. That left Adams a clear twenty-four hour window. He had everything timed to perfection. He flew to Bournemouth late that afternoon, taking a return flight on the Saturday afternoon, just after dumping Derek's body at Burton Cliffs. Military police found some residual rohypnol in Adams's quarters at Bielefeld, along with some of the benzodiazepine that he used on Paul Derek. He must have been busy even when he returned to Germany, because he traced where Lily lived on the internet. Will we ever get to the bottom of it all? I'm not sure we will. But we are looking into his background. There's violent stuff there against some other women in his life, including his first wife. Maybe that's why Sarah left him so soon after their wedding and never spoke about it.'

* * *

When Rosemary Corrigan and Ed Wilton arrived, Sophie tapped a fork on the side of her glass.

'I'm glad everyone could make it this afternoon,' she said. 'I have a whole list of thank-you messages to make, so make sure you've all got a drink to see you through the next few minutes.' She took a swig of beer from her glass. 'Summer Lightning,' she said. Gwen looked at Barry, but he merely shrugged his shoulders.

'It's the beer,' whispered Hannah, who was standing nearby. 'Multi-award-winning.'

'Anyway,' Sophie continued. 'Let me start with Rosemary and Ed, who've shown such forbearance and understanding in recent days. Something positive has come out of all of this.

They've found each other. It cheers me up immensely to think that I played a part in that.'

Rosemary and Ed raised their glasses.

'To Lydia, who's come across from Bath for the afternoon. I'm so grateful that she could help out with part of the investigation. She has a great future ahead of her. And to Gwen, on completely unofficial loan from Southampton, so unofficial that her boss doesn't even know about it, who supplied us with a couple of key bits of information. Thanks, Gwen. I'm sure we'll be seeing more of you.' Another mouthful of beer. 'Let me move on to the local crew. Tom Rose will be retiring very soon. You deserve a long and happy retirement, Tom. You may not know this, but you've always been one of the most widely-respected area inspectors in the county. We'll all miss you.'

Tom Rose's wife gave him a peck on the cheek.

'To Jimmy, soon off to join Kevin McGreedie's unit in Bournemouth. Thanks for all of your work, Jimmy, on this case and the previous ones, and I hope you're looking forward to the move. I'm so glad that I could help you land the transfer you wanted. To Jen and Jack, uniformed duo extraordinaire, a huge thanks. You've both been fantastic during the past couple of weeks and I can't thank you both enough.' She took another sip. 'As for the new member of our team, Rae Gregson, well, what can I say? She's done a stunning job, got herself concussed, bruised, badly cut and still limped back for more. And that performance at Gatwick was just amazing, and so brave. You've passed your first test with flying colours, Rae, so I can now officially say, welcome to the team!'

A spontaneous round of applause broke out and Rae fidgeted awkwardly before replying. 'I just want to say thanks to you all. You've made me feel so welcome and I feel I've fitted in really well. I've loved every minute of it.'

'Now have I forgotten anybody?' Sophie asked, looking around. 'Is that everyone covered?'

'Mum,' Jade said, 'Do you want me to put you to bed early with no cocoa? Because that's what happens to naughty girls.'

'Oh, I see that I've been suitably chastised,' Sophie replied, laughing. 'You've probably guessed that was the warning that Jade used to get when she misbehaved. Which was fairly regularly, I have to say. So, finally, to Barry. I don't think he knows what he's let himself in for, coming to work as my permanent number two. Barry, without you this whole investigation would probably have been a complete shambles. As you probably spotted, I still haven't fully recovered from my illness, but now that you're with me I'm not worried about it because I know we'll be fine. The biggest thank-you of the day goes to you.'

She raised her glass and another round of cheering and applause broke out. Barry Marsh blushed even more deeply, particularly when Gwen planted a noisy kiss on his cheek.

Ed Wilton turned to Rosemary. 'I know you've lost a close friend, and in the worst possible circumstances. But what she said just now was right. We've found each other, so something good has come out if it all.' He squeezed her hand.

'And you've started writing love songs again,' Rosemary answered, smiling at him. 'Maybe the world needs a few more of them. Don't you think so?'

'Only time will tell. I need to flog them to some gullible singer first.'

THE END

ACKNOWLEDGEMENTS

I would like to thank Jasper Joffe and the staff at Joffe Books for helping to add the final touches to this novel. Anne Derges, as the crime editor, has done a first-rate job in helping to smooth out my somewhat rough original.

The Beaumont Society (www.beaumontsociety.org.uk) is the UK's leading support organisation for transgender people. The society has a network of voluntary "Regional Organisers" across the country who are able to help with problems. The author wishes to thank members of the society for their assistance with parts of this novel. The author would also like to thank Bailey at the NTPA (the National Trans Police Association) for her help in supplying background information about the experiences of police officers with gender identity issues.

CHARACTER LIST

Detective Chief Inspector Sophie Allen is Dorset's acknowledged expert on murder and violent crime, newly appointed to run the county's Serious and Violent Crime Unit. She is 42 years old as the series starts, and lives with her family in Wareham. Sophie has a law degree and a master's in criminal psychology. Sophie may appear at first to be somewhat of a 'cold fish,' over-intellectual and too clever by half, but conceals a dark past.

Detective Sergeant Barry Marsh is in his early thirties and in Dark Crimes, the first novel, is based at Swanage police station. He's quiet, methodical and dedicated, the perfect foil for Sophie's hidden fragility.

Detective Constable Jimmy Melsom is also based in Swanage. He has only recently joined the CID, and is a little gung-ho in his attitude to crime investigation.

Detective Constable Lydia Pillay is a talented young officer based with DCI Allen at Dorset County police HQ.

Detective Inspector Kevin McGreedie is attached to the Bournemouth and Poole division of Dorset police. His assistant is DS Bob Thomson.

Detective Superintendent Matt Silver is Sophie's immediate boss. He helped to appoint her to lead the Violent Crime Unit but, to his regret, has a largely administrative role in the county police hierarchy.

Detective Chief Superintendent Neil Dunnett is the overall commander. He clashes with Sophie several times in Dark Crimes. The source of the antagonism is not clear.

Martin Allen is Sophie's husband. He is head of the mathematics department at a large secondary school in Dorchester. Martin has a minor, but very supportive, role in the novels. He and Sophie met while at university. He has a more prominent role in later novels in the series.

Sophie and Martin have two daughters. **Jade** is fifteen in the first novel, and appears in all the subsequent stories. She has a lively and very quirky personality. **Hannah**, the elder daughter, is a drama student in London. She is quieter in her approach to life. She appears as a minor character in the first novel, but has a more important role in later books.

THE JOFFE BOOKS STORY

We began in 2014 when Jasper agreed to publish his mum's much-rejected romance novel and it became a bestseller.

Since then we've grown into the largest independent publisher in the UK. We're extremely proud to publish some of the very best writers in the world, including Joy Ellis, Faith Martin, Caro Ramsay, Helen Forrester, Simon Brett and Robert Goddard. Everyone at Joffe Books loves reading and we never forget that it all begins with the magic of an author telling a story.

We are proud to publish talented first-time authors, as well as established writers whose books we love introducing to a new generation of readers.

We won Trade Publisher of the Year at the Independent Publishing Awards in 2023 and Best Publisher Award in 2024 at the People's Book Prize. We have been shortlisted for Independent Publisher of the Year at the British Book Awards for the last five years, and were shortlisted for the Diversity and Inclusivity Award at the 2022 Independent Publishing Awards. In 2023 we were shortlisted for Publisher of the Year at the RNA Industry Awards, and in 2024 we were shortlisted at the CWA Daggers for the Best Crime and Mystery Publisher.

We built this company with your help, and we love to hear from you, so please email us about absolutely anything bookish at feedback@joffebooks.com.

If you want to receive free books every Friday and hear about all our new releases, join our mailing list: www.joffebooks.com/free-books

And when you tell your friends about us, just remember: it's pronounced Joffe as in coffee or toffee!